A DISTANT SHORE

A DISTANT SHORE

John Houghton

THOMAS NELSON PUBLISHERS
Nashville • Atlanta • London • Vancouver

Published in Nashville, Tennessee, by Jan Dennis Books, an imprint of Thomas Nelson, Inc., Publishers, and distributed in Canada by Word Communications, Ltd., Richmond, British Columbia.

Library of Congress Cataloging-in-Publication Data

Houghton, John.
A distant shore / by John Houghton.
p. cm.
"A Jan Dennis book."
ISBN 0-7852-8228-9
1. Artists—Psychology—Fiction. 2. Spiritual life—Fiction.
I. Title.
PS3558.O847D5 1994 94-6209
813'.54—dc20 CIP

Printed in the United States of America
1 2 3 4 5 6—99 98 97 96 95 94

To

MATTHEW & SHARON

AUTHOR'S PREFACE

THIS BOOK IS the story of one man's spiritual pilgrimage.

Throughout his quest, Ewan Jones contends with the world, the flesh, and the devil, classically expressed by the seven deadly sins of pride, covetousness, lust, envy, gluttony, anger, and sloth. His tale is a parable for our times: his journey through the popularist philosophies, politics, and artistic expressions of the late twentieth century is one that will be identified with by hundreds of thousands who, like Ewan, are searching for a way through for themselves.

In seeking to portray the reality of this quest I have tried to steer a course that is honest yet avoids prurience. The presentation of this edition thus defers to the sensibilities of some likely readers while seeking to maintain the proper bounds of literary integrity. In seeking to portray life without God realistically my intent is not to offend, but only to contrast such a life with one of belief.

There are other layers to the plot. The work began life as a vivid and extended dream sequence and is shot through with archetypal symbolism and myth that evokes in us an awareness of those timeless realities which alone can give meaning to our existence. These universals find their full and true expression in the Christian faith. Thus the allegorical layer consciously finds common kinship with John Bunyan and his literary descendants.

Ewan Jones is not unique, nor is his longing; many undergo similar experiences. My hope is that all such readers will find the encouragement to persevere until they find the reality that they seek.

"I will set his hand over the sea."

BOOK OF PSALMS

❖

In the land of dreams we sometimes perceive realities clearer than in our waking state. Such experiences give birth to a deep longing in the heart and we grow restless with our mundane existence. So, perhaps, begins a journey—the search for a distant shore.

1

EWAN JONES CURSED THE SEA for the sixth time that day and then cursed himself roundly for his lamentable lack of self-control.

It was his token concession to morality. Not that he was a particularly moral man—like many fellow artists of his acquaintance, Ewan Jones was a survivor, a man doing his best to make a living. His worn out denim trousers and faded shirt said it all. He had no time for high-minded vocations or profound speculations on the mystery of the cosmos!

The one exception was art. Art mattered. Ewan candidly acknowledged his gift as a painter and for indefinable reasons felt a certain duty toward the human race because of it. Risking the charge of elitism, he believed he was supposed to live at a somewhat higher spiritual plane than ordinary mortals.

Ply him with sufficient alcohol, and he was eloquent about the artist's high calling.

"We are observers, not the observed; the doctors, not the patients; the victors, and not the victims," he proclaimed passionately. "Our gift sets us free to help people understand the meaning of life: we must depict fearlessly the overwhelming odds stacked against frail humans. And when hearts quail, we must weave the myth of Beauty to relieve the despair spawned by the cruel whim of Fate. If we fail in our task, everyone fails!"

Ewan's dark eyes blazed and his beard bristled on such occasions, but the effort of delivering the words was usually sufficient, shortly afterward, to send his lean form sliding under the table in a drunken stupor. His friends treated his outbursts with good humor and in due course carried him off to his bed.

Unfortunately, when he sobered up, Ewan seemed incapable of any such mastery over common nature, and it annoyed him intensely to discover he was truly no better than those he professed to help—hence, his verbal self-abuse late that afternoon.

"There. Seven curses. The number for perfection. So I've just endured a perfectly cursed day," he muttered grimly to himself.

"Did you say something?"

Ewan turned his face to his on-board girlfriend. Her name was Sally. She was on deck busily removing the wash from a makeshift line Ewan had strung up for her on their catamaran home. It ran from the foremast to a bent nail hammered into the corner of the cabin, whose paint, like the rest of the boat, had seen better days. A broken spar served as a prop for the line.

Ewan grimaced. One day he would do the place up for her, he decided. Sally looked very pretty against the dilapidated backdrop, a brilliant jewel winking for attention on a tatty heap of junk.

Like Ewan, she was twenty-four years old, and they had lived together on *Seaspray* for just over three years. It was something of a record for him, as his cronies wryly asserted, and he often caught himself wondering at the relative stability of their relationship.

Maybe it had to do with her physical beauty. Certainly she appealed to his artistic eye; and he would be foolish indeed to relinquish easily this blonde-haired beauty with her resolute jaw, soft lips, and clear blue eyes—features that captivated him as easily with expressions of demure innocence as much as with sultry, pouting passion. Nor did the figure disappoint the face. Sally's lithe shapeliness was the envy of many a woman and equally the object of admiration by men of her acquaintance. With such assets, she had never experienced difficulty in obtaining work as a model when the need required.

Yet Ewan's attraction was more than skin-deep. He genuinely liked her company and had no doubt the feeling was reciprocal. Most of the time she was easy to live with, and they shared plenty of happy moments—though when she did get in one of her moods, she could be foul. The firm jawline was not simply for show.

Domestic affairs Sally handled willingly, and she cooked passably well. Trading her own skills to supplement the proceeds from Ewan's painting assured a more than satisfactory lifestyle together.

Were they in love? It was not a question that either could easily answer—or even ask—so generally they avoided it. There was plenty of animal passion, and their relationship certainly contained elements of true romance. Yet they regarded their sexual relationship with the same attitude they held in living and eating together: it was merely a working agreement to satisfy a mutual need as conveniently as possible. Self-sacrificing devotion, jealousy, exclusive passion for one's partner, love in its highest (even religious) sense—all were nonexistent. Indeed, the very idea would have evinced in the two of them all the horror of the orthodox when confronted by a particularly virulent heresy. They naturally had never contemplated marriage.

"I was pronouncing the malediction," he yelled in response to her question. "I mean, just look at it. A whole day's work wasted yet again. It's enough to make you sick!"

"Maybe you should give up and do something different," she laughed. "Become a boat builder. Or even just a boat painter."

He ignored her oblique reference to the decorative condition of *Seaspray* and instead flopped into his canvas chair to scowl at the wasted remnants of his day's work. It was a mess, and the ghastly, late-afternoon light that shone through the sickly clouds did nothing to help. Ewan loathed the perpetually poor light, hated the drab-gray skies that stretched in a permanent shroud from one horizon to the other, despised the pathetic patch of pallid yellow that indicated the whereabouts of the sun. Why, he wondered, when the sun did manage to break through, was it never for more than a few tantalizing minutes before life returned to its customary dullness?

Ewan and Sally were anchored off Hallow's Deep at the base of the Rock. They were members of a sprawling colony of seaborne artists whose assorted craft plied the western waters of the old world. The Rock—its full title was The Great Barrier Rock—was an unscalable cliff that rose straight out of the sea and to such a height that the ever-present clouds permanently hid its topmost ridges. As far as anyone could tell (for no one had discovered differently), its span stretched endlessly and impassibly in either direction; and having no known landing places its drab, brown face effectively marked the end of the voyage for those who wished to journey west. To the best of available knowledge the Rock was totally devoid of life, supporting neither people, animals, nor vegetation.

Ewan glowered at the soaring cliff. He hated the Rock more than anything else in the entire world. Everyone hated it. Anger and frustration at its ubiquitous presence had become an obsession with the entire seaborne community that dwelt in its shadow.

Many years ago their ancestors, a group of artists disillusioned with the constraints of life on the Inner Isles, had set out to chart a new course beyond the known boundaries of civilization. More by luck than by judgment, they discovered a channel that led to the open seas, and high with the spirit of adventure they began their quest for fresh shores. Eventually, after many wanderings and numerous losses, they spied land. It was the Rock.

Flushed with their success, they searched eagerly for a landing place on what purported to be a fresh continent simply waiting to become (under their inspiration) a land of true freedom. They found no place.

At first the voyagers were unconcerned, and hopes of a landing remained high. It was only a matter of time, they said. But years passed without progress, and their sweet dreams grew increasingly bitter with age. A new generation was born, and another, without success. Eventually, as a concession to the reality of the situation, they established regular channels of communication with the Inner Isles. Some in their community even returned, preferring to accept the constraints of the old rather than struggle with the futility imposed by the Rock. Many stayed, too proud or too angry to go back. To these the Rock posed a challenge: somehow, one day, they would defeat it and open up a new world. Such people and their descendants evolved into the disparate colony now inhabiting the waters of Hallow's Deep.

Ewan had been born and bred in the community. The identity of his father remained a mystery to him, though, and he seemed scarcely to know his mother. Accepting (as most of the children did) his lot in life, he grew up surrounded by artists and their coterie and, showing considerable talent himself, embraced unquestioningly their ideology and way of life.

Their philosophy was in essence simple: Join the Cause—find your own way of despising, hating, and challenging the existence of The Great Barrier Rock. For it is the Rock that bars all progress and blocks out all vision. The Rock is the dead end to human evolution, the ultimate wall, the impasse against which the sea continually drives us. Maybe one day someone will discover a way of smashing it. Until then, we must maintain the Cause. Once you allow yourself to grow used to the Rock's blinding existence, once you accept its reality, you are lost. Thus they taught him and thus he believed.

The lifestyle of the community, as befitted radical artists, was bohemian. Morality had mostly to do with survival, but without trying too hard. In theory the people governed themselves democratically through a community moot where everyone could say their piece, but the practice had long since declined. Like so much else, it had suffered over the years from ideological decay. Nowadays, what little social organization they still possessed could best be described as a benign anarchy marked by occasional violence to provoke change.

Food and water and commodities arrived periodically from somewhere across the sea. The artists traded artifacts for goods. Such wares, naturally, were thought of not as genuine art but as the despised stuff necessary until society realized it should support artists free of charge. Only then could they produce the real masterpieces of which they were capable. Meanwhile the trade continued. Like most in the community, Ewan had a cultivated indifference to the utilitarian world and neither knew nor cared how the traders obtained or disposed of their goods. The same indifference marked his attitude to the origins of the Rock. It was there, and that in itself was sufficient to tangle with. Philosophical speculation about its roots was a luxury he could ill afford. He would survive and do his bit for the Cause.

Yet "doing his bit" was the reason for his current frustration and annoyance. For several days now he had been perched on a rickety, homemade gantry projecting from the foredeck of their boat, attempting to paint a mural on the smooth face of the cliff. It was a dangerous exercise, but one that almost every artist attempted at least once in his career as a way of expressing his personal loathing for the Rock. A few succeeded, and those who did were widely hailed for their success. Ewan wanted to be one of that number, but he was fast recognizing that such permanence required luck as well as skill, and he seemed remarkably short of the former.

Each day, while the sea was calm, he and Sally hauled as close to the Rock as possible, let down anchor, and swung out the gantry so he could reach the cliff with his brush. The difficulties were considerable, and more than once he almost fell from his precarious perch, much to Sally's consternation. Nor was the sea exactly a millpond; his painting technique had to consist largely of chance stabs at the Rock as the rise and fall of the waves allowed.

For all of that, however, he did manage some modest progress during a day's work. The careful observer might make out a scene depicting an artist's brush carving a path through the Rock while a mortar and pestle crushed the debris to powder. The problems came at the close of day. Each evening the sea rose and a series of waves steadily slapped his creation off the surface of the Rock before the paint could dry. By nightfall, the entire work was wasted.

It was the point behind Sally's jibe. She thought he should abandon the idea and go back to his usual mode of painting. At least that was profitable. Well, maybe he would—but not yet. He still had the determination to make his mark on the source of their misery. The least anyone could do was to try seriously. After all, some of the more highly motivated artists had died in the attempt; and while he did not profess to have their courage, he did draw sufficient inspiration from their example to persevere with his modest efforts for at least a little longer.

Sally moved to his side. She was more sympathetic now and gently massaged his shoulders.

"It's getting dark," she said. "We'd best be pulling back."

He grunted and continued gazing at the watery remains of his day's work.

"It's a shame," she added. "I really liked it."

Her appreciation relieved the gloom. He twisted his neck and smiled up at her as the tension eased under her skillful manipulation. "There's always another day, I guess," he said with quiet resignation. "Come on, then, let's get moving while we can."

The sea had risen and become choppy. They didn't have too much time. Assisted by Sally, Ewan swiftly dismantled the gantry and stowed his gear. While he raised the anchor, she unfurled the foresail and set it to catch the light evening breeze. Then, pulling the helm round, they moved away from the Rock to the relative safety of the open sea. Other craft nearby were taking similar action.

It was a daily routine, and in the morning they would reverse the process so Ewan could continue his efforts. Only the foolhardy risked anchoring close to the Rock after dark, and many who had done so had paid for such folly with their lives. Hallow's Deep had a nasty habit of dashing unwary craft against the impassive cliffs and sucking the occupants to a watery grave. It was a common way of dying, and the anxieties of sailing near the Rock were well-founded. One dark stormy night, an anchor rope frayed and you were gone, smashed to smithereens, nothing left except matchwood drifting in the morning light as a passing memorial to your transitory life.

Death by shipwreck provided a perverse inspiration for Ewan's talents, so much so that he specialized in graphically depicting the tragedy and grief caused by the Rock. The subject at once repelled and attracted him. It eventually had led to his series of paintings, which consisted mostly of haunted and contorted faces overshadowed by images of bodies and boats being hurled against the Rock—drowning people clutching in vain at the straws of life.

It was depressing stuff, but there was one ray of optimism among it all to offset the gloom. Having portrayed the carnage wrought by the Rock, Ewan then would paint its destruction. Typically, the scene showed the sea swirling between the crumbling, sinking remnants of the Rock, revealing a realm beyond—another, distant shore where his friends dwelt in naked, epicurean ease and the sunlight beamed eternally upon their blissful revelries. He called the theme "Hope."

"I THINK I'll have an early night," Sally said at the close of their evening meal. "Do you mind?"

"Not at all," Ewan replied. "But I won't join you just yet. I need to unwind a bit more, otherwise I won't sleep." He pushed back his plate and stretched. "That was very enjoyable, by the way. What was it?"

"Oh, just some new fish pie from the Inner Isles. I got it from Sam when his ketch called by yesterday. He was selling it to everyone. It cost me two dozen freshly decorated sea shells," she laughed.

"Hah! I bet he caught the fish on the way here and knocked it up himself. Cheating scoundrel! Still, there you go. We didn't do too badly out of it, I guess. See you in the morning, then."

He kissed Sally good night and stepped out of the cabin and onto the deck. The sea had settled to a steady swell and the wind was light. Finding his favorite chair, he settled back to enjoy a pipeful of tobacco before retiring.

For a long time Ewan stared blankly into the darkness, enjoying the savory mixture of salt breeze and rich tobacco. In the distance he could see the faint lights of his neighbors' crafts. One or two had ventured close to the Rock, he judged. Jason was sure to be among them.

Jason liked to paint by ghastly lamplight. It set the right mood, he said. Most of his pictures consisted of garish sea monsters crawling from boreholes in the Rock. They had huge, yellowed, bloodshot eyes and vicious fangs, and a young woman always lay helpless in their path. Jason's wife had vanished several years ago—washed up against the Rock and never seen again, so the story went. Poor Jason!

Ewan concentrated his gaze on the Rock. Although it was rendered virtually invisible by the darkness, he could sense its overshadowing presence as a kind of heaviness in the atmosphere. He pondered the meaninglessness of this brooding mass that represented to him everything that stank of death and alienation. The senseless destruction of his friends had been bad enough, but worse was the silence. An empty, faceless barrier, inaccessible and devoid of all life, the Rock personified impersonality. If you weren't careful it could neuter you, too. That was why you had to fight it.

He considered his fate. What blind chance had pitched him into this community, adrift on an endless sea and imprisoned by the pitiless, lifeless mass before him? Art was the only escape—that and the satisfaction of fleshy passion. There was nothing else. You just had to make the best of what there was.

He glanced into the bowl of his pipe—the tobacco was almost gone. It was time for bed. Maybe Sally was still awake.

He was at the point of rising from his chair when something unexpected caught his eye. A green light glimmered suddenly in the darkness. Under normal circumstances, Ewan would have dismissed it as the port riding light of a nearby vessel; it would have aroused in him no more than idle curiosity. But there was one fact about this particular light that made a commonplace interpretation quite impossible, and it was sufficient to freeze him to his seat in stunned, open-mouthed disbelief. It was the altitude of the light. At that height—however incredible it might seem, however incomprehensible—there could only be one explanation: the light was emanating from the Rock!

Ewan felt the hairs prickle on the back of his neck, and he shivered with sudden apprehension. This was absurd, uncanny, awesome—like encountering the ghost of a long-lost relative. Slowly he laid aside his pipe and rose unsteadily to his feet, mesmerized by the inconceivable fact of this light. He blinked and shook his head. It made no difference—the light was still there. The implications were mind-shattering.

What happened next was even more incredible.

The light began to move. Someone—or something—had cast it from the Rock unmistakably in his direction. He stood rooted to the deck, frozen in wonder as it curved toward him in a slow, graceful, shimmering green arc. Then he knew he must catch it. Rousing himself with a start, he ran forward—his body bent in earnest concentration, hands ready, eyes fixed on the light as he tried to anticipate the trajectory.

It was there, falling, just in front of him—just out of reach it appeared. It would miss the boat. He dived forward and stretched out his hand.

He was too late. Tantalizingly, electrifyingly, his fingertips brushed the glittering orb as it plunged into the sea. Powerless to stop it, he could only gaze after the shining object as it traced a wavering, phosphorescent path into the water's depths and then vanished into the darkness.

Ewan lay staring at the sable water lapping against the hull. Twice—three times—he glanced up at the somber Rock. Then he dropped his gaze and pondered his fingertips. They still tingled from the fleeting contact with the shining jewel. He returned his gaze to the sea, and suddenly a huge sense of inconsolable loss overwhelmed him. For a few fleeting seconds a window had opened and revealed the unthinkable: there was intelligent life on the Rock, and it had communicated with him. Indeed, from that seemingly dead mass had fallen (or had been cast; he was convinced it was the latter) the most brilliant, living light. It was no illusion—of that he was undoubtedly convinced. He had read of the pull of distant blue mountains; he had dreamed of unreachable islands faintly visible through the golden mist; he could imagine the yearning for a touch from a loved one; but this was *reality*.

A sob rose unbidden in his throat and racked his manly frame. He hadn't cried since he was a child. But now the floodgates burst, and uncontrollable tears poured down his cheeks as he wept for he knew not what—the brief passing, perhaps, of the one and only moment of truth in his entire life.

He had no idea how long this state of sorrow lasted—a few minutes, perhaps; maybe hours. Whatever the duration, he was tormented in turn by fear, guilt, devastation, and damnation until at last his sense of loss was absolute and his grief all spent.

Only then did he become aware of a gradual mutation in his feelings.

Something began stirring in the depths of his being—a strange conception was taking place. In the womb of desolation a desire was engendered, such as he never before had experienced. This was not a common desire, such as to possess or to achieve—but rather a primeval longing which might only be described as the immortal homesickness of the soul. The *Hiraeth* that can never forget the rugged hills and green valleys of childhood—the *Sehnsucht* that sighs with the west wind in the trees and shivers to the haunting cry of seagulls above a lonely shore—grew and came violently to birth as an ache that he knew would be with him the rest of his days.

He arose a changed man—not morally or spiritually, as such, but in regard to purpose. Whatever else Ewan did with his life, whatever little meaning it had possessed until now, he knew his destiny was to search for the source of that brightness until he found it.

Ewan spent the rest of the night gazing in the direction of the Rock with his new insight. There were no more signs; he did not expect there would be. The one had been sufficient. The call was firmly lodged in his heart now, and he knew he would not rest until he had answered it. Nobody would believe him, of course. They would say it was his imagination or the effects of alcohol. He decided he must tell Sally first. She would probably laugh.

As the night passed he attempted to work out a strategy. His first task must be to search for anyone else who had experienced anything similar. He needed clues. Where on the Rock could he land? Were there signals he could make in return? Was there any means by which he could say, "I've received your message and I am coming"?

Dawn wasn't far away; he could discern the tall shadow of the Rock. Quite evidently, there was no place to land around here. They would have to travel. He hoped Sally would come with him.

We must set out at once, he decided as the first chilly light of dawn revealed the familiar bleak scene.

He rose stiffly from his seat and shivered. It had been the most intriguing night of his life, and he was more than ready for some coffee. There was a busy day ahead.

❖2❖

A FRESH MORNING HAS THE TREACHEROUS HABIT of quenching the fervid passions, visions, and vows of the previous night. And Ewan, in the emotional trough that followed his experience, felt far less confident of himself in the cold light of day. When Sally awoke he hesitated to tell her what had happened. The Rock gave him no help; he scanned its cliffs in vain for further signs of life, but nothing was forthcoming. Unscalable, aloof, and impassive, the Rock was its usual dead and repulsive self.

With nothing to encourage him and unable himself to stir more than the merest glow from the ashes of his earlier fire, it hardly surprised him later when, seated on the bed, he tried to explain to Sally why he hadn't slept that night, and it all came out flat.

"I was on deck staring into the darkness when I saw a light shining from high up on the Rock," he told her. "Impossible, of course—but there it was. Then it began to fall toward me. I tried to catch it and missed. It sank in the sea. Green it was—a shining green orb."

Sally's steady, sardonic gaze did little to ease his awkward feeling. "How big was it?" she asked.

"Didn't I tell you? Oh, about so big. You know, would fit into the palm of your hand. At least, I think so. Maybe it was bigger." Sally arched her eyebrows in mock wonder the way a teacher would indulge a very young pupil his fanciful tale. She wasn't making it easy.

"No, I don't think I dreamed it," he said. "In fact, I'm sure I didn't. And I wasn't drunk, either. It was real." He sighed in resignation and concluded his story with more than a hint of petulance. "Believe it or not, I've been up crying most of the night because of what's happened. Me—crying! I don't think life will ever be the same again!"

For all her incredulity, Sally at least didn't laugh him to scorn, and for that he was grateful. It's hard for a grown man to say that seeing a light made him cry. And Ewan was well aware that by exposing such feelings he was exploring the dangerous territory marking the boundaries of their relationship.

But the matter could not rest there, and their conversation continued over breakfast. By this time Ewan's emotional batteries were picking up, and the more earnest and agitated he became, the more serious Sally's expression grew. When he suggested they should commence a quest at the earliest opportunity to find the meaning of his experience, Sally became pensive. She didn't ask any more questions and eventually insisted that they drop the subject. In consequence, he had difficulty getting anything out of her other than the necessary domestic grunts for the rest of breakfast. It was the first, faint hint of an impending storm.

Fortunately, Wednesday was the day they tidied the boat, and they both had plenty of activities with which to occupy themselves. Ewan had sense enough to realize that Sally needed time to absorb the implications of what had been, after all, an odd experience poorly shared; so he left her to her own devices and spent the morning by himself, pottering with his paints and brushes as his contribution to housework.

"I suppose we're going to move on, then, are we?" she said abruptly during their late-morning coffee break together. "Where to?"

"Do you really want to?" he asked. He had been caught off guard by the directness of her question.

"No, but it's not really a case of whether I want to or not. I can see you've made up your mind to follow this crazy notion. And either I go with you, or I have to leave you."

Catching his anxious glance, Sally gave a brittle laugh and shook her head in subtle reproof.

"You don't need to look so worried. I've no intention of going away—at least, not yet! It'll take more than a mad artist's dream to make me give up three years of what, I may say, has been more than a tolerable existence with you."

Ewan rightly took her sarcasm as a concession. He gave her a rueful smile. She was tense, edgy, but not antagonistic. Sally liked to be in control of her situation. She would relax, he assured himself, once she had come to terms with his experience and had secured her own role in it.

"I suppose it does seem like some sort of wild dream," he acknowledged. "Though if it is, it's the strangest one I've ever had. I was awake, you know. Wide awake. And everything was real and in its proper place. Not odd like it is in dreams. I could feel the deck and the water. And if I'd caught it, I would have felt the shining orb as well."

"It's a pity you didn't," she said a trifle unkindly. "At least that would have been real proof."

Ewan shrugged his shoulders and pulled thoughtfully at his beard.

"Perhaps I wasn't meant to. I don't honestly know, Sal. I mean, I suppose it could have been a freak of nature, but—no, there must be somebody there! You may feel it's wishful thinking on my part, but I'm sure someone or something was trying to get my attention. Perhaps they did misjudge their aim, but maybe it was more clever than that. You see, if I had caught the glowing thing, that could have been it. I might not have wanted anything else. But it's the very fact of losing it that's had such a—such a devastating effect on me."

He hesitated, struggling with his thoughts, as Sally gave him another sardonic look.

"I know, it sounds stupid put that way. Obviously, if I had the message it might make it easier to find the messenger. But I've been trying to work out my feelings all morning. You see, I was amazed when I saw a light high up on the Rock. Couldn't believe my eyes. Then when it fell—well, it fascinated me, of course. But don't you see, it was my *not* catching it that started off this—this yearning and longing inside of me. That's something deeper than I can explain. Not only am I now convinced there's life on the Rock, contrary to what we've been taught—but I desperately, more than anything else in the world, want to find a way of making contact with it."

Sally had been toying with her coffee cup as Ewan spoke. Now she leaned back in her chair and surveyed him quizzically. "You're really serious about it, aren't you?" she said.

Ewan's eyes blazed. "Yes, I am. It's the most exciting, challenging, and, I don't know—*awesome* thing that's ever happened to me."

She heaved a great sigh of resignation. "I think the only way I can live with it is if I just call it an artist's vision," she said. "And it's not the first time you've had one of those!"

"But it's not a vision. It was real," he insisted. He realized too late that he was pushing her too far.

"Yes. All right," she answered shortly. "That's enough. As you say. But just remember, I didn't see it, and there's nothing to see out there now. I looked." She took a deep breath. "Anyhow, when do we start out? For that matter, where are we going? What are we going to do? The only consolation prize I can see is that this will give us a temporary break from your mad obsession with painting a mural on the Rock."

"I don't know—where we're going, that is," he said, ignoring her barb. "Probably our best bet is to try finding out if anyone else has had a similar experience. We could work our way along the shoreline, at least for starters. Maybe someone knows how to make contact. What do you think?"

"OK," she agreed brightly. Her sudden change of mood indicated to Ewan at least a temporary acquiescence. "Anything you say, my mystic liege. We'll start this afternoon." She rose, flicked back her long blonde hair, and kissed him lightly. She added with a grimace, "Don't go getting too many visions in the night, will you? You look absolutely awful! Anyway, I don't like sleeping alone."

"MOLECULES!"

"I beg your pardon," said Ewan, somewhat thrown by this strange greeting.

"Are you deaf, or what?" bellowed the giant in reply. "I said, molecules. That's what you are. Come to think of it, that's what I am, too! It's what we all are. Random molecules drifting in the electrochemical sea of life." He threw back his head with a roar of laughter. "Are you coming aboard then, or what?"

"Don't worry," Sally whispered. "He's always like this. A self-made philosopher!"

Seamus Ferguson was an old acquaintance of Sally's, and it had cheered her considerably when a light, easterly breeze brought them alongside his ramshackle boat during the early afternoon. A bushy-bearded giant of a man, he welcomed them aboard with an ebullience that left them both temporarily gasping.

"Rationality, my friends. That's what we need," he bellowed, assuming without question that his now captive audience deserved an impromptu discourse on his work. "None of your airy-fairy nonsense. Life is all about logical structures. All feelings are illusion—superficial, mystical nonsense. I'll be having nothing to do with them myself. No, 'tis cool common sense we're needing today."

He paused from making some fine-tuning adjustments to his handiwork and stood back to admire his efforts. On the floor of the deck, ready for mounting on the face of the Rock, lay a complex contrivance of steel rods and multi-colored wires.

"Now take this, for example," he continued loudly, oblivious to whether or not they wanted to. "It's my own analysis of the Rock. Here I expose our Enemy for what it really is." Taking their bemused nonresponse as assent, he continued, "To you and me the Rock appears as a faceless, homogeneous mass, does it not? Our impenetrable, indestructible, impassive foe!" He straightened up and waved his finger like an old-time politician promising paradise to the punters. "But it's not so, my friends. And I can prove it! That Rock is weak, full of holes."

"What do you mean?" Sally ventured tentatively.

"Why it's simple, my girl," he said, fixing his eye on her and contriving the condescension of a tutor to a child. "The Rock may be a great structure, but it's only made up of molecules like everything else. That means it's all lines and spaces. It may look solid, but it really isn't. So why are we all so intimidated by it? Who needs to be afraid of a rock full of perforations?"

Sally glanced at the Rock unconvinced. There seemed to be little evidence of any vulnerability.

"So is that how you see it—like a type of rigid sponge?" Ewan asked.

"That I do, young man. For sure, 'tis not a bad analogy," laughed Seamus, turning his attention to him. "Aye, and if people will only be getting the message and stop a-fearin', maybe they'll find a way of busting through the bloody thing. After all, that's what life's all about, isn't it?"

He dropped his pose and gazed at them with a mock-serious eye. "But it's thirsty work, is all this talking. Take yourselves a seat. Good beer is what we're needing, is it not?"

Sally placed her hand on Ewan's arm and smiled reassuringly. "He'll be all right now," she said as their host disappeared to fetch some drinks. "He can't help it. He just loves being theatrical when he meets new people."

Ewan gave her a wan smile. He wasn't too sure that he was ready to risk sharing his experience with this larger-than-life rationalist. He looked dubiously at Seamus's contrivance lying on the deck. There wasn't much place for longings in a molecular world.

Seamus hadn't seen Sally for several years, and they spent a leisurely hour reminiscing about the good old days. At length Ewan felt more at ease and prompted Seamus to enlarge on his personal philosophy, and he happily eulogized the uniting of art and science and the triumph of reason over superstition.

"You see, my dears, the divide between art and science isn't all it's made out to be," he confided, gesturing expansively with his tankard. "Science is after giving us the measurements, but it takes art to provide the models for them to measure in the first place."

"You mean, like the notion of using a grid to map empty spaces?" said Ewan. "It could as easily be the outline of a whale."

"Aye, and more interesting no doubt," Seamus agreed. "And isn't that what the old astronomers were doing in the first place? The trouble was they became scared of their own models and started worshiping them. Took us centuries to debunk the illusion of religion. Thank God we've come to our senses at last!"

"It's a bit like the way some people used to worship the Rock in the hope that it would stop the shipwrecks," Ewan suggested.

Seamus spat disdainfully, then apologized to Sally. "Sorry, but it makes me angry, it does. To be sure, we don't worship it any longer, but we're still afraid of it, and I don't see there's a lot of difference. When are we going to see through the mystique and treat it like the mere matter it is? Then perhaps we'll find a way of blasting the living daylights out of the wretched thing!"

Sally glanced out to sea as a couple of seagulls squealed past. She wondered idly if they nested on the Rock.

Ewan looked doubtful. "So, as far as you're concerned, Seamus, there is no possibility of life on the Rock?" he asked.

"Preposterous suggestion!" their host expostulated. He banged his tankard on the table and splashed his beer. "And even if there were, I could demonstrate that it's just an illusion. No more than a construct of atoms and forces. Full of holes. As vulnerable as you or I. Neither to be feared nor admired."

Sally, seeing Ewan stiffen, changed the subject. "All this molecules-and-models stuff is fair enough," she said, giving Seamus her best smile. "But what about beauty and form—where have they got to? I mean, I remember when I used to model for you—you always finished up making something out of sticks and wires." She laughed. "I used to feel, well, quite mechanical. You might as well have been studying a machine as a woman."

"That's the whole point," Seamus replied warmly. He wiped his lips with the back of his hand. "You are a machine, Sally—a particularly well-made one, I should add. But we're all machines. Highly sophisticated we may be, but that's what it boils down to. All the old ideas of beauty and form were just camouflage to hide the raw truth from us because we didn't have the courage to face our vulnerability and mortality."

Their conversation drifted on in this vein for a while longer, but Ewan never rustled up enough courage to share his experience with Seamus. Reason might have the power to kill faith, but it could never replace faith—and he wasn't ready to expose his experience to possible execution just yet.

At length, Ewan and Sally took their leave of Seamus and returned to their craft. Ewan gave a passing glance to the mechanistic artifact lying on the deck. Whatever questions his recent experience raised, he knew their solution did not lie here. In any case, the seagulls had left their mark.

"Thanks for the ale," he called back as they loosened the mooring ropes.

"Think nothing of it," Seamus replied. Then he added with a lascivious chuckle, "Hey, Sally, did I never tell you? I always enjoyed stripping off your fascinating illusions!"

She responded with an insincere smile. As they pulled away, she said to Ewan, "What a con! You know, I'm not sure he really lives out a word of what he says. He used to fancy me, you know." She laughed coolly. "That man knows all about sensuality and emotion, but he's afraid to express what he feels in his art. I reckon if he ever betrays his real feelings, it'll frighten him into facing his own inadequacies—and he knows it!"

Ewan gazed at Sally with fresh appreciation. Without realizing it, she had protected him from the dangers of rationalizing away his experience. In a jovial mood, he set the sails and turned the prow eastward.

"WHAT'S THAT over there, Ewan?"

Sally pointed back toward the cliff. They had been sailing for about an hour under the uniformly ghastly light of early evening when, unexpectedly, a shaft of blazing sunlight broke through the clouds. Such was the rarity of this phenomenon that some artists based their entire work on trying to capture the moment. It was not unusual for them to drop everything else and feverishly attempt to portray on canvas the vivid hues and dazzling whites that momentarily transformed their otherwise drab world.

A resonant red burnished the Rock where the sun struck its face, and Ewan felt strangely moved by the sight. But it wasn't this that had caught Sally's eye. On a small promontory of the Rock, about a mast's height above sea level, something glistened and glittered silver in the rays of the sun.

For one affecting moment, Ewan thought it was another sign. Then he spied a yacht bobbing on the sea below and recognized its colors.

"Oh, it looks like something Carl and Colette have been doing," he replied, a trifle disappointed. "Do you want to take a closer look?"

"Oh, come on, yes, let's. We haven't seen them for ages. And you'd never forgive yourself if they had something that could set your mind at rest and you missed it. If we're going to carry on this crazy pilgrimage, we might as well do so thoroughly!"

Ignoring her lighthearted jibe, Ewan eased the tiller round and made for the headland.

As they drew near, the source of the reflection became apparent. Carl and Colette had succeeded in either painting or mounting a gigantic head of multifaceted silver and anodized colors high onto the Rock. Given the extreme difficulty of such a task, it was a superb achievement and worthy of admiration. The closer Ewan and Sally sailed, the more detail they could see. It soon became clear that the head itself was a composite of many heads and torsos, geometrically arranged in bas-relief and designed to create a noble, heroic impact.

"Welcome aboard, comrades," called a woman's voice they recognized as Colette's. They pulled alongside and were greeted by a middle-aged couple dressed in a motley fashion of workman's overalls and military uniform. Carl was a striking figure with a pointed beard and piercing, deep-set, dark eyes. Colette was lithe and diminutive with an intelligent, if somewhat stern, face. She wore her hair under a peaked green forage cap.

"Absolutely magnificent," Sally raved, indicating the sculpture, as soon as the formalities were over.

"Built to last a thousand years," Carl said proudly.

"It's our finest achievement yet," Colette explained. "The fruit and symbol of the people's struggle against the Rock. It will become the rallying point for the oppressed of the world."

"You did well to get it done at all," Ewan said, aware of the difficulty he was having with his own attempts. "I am truly impressed. What was your secret?"

"The dialectical moment," Carl answered enigmatically. "And the will of the people."

"You mean others helped you?"

"We wouldn't put it quite that way," Colette replied primly. "It was a united effort in which we all gave of what we had. It has not been without sacrifice."

Sally looked at her quizzically. "What do you mean?"

"In the great struggle, blood is shed and lives are lost," Carl answered heavily. "What you see is the triumph of the human spirit through months of labor and suffering." He hesitated. "Some paid the ultimate price. They are honored forever. Theirs are the faces you see in the finished work."

Ewan and Sally were dumbfounded somewhat, and more than a little awed by the supposed commitment of their hosts. People had died for this work? It was way out of their league! Both breathed a sigh of relief when the subject changed to the mundane issue of whether they preferred tea to coffee.

Though he professed none of Carl's or Colette's zeal for their cause, Ewan could accept the validity of their politics. He understood the appeal that the notion of a corporate materialistic soul could have. He was more doubtful, however, about the infallibility of the dialectic of progress. Life didn't seem to work out that way in his experience, especially for those who died for a cause. For a strange, fleeting instant he remembered his mother, whom he had not seen in years. Was her life progressing upward? He doubted it.

"How do you answer the charge that you prostitute your art when you politicize it?" he asked later as they sat in the cabin, sipping their drinks.

"When don't we politicize?" Carl answered promptly. "Every work of art makes a political statement, even if it's only to reinforce the status quo. You've only to look at the work of those who live on patronage. Why do people single us out simply because we want a new social order?"

"Spoken like a true revolutionary!" Sally exclaimed with a laugh.

The answer didn't satisfy Ewan. "So what happened to art for art's sake? Shouldn't we artists strive to be free from the particulars of politics and seek the universals?" he demanded.

"I've seen your work, Ewan," Colette interjected. "I like it very much. I admire the force of your attack against the Rock. You express the cruelty of the sea and the merciless oppression of the tyrant Rock better than most of us when you depict the suffering caused to our people. Frankly, we all owe you a great debt. But it's thoroughly political work, don't you see? All Carl and I have done is to respond with a call to radical social unity against this common foe. You raise the political need—we propose the political solution."

Ewan acknowledged her generous tribute and conceded the point. However, he wondered privately now about his own painting. Had he been so right in his assessment of the Rock? Was it such an unqualified enemy after all?

"Hey, comrade, don't look so glum," Carl laughed, misinterpreting Ewan's seriousness as chagrin for losing the debate. He leaned forward and punched Ewan's shoulder playfully. "*Ars longa, vita brevis*, and all that. We have to eat as well. Come on, Sally, have you got any grub? Bring it aboard and we'll share a decent socialist meal together!"

Sally rustled up enough food, and that evening the quartet regaled one another with tales of tyranny and revolution. They all gaily planned a new world order that would silence the Rock forever. By midnight all four were thoroughly drunk, and it was in the early hours when Ewan and Sally finally staggered back to their craft and fell into bed.

EWAN AWOKE two hours later. It was still dark outside, and he sensed the presence of someone in the cabin. His skin prickled uneasily with an uncanny sense of danger. Protectively, he reached for Sally, but, undisturbed, she continued sleeping soundly.

Ewan struggled to open his eyes. He was still suffering badly from the effects of alcohol. Was it his imagination, or was there a dark shadow, a deeper blackness hovering silently in the corner? He shivered, afraid and unable to move. When he tried to speak, no sound came from his mouth. Terrible apprehension seized his chest and almost paralyzed his lungs. Death seemed suddenly very close.

Then a hollow sigh emanated from the darkness. It howled like a bleak wind through a gully, full of dread—and with the menace of arcane knowledge obtained from sources unknown, it carried his name,

"Ewan . . . Ewan . . ."

❖3❖

EWAN AWOKE with one of the worst hangovers he could remember. Unable to face the day, he huddled under the blankets nursing an absolutely splitting headache and struggling to recall the events of the past night that had brought him to such a state.

He realized he must have consumed a simply appalling amount of alcohol. Little wonder his memory of the conversation with Carl and Colette had vaporized into a blur of political slogans and vain talk of socialist realism in art. What costly follies had they committed themselves to in their drunken state, he wondered?

He was in his own bed, so he assumed he and Sally had eventually gotten back to *Seaspray*, though he had no recollection of how they had managed it. He could remember one event that had occurred in the night, however—an unknown, unnatural being had been in the cabin, calling his name. He winced. It had been an unpleasant experience. He must have lain awake for some time afterward; he had vague memories of a fitful, disturbed sleep punctuated by ghostly images of flitting shadows. Then suddenly it was dawn. He wasn't sure whether to curse the cruel day for waking him or to greet it with relief for ending the rigors of the night.

He did neither, deciding death by inaction was the best option in his present condition. He rolled onto his back, put a comforting hand to his forehead, and gazed with half-focused eyes at the timbered ceiling of their sleeping quarters.

Slowly the pain eased and a quiet melancholy settled over his listless spirit. *The days of high romance surely were past,* he thought. People no longer set out on impossible quests with a holy madness in their eyes. Dreams and demons, gods and giants—they had all been demythologized and categorized by rational men. Far-off, fair lands full of soft nights and smells where lovers walked to angels' songs existed only in the imaginations of dreamers. He was a fool to think otherwise. *Why must you stick your neck out like this, Ewan boy?* Sally was right. They all were right. This is the day of the homogenized mass. Lose yourself in the corporate soul. There's no longer a place for the mystic who rants on about lights falling from the Rock!

In truth, Ewan was somewhat afraid.

Being intimidated by Seamus or politically inebriated by Carl and Colette was one thing; he could handle that reasonably well. But the night caller was another, deeper matter. If his feelings were anything to go by, then whoever—or whatever—had visited him during the night was distinctly un-human. True, it had only spoken his name; but the undertone was unquestionably malevolent, and Ewan sensed he had received a warning connected with the uncanny event of the previous night.

There would be trouble if he persisted with his quest.

It was a difficult thought for Ewan to handle. Not since childhood had he believed in the existence of the supernatural. *Is this what happens when you start seeing lights before your eyes,* he wondered? *Just when we think we're safe—*

A resounding crash from the galley broke his torpor and told him Sally was very much up and about. Unlike Ewan, she never suffered from hangovers. He winced and pulled the covers over his head. But there was to be no escape: in the next instant, dressed in a pair of shorts and a tank top and Carl's forage cap set at a rakish angle on her head, Sally bounced gaily into the cabin and ripped the bedcovers away. Ewan gazed up at her bright face in bleary despair.

"Good morning, comrade!" she laughed, clattering a plate and a mug onto the bedside table. "It's bacon and eggs for the masses, courtesy of Carl and Colette's fair-shares-for-all larder and a passing supply boat. Sheer luxury, but then we must feed the workers or the revolution will die of starvation!"

It was all Ewan could do not to retch. He groaned audibly. "Sorry, I can't face anything this morning. Had a terrible night," he croaked.

"Ah well, there you go, you shouldn't drink so much," she replied, unperturbed. "I didn't think you'd want it, so I'll eat it for you. I haven't done any for myself. Wise planning and good economy, you see."

With that she plonked herself on the bed and, to Ewan's dismay, began with cruel relish to lunge into the hearty breakfast. Finally, acknowledging with regret that he would have to live after all, Ewan made a supreme effort to down some coffee. It helped.

"So what are we going to do today?" she mumbled through a mouthful of food. "Do we stay and join the revolution or continue in our quest for the Land of Green Lights? Just give the orders, my ever-inspired captain!"

Ewan took another gulp of coffee. "No, I don't think I want to stay here. Couldn't stand being drunk every night," he replied ruefully. "Anyway, political ideals never last long. A thousand years, they reckon! Why is it always a thousand years? Huh, it'll all change by next month, if the weather doesn't get to it first."

He took another swig and coughed. "Same as advertising," he continued, in an effort to talk himself back to life. "One moment this or that's all the fashion. The next, everyone laughs at it. Politics, advertising, it's all a con. No, much as I like Carl and Colette, they haven't got what I'm lookingfor."

"Okay. So we carry on then?" She arose, collected up the crockery, and left him to attempt the faint possibility of standing upright.

The weather looked decidedly foul when Ewan staggered onto the deck. He sniffed the air and gazed at the Rock. Carl and Colette's creation appeared distinctly unimpressive in the dreary light of the impending squall. He was glad he and Sally had agreed to move on.

Within a quarter of an hour of taking their leave, the weather hit. Squalls of this nature were not uncommon, and on such occasions experienced sailors like Ewan and Sally kept well clear of the Rock. Too many a hapless craft had foundered against the merciless cliffs under these conditions, their occupants never seen again.

Although Ewan cursed the weather, the bracing effect of the wind and rain soon cleared the remnants of his hangover, and he began to think life was worth living after all. The disturbing memories of the night passed, and the notion of his quest began to revive. Maybe this was the way of such things, he thought—like a wine cork on the sea, always bobbing back up just when you thought you'd lost it. He hoped so.

By the time the squall finally abated, it was past midday. They had enjoyed an exhilarating but exhausting morning riding the waves, and Ewan had gotten his appetite back. Satisfied they were out of danger, he lashed the tiller while Sally reduced the sail to keep them coasting eastward under the diminishing wind. They ate a generous lunch under cover, after which they took a nap.

An hour or so later, satisfied and happy, they emerged on deck to discover they were unexpectedly within range of what appeared to be a moderate-size community.

"We'll make for there," Ewan suggested. "I've never met these people before, have you?"

Sally shook her head, comfortably snuggled under his arm. "I don't mind where we go, so long as it's together," she sighed.

"Even to the Land of Green Lights?" he murmured.

"Even to the Land of Green Lights," she repeated dreamily.

Ten minutes' sailing brought them alongside the commune. They berthed at what turned out to be a series of steel-decked pontoons, joined to form a broad, floating plaza fringed by sheet-metal cabins. Ewan and Sally's catamaran was quite spacious as boats went, but they always enjoyed the pleasure of real space when they had the opportunity. Once on the jetty, Sally began to dance with delight. Ewan ambled after her, hands in his pockets, a good-natured smile on his face. There were times when life seemed *really* worth living, he decided.

Just then, a morose-looking man in his mid-twenties shambled out of one of the cabins nearby. He had dark, shoulder-length hair, and a long, drooping moustache hung lankly from his sallow face. He wore a limp gray T-shirt and sagging trousers. Altogether he conveyed a pervasive air of pathological depression.

"Hello!" Sally cried. Ewan immediately was struck by the contrast between her rude health and vitality and the sickliness of the young man.

"Oh, hi," he responded in a monotone. It conveyed neither acceptance nor rejection. An awkward silence followed as the young man stared vacantly at the deck. Clearly, he had nothing more to say.

"Um, well, see you, then," Ewan said as he took Sally's hand.

There was no response. The young man shuffled on his way as though they hadn't existed.

"Good grief!" Sally exclaimed once they were out of earshot. "I hope they're not all like that. Otherwise, I'm going back to Carl's and Colette's!"

As they proceeded along the floating plaza—it was longer than they'd thought—they became conscious of more signs of life around the perimeter cabins. Nobody, however, bothered to greet them or to inquire as to their business.

"Arrogant lot, aren't they?" Sally muttered.

"Shh! Maybe they just don't like strangers," Ewan hissed. "Behave yourself!"

Sally giggled.

At the far end, they came upon a scarlet curtain stretched straight across the thoroughfare. Peering behind it, they discovered a circle of about thirty people seated on steel chairs. Most of them wore dark leather jackets, and quite a number of the men and women wore short, cropped hair. A fiery-looking young man with a fleshy face had just risen to his feet. He held a sheet of paper in his hand.

"Ah, signs of life! I wonder what this is all about?" Ewan whispered, his tone tinged more than a little with irony. "Shall we join them?"

They slipped round the curtain and unobtrusively took two vacant seats on the outskirts as the young man began to read.

Death, dark death;
Merciless.
Unforgiving edge
Cuts deep to the heart;
Blood runs to the ground.

Death, dark death;
Strangling.
Like poisonous gas
Denies us our breath;
Sears holes in our lungs.

Death, dark death;
Negating
The truth about life;
To hope is to dream;
To wake is to die.

ENTHUSIASTIC APPLAUSE ACCOMPANIED HIM as he resumed his place in the circle. Ewan and Sally sat in horrified disbelief.

"Superb!" exuded a large, leather-clad woman to Ewan's left. "I was stirred by that last couplet especially. 'To hope is to dream; to wake is to die.' That expresses it so well!"

"I agree," said a fair-haired young man. "You've captured the nihilistic essence there, Frederick. I identify immensely."

The poet nodded in curt acquiescence as others agreed readily, encouraging him to produce more in the future.

Much earnest discussion followed about death's being the only reality. Only a few days before, Ewan might have shown some sympathy for their views; on several occasions he had painted these themes himself. But now it irritated him to hear such talk. In spite of Sally's warning glance, he couldn't contain himself.

"Excuse me—we're visitors here and maybe we shouldn't speak," he began, suddenly rising to his feet with a demanding tone in his voice. "But is what you are saying all there is to it? I mean, do you really believe death is the ultimate truth about life—that there's no point in hoping for anything better? How can you say that?"

"Aha!" cried a thickset older man. The others had been deferring to him, and he obviously was leader and mentor of the group. "A fool and his maid have ventured into our midst, I perceive. A dreamer, perchance? Welcome, Sir! Pray be seated and become our teacher, if you dare. Though

I fear you will find us not easy converts to the views of enchanted idiots!"

The man's sarcasm was not jovial but rather was clearly calculated to intimidate and belittle his opponent. He undoubtedly possessed a very powerful personality, and Ewan found his confidence unexpectedly shaken by the force of it. He sat down and felt Sally shift a little closer. All eyes fixed on Ewan as he took a deep breath before replying.

"If what you people say is true, then life itself is entirely without meaning or purpose," he argued. "There's no point to love, or anything—not even in a baby's birth. In fact, why even have children at all? The only honest thing would be for each of us unfortunate enough to have been born on this miserable planet to commit suicide. Let's all give up and die!"

To his amazement, some in the group applauded his suggestion.

A quiet-spoken woman answered with evident sincerity. "There are those who do elect to take that path, and we honor them for their fearless strength."

Before Ewan could protest, the thickset man jumped in again. "You mock such courage because you yourself are a coward, and like all moral cowards you hide behind myths. Love and hope—pah! Such words are gibberish—the futile refuge of those too weak to face the truth!"

"So why haven't *you* followed the suicide pack?" Ewan rejoined, heartily provoked by the man's aggression.

"Because, my despicable young weakling, there is a higher path requiring greater courage, and evolution demands that some of us stay alive to take it." He gestured toward the Rock. "Take a long, hard look at it, you blind idiot. It typifies meaninglessness. So what do fools like you do? You dream of smashing a way through it in the vain hope of finding meaning. You imagine worlds beyond, but there are no worlds beyond. You hang on to paltry rags of morality and what you laughably call values, without a scrap of objective evidence to support them." He intensified his tone and looked Ewan squarely in the face. "We at least have the courage to embrace despair for what it is."

"We've stopped pretending, we have," piped in a doleful voice. Sally saw that it came from the depressed young man whom she and Ewan had encountered as they disembarked. He had joined the group without their noticing and sat toying with a vicious-looking knife. She wondered with alarm if he was about to commit suicide on the spot.

For a moment Ewan was unsure how to respond. Sally came to his rescue with a question. "How do you propose that we embrace despair, then, if we don't choose to commit suicide?"

The thick-set man leaned toward her and fixed her with a steely gaze, seeming almost to overpower her. "The maid has a tongue, too, does she? And uses it as foolishly as her man, by all accounts. Well, I'll tell you how. By triumphing over the weak, petty sentimentalities we call feelings, values, and humanity. We root them out of ourselves and others ruthlessly." His voice grew strident, and the back of his bull neck bristled. "We toughen ourselves, set our faces like flint, deny the myths that make us weak. All infirmity must be crushed without pity. There must be no compassion, no tolerance, no mercy." He drew back with clenched, upraised fists, his body trembling with cold passion. "Triumphant despair alone will conquer all and survive!"

Suddenly, Sally felt very afraid. She wished they had not landed here. Her hand slipped into Ewan's and gripped it tightly.

"You mean survival of the fittest, no less," Ewan said steadily. "And the fittest in your opinion are those who can face death and suffering without fear or any other emotion. You deliberately set out to destroy the higher emotions and virtues by calling them weaknesses! I think you're mad."

"Is it madness to purify the human race of its imperfections?" demanded his antagonist. "No, it is the victory of the spirit to obliterate the useless rubbish that clutters true progress."

Ewan was stirred. He could see where this mentality would lead.

"Your philosophy will turn people into dispassionate killers!" he cried angrily. "You'll justify every imaginable atrocity in the name of progress." He glowered at those around him. "Well, you're welcome to it. I want something better."

Caught in the torrent of emotion, Ewan took the plunge regardless of what his opponent might think.

"Listen! The other night I saw a light fall from the Rock! I wasn't expecting it, and I don't pretend to understand what it means. But I intend to find out. As far as I'm concerned it has shown me there is some kind of life there. If that's the case, then your philosophy of triumphant despair is a false one, and hope is not a delusion after all."

Ewan was shouting now. The group responded in hostile silence. The tension mounted. He could feel Sally's nails digging into his hand.

"Come on," he said to her. "Let's leave these people to their despair! When he's destroyed everyone else, the last one left will call himself superman and then commit suicide to prove it!"

Sally rose quickly to her feet, only too willing to depart.

"You are more deluded than I thought," the leader intoned. "The worst kind, in fact. Highly dangerous." There was a sinister edge to his voice. "Worthless scum like you shouldn't be allowed to exist. You are a menace to society. We judge you unfit to survive."

Sally shivered, unable to miss the import of the last veiled threat. "Let's get out of here, Ewan," she muttered. "And quickly!"

THEY NEVER MADE IT to the boat. Ewan's last recollection was of Sally screaming. Then a fierce blow on the back of his head sent him tumbling into a pit of endless darkness.

❖4❖

HE COULD HEAR SALLY WHIMPERING with fear. She was somewhere in the darkness, a long way off, it seemed. He struggled to reach her but something held him back. Suddenly, there was light—blazing, painful light that seared into his brain like a white-hot knife. Sally was much closer; he could hear her clearly, but his eyes hurt too much to look and he had to turn away.

Now her cries were urgent, pleading. He must reach her—somehow break free from whatever held him and cope with the terrible light. Slowly and against the pain, he forced his eyes open.

They focused on hell.

Horror jerked him into full consciousness. Sally was manacled to the wall opposite him, helplessly spread-eagled and quivering with terror. Ewan quickly discovered he was in a similar predicament. The young man with the knife stood before Sally. He had cut the right shoulder strap of her top. A trickle of blood ran where he had nicked her, and he was about to start on the other strap. Ewan forced himself to cry out.

"No! Stop!"

The young man paused and turned. A mixture of lust and cruelty contorted his gaunt features. The presence of overwhelming evil was tangible in the room; Ewan knew then beyond doubt that the unseen malevolence of the previous night had returned. Too late he realized his folly in not heeding the warning. Now he struggled frantically against his bonds as the man approached him.

One glance at his captor's glittering eyes and fanatical leer convinced Ewan he was dealing with a full-blown psychopath. The words the man spoke left no doubt.

"I'm going to kill you both," he sneered. "And I'm going to enjoy it!" Then he spat in Ewan's face.

Ewan tried desperately to stall. "Why do you want to do it? What have we done to you? Why can't you just let us go? You don't have to kill us."

"Oh, but I do," the man replied huskily. "I must. It is necessary."

"Why is it necessary?"

"You are inferior. I have proved it by capturing you. The weak must be conquered, or we all will be destroyed." A look of painful irresolution momentarily passed across his eyes. "I must destroy the weakness in myself. Show myself to be strong by killing you."

"You would be stronger if you spared us," Ewan tried—but the thought was lost on the young man, for the gleam returned to his eye.

"I'll start on the girl. She will die slowly. I shall triumph over her cries for mercy," he gloated. "I won't, I mustn't pity her screams. They have given me the chance to prove myself."

Ewan fought to keep his panic under control. Sally was alternately sobbing and screaming. There were instruments of torture lying round the room. He mustn't crack. The young man was sweating profusely, evidently close to breaking point himself.

The extremity of the situation forced a desperate plan into Ewan's mind.

"You're right!" he cried. "They have given you the chance to destroy your own weakness. But I want that chance, too. I want to join the new breed with you."

The young man hesitated at the unexpected words of his captive. He seemed unsure how to respond. Ewan pressed his advantage.

"I see it all now," he exclaimed. "Strength must triumph over weakness. You have converted me. Despair has conquered hope. I am free! I am free!"

His captor approached him quizzically, his eyes searching Ewan's face.

"Let me help you," Ewan pleaded earnestly. "I want to hurt the girl with you. We can take turns making her writhe in agony while the other watches. When one of our wills falters, we'll encourage each other. We'll harden our souls to every scream until we are invincible. You and I will become supreme masters over pain and pity!"

Indecision confused the young man's features. His body shook with tension, and he breathed in short, tortured gasps. His eyes pleaded to be convinced—and Ewan had one more card to play.

"Listen," he confided earnestly. "I know things about her that you don't. How to increase her pain—the best way to make her plead and beg for the mercy that we'll refuse to give. I can help you reduce her to a quivering mass. That way there will be no doubt. You'll walk out of here a true master."

It worked. With trembling, eager fingers, the young man loosened Ewan from his bonds. They looked one another in the eye—Ewan dominant, the young man craving reassurance. Then Ewan nodded curtly. They turned and advanced on Sally. Her face was a mixture of uncertainty, fear, and incredulity.

"Give me the knife," Ewan said grimly to the young man. "I want to start on her first."

"No! Ewan, no!" she screamed. "Don't hurt me!"

He had never been a violent man, but life at sea had given him a wiry strength and developed in him quick reactions. So, the moment his fingers closed around the knife, he slammed his right elbow hard into the unsuspecting young man's stomach and doubled him over. Ewan brought the handle of the knife down sharply on the back of his head in a two-handed chop. Their captor fell unconscious to the floor.

Swiftly, Ewan released Sally's bonds. It was all he could do to keep her from collapsing in his arms.

"Come on," he said briskly. "Let's get out of here."

He opened the door a fraction and peered through the crack. Someone was coming. He closed the door swiftly and bolted it.

"Start screaming," he urged Sally. "As loudly as you can."

Sally needed little encouragement in her traumatized state. She shrieked and screamed at the top of her lungs. A few moments later, a coarse laugh penetrated from outside. Then Ewan heard footsteps receding.

Ewan took one last glance at their unconscious captor and, assured that the coast was clear outside, he opened the door. Taking Sally by the hand, he led her swiftly round to the rear of the cabin. With nerves as taut as bowstrings, they began to inch cautiously from cabin to cabin toward where *Seaspray* was moored. Ewan hoped desperately that their boat was not under guard; he was aware that at any moment the alarm might be raised.

Fortunately, the day's light was fading fast and, in spite of a couple of tense moments when people emerged unexpectedly from their cabins, Ewan and Sally reached the boundary of the last pontoon unchallenged. There was no sign of activity aboard their boat.

Ewan eyed the broad jetty. "We'll have to make a run for it." He turned to Sally. "You OK?"

She was still trembling, but she nodded and smiled weakly.

They were halfway across the open space when a raucous Klaxon sounded. Immediately, people poured from the cabins and came running. Many brandished clubs and knives. There was no mistaking their murderous intent.

Not a moment too soon, Ewan and Sally reached their craft and scrambled aboard. Still clutching the knife, Ewan slashed frantically at the moorings while Sally struggled with the small engine they kept for emergencies. Once, twice it failed, then it spluttered into life. They pulled away from the jetty just as the first of the mob reached the water's edge.

A hail of missiles clattered onto the deck. "Keep your head down!" Ewan yelled to Sally as they maneuvered for the open sea. One or two objects were incendiary devices, and if it hadn't been for prompt action by Ewan, the boat might have gone up in flames.

However, within a few minutes they were safely out of range and able to hoist sufficient sail to catch a fortuitous brisk breeze. To their immense relief none of their pursuers was sufficiently prepared to put to sea, and so they made clean their escape without further ado.

THE ORDEAL LEFT THEM both weary and dispirited. Sally cried a lot. Ewan held her tightly for many hours, soothing, comforting, reassuring her. If either of them slept at all that night, it was only fitful and often punctuated by Sally's sobs. Ewan felt wretched. He'd never intended to get her into anything like this. It was all because of his foolish quest.

Yet still he knew it wasn't foolish. The real folly would be to abandon it. Then what would he have left? Nihilism was indeed the logical option to those who abandoned hope. He shuddered at the thought. Somehow they had to press on.

Breakfast was a somber affair, eaten in silence and with downcast eyes. Sally merely picked at her food.

"I know we've got to go on," she said suddenly. "I understand that, and I don't mind. Really, I don't." Her voice was edgy. She promptly burst into tears again. "I'm sorry. Stupid of me," she sniffed. "I guess I'm just tired."

There was little Ewan could do but agree. Sleep was a great healer. He would manage the boat—she needn't worry. He was sorry he had gotten her into such a mess. It wouldn't happen again. They would be more careful. The world was a treacherous place, curse it!

Sally returned to bed and slept soundly the entire morning. She appeared on deck again at lunchtime, and Ewan was amazed at how quickly the haunted, hollow-eyed woman was transformed back to her usually radiant, lively self. He kissed her, relieved to see that the nick on her shoulder was superficial. He marveled at the resilience of women.

The sea was light but offered sufficient breeze for them to continue eastward along the coastline. With no more sense of urgency and now feeling they had earned a rest, the couple enjoyed a leisurely lunch and afterward settled easily into their deck chairs.

Exhausted by all the events, Ewan slept.

He dreamed he was crawling up a gully on an unfamiliar surface of rough, broken rock. Reddish brown dust covered him from head to foot. His lips were parched and cracked, his fingernails broken, his clothes in tatters. He must have been crawling this way for a long time.

Somewhere ahead he glimpsed water, clear, blue, and inviting. The sight intensified the terrible thirst that tormented his exhausted frame, and in spite of the pain he drove himself onward.

Then a shadow fell across his path—and he was suddenly aware again of the malevolent presence that had begun to haunt his life. He stopped and hung his head for a few exhausted moments. Then, slowly, with a mixture of curiosity and fear, he twisted round to gain a glimpse of his adversary.

It was eerie. There was no one in sight, but the shadow remained. He heard a voice.

"Go no further," it commanded. "This is not for you."

"But I am thirsty," Ewan croaked.

"It is not for you," insisted the voice. "You shall eat dust, for from dust you are. On your belly you shall dwell all the days of your miserable life!"

"No! I must have the water. I will have it," Ewan fought back. At once with renewed determination, he began to scrabble forward. To his amazement he broke through the shadow with surprising ease, and gasping with success he soon came within touching distance of a pool of water. A few more meters, a couple of body lengths, and he would be there. He stretched out his hand in eager anticipation.

To his dismay, the water retreated. Desperately, he crawled another meter and repeated the action. Again the water drew back. Faster now, he reached out. But just as quickly the water withdrew. It was a cruel game, and before long he was spent with exhaustion. Taking his breath in great gulps, and with his growing thirst unbearable now, he conceded defeat and wept. Great, parched sobs racked his frame. He was too thirsty for tears and hopeless beyond words.

Then, from far off he heard the long, mocking, cruel sound of his adversary laughing. The sound echoed interminably in his ears until the oblivion of madness seemed the only escape from his torment.

The laugh turned into the noise of a wailing banshee, intermixed with the irregular clatter of falling tin cans and a sound of breaking glass.

Ewan awoke with a start. A curtain of fine mist had fallen across the sea while he'd slept. In spite of an appalling racket—which evidently was not part of his dream—he breathed a momentary sigh of relief at being surrounded by the familiar and refreshing presence of water.

Sally must have awakened at the same moment. "What in heaven's name is that row?" she gasped loudly, sitting bolt upright and looking about her with considerable agitation.

"It's coming from over there," Ewan said, having obtained his bearings. He pointed through the mist to a vague shadow on the water.

"Whatever it is, it sounds crazy," Sally answered crossly.

At that precise moment, Ewan's skin prickled uncomfortably. The haunting presence was there again. This time the warning was different—more like an omen. *They would be safe if they visited the source of the noise—otherwise, there would be trouble.* The Haunter—Ewan had decided to call him that—suggested it would be wise to cooperate.

For the first time in his life, Ewan behaved superstitiously. Under normal circumstances he would have berated himself for such momentary cowardice—it was irrational, primitive, and all that. But right now his instincts told him it was better to be safe than sorry. He couldn't cope with another risk to his and Sally's lives—at least, not just yet.

"Why don't we go take a look?" he suggested to Sally, never revealing an inkling of what had been running through his mind.

"What? We're surely not going closer to that racket!" she exclaimed.

"Why not? There might be something to learn here. You never know, they may have information that could help us in our quest."

Sally snorted derisively.

"We'll be careful," he assured her. "I'll go aboard first, if you like."

She gave a scornful laugh. "Thanks for your concern, but somehow I don't think there will be much danger here. I mean, listen to it!" Then, seeing the seriousness on his face, she shrugged and uncurled herself from the chair. "Oh, well, if you insist, my happy wanderer! Come on, then. Give me a hand with the sails."

They drew alongside a ramshackle, garishly painted collection of boats roped together haphazardly with apparent disregard for symmetry or seaworthiness. The sight provoked from Sally a stream of sarcastic invective, but, undeterred, Ewan made fast and clambered aboard. With a resounding crash and a yell of pain, he fell over the moment his foot touched the deck. Looking down he discovered that what should have been solid wood was, in fact, a cunningly concealed flight of stairs.

"This is some kind of nuthouse!" Sally expostulated as she climbed aboard more circumspectly. "Come on, let's leave it before you go and break your neck. Anyway, that noise is giving me a headache."

Ewan struggled to his feet. "At least give us a chance to find out what's going on," he replied irritably, rubbing his aches and pains. Sometimes, she really got on his nerves!

They entered the nearest cabin only to find it wasn't a cabin at all but a mere sham wall. Each momentarily disoriented, they failed to notice someone was seated on the deck with his back to this wall.

"Good night. Horrible to see you, but don't go away!"

Sally yelped, nearly jumping out of her skin. The strange greeting had come from a man who, as he rose, appeared to be dressed half as a pig and half as a cocktail waitress. He observed them with an expression of vain amusement as they stared agape at the bizarre sight.

"Oh, hello," said Ewan nonchalantly, trying to recover from his surprise. "Er, we're just on our way through. Curious really. Wondered who you were."

"Us? We're whatever or whoever we want to be, or what you don't want us to be, because who knows? It'll all change tomorrow. So who cares? At the moment, we're the CME—Chaos Music Ensemble." He pointed out this last fact with a high degree of urbanity.

"Is that what the noise is all about?" Sally gasped, making no attempt to mask her incredulity. "You call that music?"

"Does it matter?" the man replied with an effetely dismissive flick of his wrist. "There's no form or order in the universe, so let music be whatever we want it to be. Or, for that matter, whatever we don't want it to be."

The constant ambivalence in the man's speech was bewildering. Neither Sally nor Ewan was sure what to say next. Just then the noise ceased, and Sally seized on the opportunity.

"Is that the end of the, er, piece?" she asked.

"No, it's the quiet movement," their host explained. "Total silence. The chaos of nothingness. Listen to the sound. It's wonderful!"

In the next instant the silence shattered, and Ewan and Sally jumped to an energetically renewed racket of clattering cans and squealing pigs. Their amiable host appeared unperturbed and looked upon them with slight amusement.

"Come and meet the troupe," he beckoned. "Oh, and you can call me Harp," he added with a laugh.

"Ewan and Sally," the couple replied lamely.

He led them through a veritable forest of spars and timbers, tangled with randomly strewn ropes and barrels, until they came to the adjacent boat. There they passed a group of children who were using a painting of the martyrdom of Saint Anthony as a dart board. Neither Ewan nor Sally was in any sense religious, but this conscious blasphemy was nevertheless strangely disturbing to them. However, before either could comment, they came upon the music ensemble.

The group consisted of five people. A wizened old man hung upside down, swinging by his knees from a horizontal bar while banging two tin cans together. The randomness of his rhythm was due to the construction of the swinging apparatus: a line connected the bar to the boom so that every movement of the wind threw him out of time. Two women, both wearing pigtails and voluminous, bright-yellow polka-dot dressing gowns, sat back to back on the deck, wailing like banshees. Each held the other's hair and periodically gave a yank causing the drawn-out wail to be interspersed with random yelps. A young man, who had obtained somehow the iron frame and strings of a piano, was attempting noisily to cut the strings with a handsaw. Another man had punched his fists into two round and otherwise intact melons, and was using them vigorously to break sheets of glass that increasingly lay in fragments before him. He seemed not to have noticed that he had cut his arm in the process.

"They're complete lunatics!" Sally whispered.

"I'm not so sure," Ewan answered. He tried to ignore her raised eyebrows that suggested he might be as loopy as they were. "I think they're trying to say something. I'd like to ask them." He yelled to their host, "Can we talk?"

"Sure," Harp replied, at once signaling the ensemble to stop their antics. They did so without any sense of having been interrupted in their performance. The old man on the bar swung down to the deck with surprising agility and, to the young couple's relief, tied a towel about himself.

"Hi, I'm Ewan, and this is Sally," Ewan explained. "We're on a search."

"*Ewan* is on a search," Sally interjected matter-of-factly. "I just came along."

Their audience seemed to consider this outrageously funny and fell about in hysterics for a full minute, much to Ewan's chagrin.

"We're looking for anyone who has had any experience that suggests there might be life on the Rock," he said, recovering his composure.

"Oh, you've come to the right place, then," replied one of the pigtailed women. "Of course there's life on the Rock."

Ewan gazed at her in amazement. He couldn't believe his ears! *These apparently crazy people agreed with him!* He was about to give Sally a smug glance when the other woman piped in.

"Yes, my sister is completely wrong. No, she is," she said. "The Rock defies rationality, you see. It is madness. So why shouldn't it be alive or dead? Or both, but neither?"

Ewan began to feel his head spinning. He sat down and nearly wept with frustration as the two sisters continued in this vein.

"You find us disturbing," Harp noted.

Ewan nodded. "I just can't make any sense of what you're saying."

"That's the whole point. There is no sense," their host explained. "The universe is mad. Chaos. We just articulate the silent voice of the unreality that is reality."

"I couldn't live like this," Ewan said, shaking his head in disbelief.

"Of course you could," Harp replied. "Join us. Let go of your false security. Embrace the sanity of madness!"

Sally snickered in the background.

"Tell me, what brings you here asking such sanely insane questions about life on the Rock?" explored their genial host.

With some difficulty, Ewan attempted to explain his experience of the falling light and tried to express something of the longing that had been born within him as a consequence.

"There you are, then," said Harp. He spread his palms and shrugged with a look that said the explanation was obvious to anyone. "You have this safe framework which says the Rock is dead. Then you have a random experience of some light or other. Immediately, you slip into another equally safe, but opposite, framework of rational explanation. The Rock is dead—now the Rock has life."

"But what's wrong with that?" Sally interjected coldly. "I might not agree that Ewan actually saw a light—I think it was a vision—but if he did, then it's perfectly reasonable for him to believe the opposite of what he used to believe. I mean, the Rock has to be either dead or alive. It can't be dead and alive any more than the same wind can blow from the West and the East at the same time."

"Ah, but that's where you are mistaken," said the man who had been breaking glass. He still wore the melons as mitts. "Where does East meet West? What is East and what is West? Turn around and they turn around. Left becomes right. Stand on your head like Papa here, and up becomes down. If I stand the opposite way to you, then we'll have to agree the wind is coming from East and West at the same time." He waved a mitt is Sally's direction. "Your problem is you want life to be objective. But it just isn't.

"There is no reality, no order, no meaning," said Harp. "People only put things into categories in an attempt to control chaos. But chaos is the only reality."

Sally turned her back on them and folded her arms. She was seething. *Navigate like that, and you'll find chaos soon enough—at the bottom of the sea*, she thought to herself.

"I was like you once," said Papa, the wizened old man who had been hanging from the bar. "I wanted order to my existence. I thought life made sense. The Rock is there, attack it rationally, I said. Then I realized that this was precisely what the Rock wanted. It was dictating the terms of the battle. I learned better. So now I attack it with the invincible weapon of folly and of irrationality. Chaos reigns, and the Rock to me is simply part of the chaos, no more, no less."

"So could there be life on it, do you think?" Ewan persisted.

"What would it matter, and what would it mean?" replied Papa.

"Ewan wants to find it, if it's there—don't you, Ewan?" Sally retorted acidly over her shoulder.

"But why?" Harp responded. "Even if there is life on the Rock it has no reality, no value or ultimate meaning. It will only be a chance affair."

"Like the chance that I saw a shining green object fall from it?" Ewan challenged.

"Random," said Papa. "A small incident in a world of chaos. Forget it. I can see your lady thinks we're mad," he observed, gesturing in Sally's direction. "Let me tell you that I consider your quest to be equally mad. My advice is that either you embrace madness of one kind or another, or settle back for the myth of order in which people imprison themselves."

"Thank you," Ewan said thoughtfully. "I'll consider what you've said."

Sally turned and looked at him with shocked disapproval. "I think I'll stay in prison," she said, and with that she took her leave and strode off purposefully in the direction of their boat. It was a careless move—for in the next moment she cursed loudly as her shin caught a stray spar.

"I'd better be going," Ewan explained with an apologetic smile.

Back on *Seaspray*, Sally was incensed. To make matters worse, her shin now sported a large bruise.

"Just what are we playing at, Ewan?" she demanded. "I mean, so far all we've done is visit drunken political lechers, psychopaths who want to torture us to death, and now complete raving lunatics! I've had just about enough of this."

Ewan was suitably sympathetic about her shin, but he was adamant that they had to go on.

"Sally, listen to me," he said earnestly. "I know it sounds crazy, and I know you don't believe I saw a real object that night. But I think I did, and—I've just got to test it out. I can't explain this longing I feel. It's like being homesick, I suppose. It just overwhelms me." He ended lamely with a shrug of his shoulders. "Sorry, and all that."

Sally nodded thoughtfully, her indignation spent. "All right. I'm sorry, too. Just overreacting, I guess. Stupid really. I should be enjoying the adventure. After all, not every girl gets a chance like this!" She looked him in the eye and shook her head wonderingly. "You're a pain, Ewan Jones, but I can't really live without you."

He smiled wanly and put his arms round her. "Let's hope it gets a bit better, eh?" he said.

THAT NIGHT EWAN AWOKE to find his pillow soaked in tears.

Sally sat awake beside him, looking at him with great concern. "What's wrong?" she inquired sympathetically.

For a moment he couldn't quite orient himself. He lay in silence.

"Bad dream," he said at length. "All tied up with this longing I feel. I should have told you before, Sally. There's more to it than I've said. Someone there. A threatening presence. I call him the Haunter. To be honest, he frightens me. That's why I made us visit those people today. I felt we'd be in danger if we didn't—but now I feel in danger because we have. They've made madness seem a real option for me." He shivered in apprehension.

Without a word, Sally drew him toward her and for the next half hour drowned his fears and sorrows in a soft sea of feminine comfort. Haunted or not, someone had to take care of him, and, secretly, Sally was glad it was her.

5

THEY AWOKE the next morning to find their boat becalmed amid a mellow mist that had settled like a silver blanket over the ocean. Visibility was almost zero and a fine, dewy sheen bathed everything in sight. Only an occasional creak in the rigging or the lazy slap of a random wavelet against the hull broke the muffled stillness.

This kind of weather suited Ewan's mood. He sat alone on deck in quiet meditation, pondering his destiny, content to let the mist caress the tension from his troubled psyche. Madness might be a valid option in a meaningless universe, he decided, but it wasn't for him. A smile touched the corners of his mouth. Sally's nocturnal ministrations had done the trick. If chaos really reigned, then it was either too organized to merit the title or too ineffectual to claim the right to the throne! He sighed, satisfied, and was determined to remain sane—but searching.

Sally waited until she saw him smile, then slipped her arm round his shoulders. He hadn't noticed that she'd joined him.

"Feeling better?" she asked, ruffling the coarse wool of his sweater with her fingers.

He nodded and smiled, reaching out to give her arm a reassuring squeeze.

"When are you going to paint again?"

It was a leading question, perfectly timed to his easy mood. Yesterday, he would have met the idea with an angry rebuff and intense talk about glowing orbs and impossible longings—and, however perilous, they would have had to press on with all possible haste. Now, his passions spent, at least temporarily, he was open to considering an alternative that didn't require abandoning his quest yet would provide a creative diversion for his energies.

"I'm not sure," he replied. "Maybe in a day or two, if the weather brightens."

Sally stared serenely into the mist.

"I'm glad," she said. Then she added, "Breakfast is ready if you want it."

An hour or so later Ewan called Sally onto the deck. He pointed vaguely to starboard. She peered through the mist but could see nothing, and said so.

"No. Listen. Somebody's singing," he explained.

This time there was no mistaking the haunting strains of a beautiful melody, sung with passion by a magnificent baritone voice.

"I can't make out the words," said Sally.

"That's because they're German," Ewan laughed. "I'll bet that's old Siegfried. Come on, let's start the motor and see if we can find him."

Most catamarans like *Seaspray* were equipped with a basic motor that, while not powerful enough to take their occupants far, could in a pinch get them out of trouble or manage short maneuvers. The cost and difficulty of obtaining fuel meant that most of the artists seldom used them, relying instead on sail and tide.

The burble of *Seaspray's* engine all but drowned out the sound of the singing, and it wasn't long before Ewan was convinced they were going in circles. He began to wonder, too, if they weren't coming too close to the Rock, and he scanned watchfully for its dark mass to loom suddenly out of the mist. He ordered Sally to cut the engine.

To their surprise, the sounds of the singing came across the water now to the stern of their vessel. They hove to, and within a minute they could see the dim shape of a boat emerging from the mist. It bore the unmistakable lines of a Viking longship, and at its dragon-head prow stood the solitary jerkin-clad singer, one booted foot on the gunwale, his arms outstretched expressively. A pale lantern swung from the single mast, pervading the scene with an air of noble tragedy.

The singer spotted them and broke off his song mid-stanza. "*Guten Morgen!*" he cried. There was no mistaking the guttural accent and stentorian voice.

"Good morning, Siegfried," Ewan answered. "May we come alongside?"

"I host all the inconsolable wanderers of the world, yet you know my name!" he replied. "Come aboard, whoever you are, and let us comfort one another on our weary journey!"

He recognized Ewan the moment they emerged from the mist and flung his arms about the younger man in a warm embrace.

"My old friend! Ewan, it is you!" he cried. "How did I not recognize your boat? It is so very good to see you again." He spoke with a poignant sincerity that Sally found touching. "And you, *Liebchen!* What a beautiful, beautiful girl." He took her shoulders and gazed at her with appreciation.

She felt herself blushing slightly, but the unaffected manner of this charming old man instantly drew from her a fondness for him. She accepted the compliment happily.

"Come out of this murk," he said, ushering them into the cabin. "It is time for some refreshment, I think, *nein?*"

As soon as they had settled comfortably in the snug of Siegfried's living quarters, Sally took the opportunity to study their host as he prepared the drinks. In spite of his age and his graying temples, he was still a powerfully built man possessed of strong, almost operatic features. His face was etched with lines of profound emotion. He had known suffering, she thought, and yet apparently had overcome it with a nobility of character that had preserved him from the ravages of despair. Glancing round the cabin she saw that, though cumbered with many keepsakes, it was, nevertheless, clean and tidy—like his well-kept beard which framed a full-lipped, mobile mouth, the mark of a man who had refused to let the misfortunes of fate discourage him.

"Well, it has been a long time," he said to Ewan. "How many years?"

"I've lost count," Ewan replied. "Too many."

"Hmm, also too many since Hilda passed beyond," he mused. He raised his glass. "Your health, my friends, and the memory of my Hilda."

"Your health," they acknowledged.

"Siegfried is a widower," Ewan explained to Sally. "Hilda was washed overboard in a storm several years ago. It was a terrible tragedy."

Siegfried turned to Sally and took her hand. "She was a wonderful woman," he said earnestly, as though seeking to convince her. "And such a beautiful singer."

"It was your singing that attracted us," she replied. "Ewan heard you first."

"Ah, well, he always had a good ear for a tune," Siegfried laughed. "But his singing! No, that is not his gift."

Ewan nodded with good humor. He had always liked Siegfried. They'd first met when Ewan was in his early teens. Hilda was still alive then, and the couple gave him shelter during one of the many periods when his mother had found it convenient not to have him around. He owed to them, apart from the warmth of their hospitality, the ability to express his feelings openly—something, he claimed laughingly, that had helped both his sanity and his art.

Siegfried and Hilda sang splendid duets, as well as solos, and made a living, as Siegfried once put it, by being "an inspiration to the inspired." Their concerts always played to packed houses, and on many occasions the evocative power of their singing moved the entire audience to tears.

Hilda's death had devastated Ewan. By then he was living with a coterie of experimental artists, and it had taken several weeks for the news to reach him. Such was the depth of personal loss he experienced, he recalled, that he spent days on end doing nothing but ranting and raging interspersed with long periods of morose silence.

Yet now that he once again had met up with Siegfried, he was amazed at the way the man had coped with his bereavement. True, the lines in his face were etched deeper and his hair had receded, but there was an air of indomitable strength about him, as though the very tragedy itself had forced an unwitting victory from the depths of his spirit. Siegfried might be lonely, he might pour out endless pathos, Ewan thought, but that would be his triumph, not his defeat.

"I'm glad our paths have crossed again," Ewan said. "Maybe you can help me."

"It will always be my pleasure to assist you in any way I can," Siegfried replied. "What can I do for you? It's not money, is it? I have precious little of that!"

Ewan laughed and sipped his drink. Money was a standing joke among the artists, often referred to as 'precious little.' Although it existed on the Inner Isles, precious little of it ever reached the seaborne community, which relied instead on barter as their most common form of trade.

"No, not at all," he said. "It's to do with something that happened to me a few days ago."

He recounted the event that had set him on his quest and all that had happened to date, including the advent of the Haunter. All the while, Siegfried nodded sagely, except when Ewan came to Sally's ordeal. Then he bestowed on her a look of genuine pity and cursed the nihilists for their madness.

When Ewan finished his tale, Siegfried looked at him expectantly, sympathetically, fully engaged. "And what did you feel?" he asked.

"I—I wept at first. Often I still feel like weeping," Ewan answered candidly. "Silly, really. Not like me at all."

"Of course you wept," Siegfried cried. He clapped his hands. "Why do you feel ashamed of that, eh? There is not a day goes by when I do not weep." He jabbed a forefinger at Ewan. "You have been privileged to have a wonderful experience, my young friend. Something has, how do you say, birthed in you."

"You mean you understand what I'm talking about?" Ewan exclaimed.

"Understand? Of course, I understand," Siegfried chuckled. "I have had a similar experience myself, of course. It is what the Nordic races call *sehnsucht*, the state of longing. The eternal, insatiable desire which has no words by which to be expressed."

Ewan was both dumbstruck and delighted. "There!" he cried enthusiastically to Sally, who by now was curled comfortably on the bunk and cuddling a cushion. "I told you I wasn't mad or the only one. There *is* something out there." He turned back to Siegfried. "So are you searching for life on the Rock, too?" he asked.

"Searching? No. I have found!" Their host spoke with such certitude that Ewan peered into his face, searching for the meaning of his words.

"I don't understand."

"I have found," Siegfried repeated simply, "the experience you have had *is* the reality."

"You mean that's all there is? That's it?" Ewan exclaimed. His disappointment was impossible to mask.

"All?" roared Siegfried in a voice that made the glasses ring on the shelves. "All? It is everything. You are one of the privileged few on this God-forsaken planet to have had such an experience. What more do you want?"

"I was looking for—for *life* on the Rock," Ewan answered. "I thought there was someone or something there."

Sally smiled wanly at Siegfried and opened her hands expressively as if to say, "What do I do with him?"

Siegfried leaned forward and patted Ewan on the arm. "Don't be so discouraged, my friend. Here, have another drink. Now listen to me and I will explain what you must do."

Ewan nodded glumly.

"What you experienced was a symbol. How or why, I do not know or care. Maybe it is just the expression of our subconscious. But do not despise it, for it is the artist's light and inspiration. All your life you have wanted to express what you feel through your painting. I, through music and song.

"I know your work. You paint what you most clearly see. The impenetrability and harshness of the Rock. The pain it causes—and nobody understands that more than I."

Ewan nodded understandingly.

"But you long for more. You wish there were something else. We all do. Sometimes that wish becomes a vision—to the favored few, that is. We see a symbol that, how do you say it, encapsulates all our hopes. You saw a jewel, a bright light that slipped from your grasp, and it awoke in you an endless longing."

"So what should Ewan do?" Sally interrupted. "He can't simply go on looking for something that isn't there."

"Precisely. You must look within, my friend. Explore this feeling. And, most important, you must express what you feel through your art."

"How?" Ewan asked.

"Draw it. Paint it. Release all the passion, all the longing. Do not fear this Haunter, for he is only your own fear. Paint the symbol." He stood to his feet, swaying slightly. "I see it now. The bright jewel falling over the sick and dying world. Never able to be grasped. Always out of reach, as all beautiful things are."

A tear started in Siegfried's eye. "Like my Hilda. Paint your falling star above my Hilda, Ewan. Please, I beg you. Let it be your memorial to her life. Express for me my inconsolation. Let it speak eloquently of the love I yearn to give but never can."

Siegfried's feelings moved Sally deeply, and she too felt tears welling up.

"You must do it, Ewan," she implored. "Paint the picture. Siegfried's right. I think I understand now what your experience was all about. I—I'm sorry I didn't take you seriously before."

Ewan looked first at Sally, then at Siegfried, unsure whether they were pulling his leg. Their gazes of intense pity, coupled with their earnest pleadings, were difficult to resist. And he could detect no betraying flicker of humor. Perhaps he had been mistaken, after all. He was chagrined to think so, not to say somewhat disappointed. But if there was one thing he had grasped in his twenty-four years of existence, it was the fact that life often did the dirty on you and you just had to make the best of it. If he was wrong, then the sooner he faced it like a man and expressed his gratitude to his companions for setting him on course, the better it all would be.

He made up his mind.

"I guess you're right," he smiled bashfully. "Why didn't I see it? I thought there was something more to my experience. An external reality. What an idiot! I've been chasing the wind." He looked at Sally, suitably shame-faced. "Yes, of course I'll paint the picture. In fact, I'll start as soon as possible. Siegfried, do you mind if we anchor alongside?"

"Mind? I am overjoyed!" he sniffed. "Fate has brought us together. We are brothers in a common feeling. I shall sing to inspire you. And you, Sally, *Liebchen*, you shall model for my Hilda."

Thus Ewan ceased the quest—he devoted himself instead to the painting. Day after day Sally donned Hilda's old, heavily embroidered clothes and composed herself to lie on the deck amid the carefully arranged flotsam depicting a storm's aftermath. Her face appeared pale and cold, and Siegfried would weep upon seeing her. "Ah, so like her. So deathlike. My Hilda." Then he began singing in a minor key haunting songs of lost love.

O, lost dream;
Faded hope beyond despairing;
Love burns strong,
Though unrequited.
Gone forever;
Bright laugh by lamplight glowing;
Quenched in watery depths;
Beyond the knowing.

Ewan painted furiously. The muse was upon him, he sensed. His brush drew out Hilda's tortured death and the implacable harshness of the Rock. He made the latter tower like a ravenous bird of prey over Hilda's pale form. Then he painted his star, the iridescent orb, tracing its lucent green path through the dark-clouded sky and letting its glow cast across Hilda's pale face before plunging it into the sea, a finger's reach from her outstretched hand. Hope forever beyond the grasping, yet, like the lonesome seagull, always calling.

He wept as he painted and often was too overcome to continue. Every brush stroke evoked memories and yearnings too profound for words. His own experience became inextricably woven into the picture. Exhausted, he would retire for a while, only to struggle back, inspired by Siegfried's songs to squeeze the last dregs of pathos from his heart and onto the canvas.

When the work was finished, both Sally and Siegfried acknowledged it to be Ewan's finest yet—possibly a masterpiece.

Yet Ewan was strangely unsatisfied. He confided in Sally one evening as they lay in bed.

"It's not enough," he said. "The more I painted, the more I felt the longing to reach into the Rock. Instead of providing an outlet, it only intensified what I feel. It's like a thirsty man who paints cups of water. The more he expresses the freshness of the water, the worse becomes his desire to have it. Do you understand? We can't stay here, Sally. I simply must go on."

"Listen to me, Ewan." She spoke earnestly, sitting up on one elbow to face him. "You have the makings of a genius. Of course you aren't satisfied. You must paint and paint. That's what Siegfried said. You'll never be satisfied, but that—that longing inside you will produce masterpieces all the while it is unsatisfied. Even your battle with the Haunter is part of it. Each time you break through this fear, this oppression you feel, you produce great art. You could become famous as the one who gives the finest expression to all the pathos of our existence. It would be a great service to the human race. Don't you see?"

"I understand what you're saying, all right," he replied. "I know I could settle here and with Siegfried's singing keep painting. There's something terribly attractive about it. But it's not what I'm looking for. I want to satisfy this longing, not just express it—not even for the benefit of others."

Sally heaved a sigh of exasperation and promptly turned her back on him. It was no good arguing when he was in this mood. "Well, if that's what you want, that's what you want. We might as well move on tomorrow, I suppose," she said resignedly. "Good night."

"Good night," he said absentmindedly. For a long time he lay staring vacantly at the cabin ceiling. Was he mad? A fool on a fool's errand? What was he giving up? A chance for fame. He had discovered under Siegfried's tuition the meaning of inspiration, and there was no doubt that *Morte d'Hilda* was his finest work. What was it, then, that jarred him, left him feeling unresolved within? It came to him at three in the morning.

"The Rock. There is nothing I can do other than express my antipathy toward the Rock at the moment." He spoke aloud and Sally grunted in her sleep. "Yet, if the Rock gave me hope, how then should I hate it? But if I cease hating the Rock, then expressing inconsolable hope becomes meaningless—because then I'm believing there is something there to *fulfill* my hopes." He sighed. "The only real option is for me to embrace the Rock. Yes. And that means I must go on until I find out how."

Filled with fresh resolve, Ewan drifted off to sleep.

The next morning they bade a reluctant farewell to Siegfried. And, apologizing profusely, Ewan left him the painting.

"I shall treasure it," Siegfried said. His voice was thick with emotion. "Thank you for what you have done. Always when I sing I shall remember you. And though I think you are mistaken, I wish you good luck, my friend."

Sally was sad to depart. She had grown very fond of Siegfried. With tears in her eyes, she kissed him warmly on the cheek.

"Good-bye," she said sorrowfully.

"Farewell, *Liebchen*. I shall always see you, of course, as I see my Hilda so beautifully tragic, child. Farewell. And look after him won't you? He needs you."

Sally gazed wistfully after Siegfried as they drew away from his longship. "We could have stayed there," she said.

"I know," Ewan replied. "I know."

6

LIFE SEEMED STRANGELY DEVOID OF FEELING once they had left Siegfried. Both succumbed to that peculiar emotional flatness experienced by performers when the act is over and the applause has died away. They spoke little to each other for several days afterward.

It was then that Ewan began to go mad.

For want of an easier or even safer explanation, that was how Sally interpreted it. Being reasonably level-headed and practical—a good foil to a mercurially moody artist—she was well-used to coping with the unexpected from her consorts. She recalled the time a former acquaintance had insisted that, to be able to sculpt a figurehead, he needed her to pose by actually being tied to the bow of the boat. She had complied for one session, gotten soaked to the skin, caught a chill for her pains, and, quite sensibly, refused ever to do so again. The sculptor had agreed it was folly and penitently turned to carving goblets instead.

Crazy ideas Sally could handle. Emotional peaks and troughs were the stock-in-trade of life among artists, and she was adept at dealing with either. However, what was happening to Ewan did not fit those familiar categories, and, for reasons hard to define, the matter disrupted her customarily flexible equilibrium. Her best refuge seemed to lie in attributing it to mild temporary insanity on his part.

Sally had grown up in the bosom of a successful family specializing in frankly commercial art. It was an easy life, and upon reaching maturity, she had taken wing for the wide world confident all would work in her favor, if simply for no other reason than because it always had. However, once she had distanced herself from the family nest, matters proved to be not quite as simple. Unable to settle down, she had ventured on a series of transitory liaisons, none of which satisfied either her financial or her personal needs. Cynics described her as an economic moll, providing as she did for the various sequence of men of her acquaintance a small livelihood from her modeling, along with domestic duties and the pleasures of a bedmate. In return for these services she obtained both shelter and a measure of acceptance and social stability in the artistic community.

Ewan had entered her life at a time when she was, as she put it, in between situations. This lean, dark-haired man with earnest brown eyes had proved to be charming, sensitive, and genuinely caring. For the first time in her life she saw the possibility of a long-lasting relationship, and indeed the past three years had not disappointed her hopes. Yet that made his present state of mind all the more unsettling.

She disclosed her dilemma one morning aboard the yacht of a passing friend.

"It's not just this quest of his, Deirdre," she confided, pausing to sip her coffee. "Artists get these obsessions—I know that. It's what's happening to him in his sleep that worries me."

"What do you mean?" Deirdre asked.

"He cries out. Suddenly. You know, as though he were being attacked by some awful monster. To be honest, it frightens the life out of me. I wake up feeling like screaming myself."

"Very disturbing to you, I'm sure," Deirdre replied, drawing deeply on a cigarette. "Is he aware of this? Does he talk about it?"

"Oh, he's aware of it all right," Sally answered with a hollow laugh. "That's what makes it worse. He says he's haunted."

"Haunted?" Deirdre pouted her lips in disbelief.

"Yes. He keeps saying there's somebody there. In fact, he calls him the Haunter. He comes to him in the night mostly, but sometimes even in the daytime as well, when he's sitting quietly. Then Ewan's face goes all ashen and I can see him trembling."

"What does this Haunter-thing look like?" Deirdre shifted in her seat and eyed Sally quizzically.

"That's part of the problem. Ewan can't describe him. Just a shadowy presence, he says. No shape, no color. An influence that keeps threatening him. He thinks the thing doesn't want him to continue with this quest of his."

"Why doesn't he give it up, then? Perhaps that would solve the problem and his nightmares would go away."

Sally laughed.

"You might as well tell him to stop eating," she retorted. "He's quite obsessed with it. You know, I'd thought we had found somewhere to settle. Everything looked fine, and Ewan was painting brilliantly. Then, just as I start to relax, we're up and off again. 'There must be life on the Rock. I've got to find out,' he says."

"What? You're joking! The Rock's dead. Everyone knows that," Deirdre exclaimed. She puffed on her cigarette.

"Except my Ewan," Sally said glumly. "Trust me to land up with a man who wants to be different from everyone else." She took another mouthful of coffee and stared gloomily into her cup.

"Get yourself another man, you should," Deirdre sniffed. "That's what I did when Albert decided we should stop wearing clothes. I mean, *you* might get away with it, but with my figure—huh! Anyway, it's too cold. I left him."

Sally cupped her chin in her hands and sighed. "I don't want to do that," she replied. "I really am fond of Ewan, and the last thing I want is for him to go out of his mind and for me not to be able to help him."

"Don't know what to say, then," Deirdre answered dryly. "Let's hope it's just a passing phase, eh?"

"Yes, let's hope," said Sally.

EWAN DID NOT PAINT during those days immediately following their departure from Siegfried. It was understandable. *Morte d'Hilda* had taken a lot out of him, and he needed time to recharge his creative batteries. Yet Sally knew the enforced idleness was not helping his state of mind. Consequently, she awoke late one morning delighted to find him on deck busy with his brushes and easel. Not wanting to interrupt the flow of his work, she left him until well after lunch and contented herself with quietly tidying their living quarters.

Finally, judging the moment to be right, she approached noiselessly and peered over his shoulder. At first she could make little sense of the distorted and fragmented surreal shapes that covered the canvas. Ewan had consciously twisted and elongated all the perspectives so that it was impossible for a single observer to relate the elements of the picture. A unity of discontinuity was how Sally later described it—a form quite unlike anything he had ever painted.

"Oh, hi," Ewan said, sensing her presence. "What do you think?" Judging by his tone of voice, his mood was brittle.

Sally studied the work, her head to one side. The picture was nightmarish.

An attenuated man with a tormented face, recognizably Ewan, was crawling up a long series of stone staircases—but Ewan had drawn it cunningly, after the manner of Escher, so that what appeared to be up always led down. His limbs flowed like molten wax over the edge of the steps, and he crawled through a lurid pink slime of his own making. A maw-like abyss hung below, yet from its depths shone a green light. She recognized what she presumed to be the Rock. By some trick of perspective, Ewan had contrived it to be in both the background and foreground at once, making it appear as though a bloodstained set of granite teeth was about to crush the entire scene. A long, continuous shadow fell across the fragmented whole, lending it an air of uncertain, brooding menace that made Sally shudder.

"I don't like it," she said, adding hastily, "oh, not the workmanship, that's brilliant. I mean the theme. It's very disturbing."

He turned on her angrily.

"Disturbing? It's the truth!" he snapped. "That's my mind you see before you. Madness, yes! Incongruous folly, yes! Isn't that what my life is all about? I'm trapped, Sally. Trapped, and the jaws are closing!" He strode up and down animatedly, waving his hands in fluster. "I reject madness, but life drives me mad. Time melts. Up is down and down is up. I die stranded on a remorseless stair, my life juices seeping away while all the time the shadow deepens. Yes, it's a nightmare, but I can't stop it. You can't. Nobody can."

With that he smashed his palette to the deck and stomped off to the cabin.

Sally started to follow him but had second thoughts. He was right. She had nothing to say that would help. Feeling useless and wretched, she remained on deck and sat scowling silently at the hated Rock.

Scenes like this one occurred day after day, and there was little Sally could do but wait and hope that, as Deirdre had said, the phase would pass. Meanwhile, Ewan continued to turn out nightmarish canvases with neurotic frequency, alternately defending the subject matter with ferocity and then suddenly becoming lucid and treating the pictures with utter scorn. "Put them up for sale," he would say with a dismissive wave of his hand. "The punters will buy anything. Why not this nonsense?"

During such interludes their lives returned to relative normality for a few, precious hours. But the rest of the time Sally sat alone on the foredeck of their craft with her chin cupped in her hands, gazing forlornly at the ever-gray sea while Ewan moved about like a ghost, painting his surreal images in a futile attempt to exorcise the agony within. It would be only a matter of time before he cracked completely, she decided.

THE PIRATES CAUGHT THEM UNAWARES several days later. Not that they were real pirates, much to Sally's (and for that matter Ewan's) relief—though Sally wondered if he was fit to consider anything in his tormented, sleepless condition.

Since leaving Siegfried, they had drifted continually eastward with the current, keeping a steady distance from the Rock and meeting no one other than Deirdre. Then, late one afternoon, Sally spied signs of habitation on the horizon. Soon they were within range of what appeared to be a very large community raft anchored extremely close to the Rock.

"Hey, Ewan, come and take a look at this," she called.

He joined her on deck and peered through his telescope without comment.

"What can you see?" she asked. "Do you recognize anything about them?"

"Dunno," he grunted. "But we'll soon find out. They're sending a boat." He paused and fiddled with the telescope curiously. "Good grief! They look like pirates!"

Sally's brow furrowed with anxiety. Surely this crazy quest hadn't landed them in yet more trouble? She had enough to cope with as it stood!

There was little they could do except watch and wait. The boat approached rapidly under full sail and bore the unmistakable lines of a small-scale, old-fashioned pirate galleon, complete with Jolly Roger and cannon. Attempting to outrun it would be futile.

Yet their apprehension turned to incomprehension. The galleon dropped sail and drew alongside. And instead of hearing the clatter of cutlasses or the roar of cannon fire, they noted only the heavy beat of dance music. The 'brigands' were having a party, and a fancy dress one at that!

Thoroughly bemused, they watched helplessly as young people dressed in pirate costumes poured onto the deck of their boat and, without any by your leave, began to dance as though it was a stage designed and provided for just that purpose. Soon there was scarcely room to move.

Sally put her hand to her mouth and giggled at the incongruity of it all. These people were having *fun!* After the traumas of the past few days, she had almost forgotten the meaning of the word. A bit of light relief was precisely the tonic she needed—so, leaving Ewan still in a state of stunned disbelief, she began to mingle with the crowd and move with the inviting beat. It was a pleasure to have some cheerful company around again.

"Hi, baby. How you doing?" The greeting came from a good-looking young man dressed in white pantaloons and a sleeveless leather jerkin.

"Hi," Sally shouted back. "What's your name? Who are you people?"

"Jacques," he replied. "I guess we're just a fun crowd who likes to groove together. Who are you?"

"Sounds great. I'm Sally, and that's Ewan over there." She pointed through the crowd in his direction.

"What's up with him?"

"Oh, he's having a bad time. Life's heavy for him at the moment," she answered vaguely.

"Why not join us then? We'll cheer you up. Everyone needs a bit of a party sometimes." He grinned. "Anyway, a good-looking woman like you shouldn't be moping around on this old tub."

Sally laughed. "Thanks. I'll see what he thinks. Maybe we will."

The happiness of this crowd was infectious, and once Ewan got over his initial incredulity, he cheered up considerably. When Sally told him of Jacques' invitation, he responded positively, much to her relief. A diversion from his claustrophobic madness was just what they needed, he said. He hoped, too, that there might be somebody among so many people who would have some useful leads to assist him in his quest.

Sally rolled her eyes in mock despair at this but was pleased at least that he wanted to enjoy the fun. She introduced him to Jacques, and the two seemed to click. Applause greeted the news of their easy recruitment, and before long *Seaspray* was in tow while the party continued unabated on both vessels.

Ewan laughed for the first time in days. "Is life really just one long party for you people, Jacques?" he asked.

"Yes and no," Jacques replied. "We're a very creative group, as you'll see, but the party often sets the mood for us. It's where a lot of us get our inspiration. Anyway, don't worry about it. Just enjoy, man!" He gave Ewan a slap on the back and disappeared into the melee.

That evening the party continued aboard the communal raft.

As Ewan came in a long-haired hippy named Tim approached him. "Try some, man," he offered. "Release some good vibes."

Ewan accepted, and he soon drifted into a state of blissful euphoria, gently borne along by the laid-back rhythms of the music. The lights blurred and the room filled with a golden haze. Dancing figures floated with dreamlike grace. One of them, whom he presumed was Sally, detached herself and glided toward him, arms outstretched and inviting.

He awoke the next morning feeling fantastic. It took some time for him to adjust to his surroundings—he was by himself, in a strange bed, in a cabin with walls completely covered by psychedelic art. He had no idea how he got there.

Just as he was wondering what had become of Sally, a figure appeared in the doorway—Jacques.

"Hey, man. How you doing?"

"Oh, fine. Just fine," Ewan replied, running his fingers through his tousled hair. "I must have slept like a log."

"Great." Jacques eyed him quizzically. "I thought you might like to join one of our teach-ins sometime today. Just to prove life isn't one long party for us! Sally tells me you're on a quest. Is that right?"

"Yes. And thanks—I'd appreciate coming," Ewan replied. He yawned. "By the way, where is Sally?"

"Oh, she's around, you know—somewhere," he answered vaguely. "See you when you're ready."

Ewan emerged onto the deck and took his bearings. This was the largest commune he had ever encountered. The number of rafts strung together made it a complete, floating village. Yet their proximity to the ugly brown mass of the Rock surprised him; he wondered how they coped with moving such a large platform to a safe distance during the inevitable storms. Maybe they didn't.

The other thing that struck him was the colorfulness of his surroundings. The ghastly light did them little justice, but even so it seemed that every wall, and even much of the deck, was decorated with vivid, bold abstracts, some of them of wondrously complex designs. He was interested to know what inspired these artists.

He ambled along the main thoroughfare. Somebody was fingering an instrument—the music was cool and easy. A young woman played with her baby outside her cabin. She greeted Ewan with a smile. Many others did the same. He could get to like this place, he decided.

He came across Sally by accident. She wore a long, pale-blue caftan and sat cross-legged on a cushion next to a similarly clad young man with whom she was in conversation. She looked very fresh and softly sensual.

Before Ewan could greet her, she glanced up and saw him.

"Ewan! I was wondering where you were. Come and join us," she called. "This is Tim. Do you remember? He spoke to you last night."

Ewan laughed as he sauntered across. "I can't remember anything much about last night, I'm afraid. Hi, Tim."

Tim faced him with an outstretched palm. "Peace," he answered.

"I was just talking to Tim about you," Sally said. "He's interested in this quest of yours. Why don't you tell him about it?"

Ewan sat down, putting aside his slight unease at finding Sally with another man and having received no explanation as to where she had been all night. He recounted for the young man the event that had changed his life, though for reasons he couldn't explain, he omitted to reveal just how deeply it had affected him.

Tim listened with casual patience.

"Life on the Rock?" he pondered. Then, gazing at Ewan with raised eyebrows, he said in a natural voice—as though he'd heard the most obvious thing in the world—"Of course there is."

❖ 7 ❖

TIM'S MATTER-OF-FACT RESPONSE LEFT Ewan stunned.

Sally, for her part, was flabbergasted. Whatever else she had expected to encounter in this hedonistic community, it was not support for Ewan's crazy, exotic quest. She was the first to recover her voice.

"Are you serious, Tim? I mean, are you saying there really is something out there? Life? On the Rock?" she asked in disbelief.

Tim smiled at her incredulity. "Right on. Never more serious in my life." He spread his hands expressively. "Hey, where have you people been? It's time you got tuned in before it's all over! Get cool, man! Come to the teach-in and find out where it's all at. Jacques has already invited you, hasn't he?"

Ewan nodded affirmatively.

Tim rolled to his feet. "Well, got to split for now. See you later, then." He let the back of his finger stroke across Sally's cheek. "Ciao, sister," he murmured and ambled off.

Thus Ewan and Sally found themselves sitting cross-legged in a motley circle of about twenty people, mostly young, some evidently still spaced out from their previous night's activities. A few had brought along their musical instruments and were quietly tuning up. In spite of the laid-back atmosphere, an air of subtle expectancy hung over the meeting.

Looking about him, Ewan decided he would have to do something about his wardrobe if he and Sally were to stay in this community. Fashion evidently was an art form here, notably characterized by bright colors, psychedelic patterns, and exotic accessories, the latter ranging from endless varieties of beads to dyed albatross feathers. Looking at his own seafaring trousers and T-shirt, Ewan felt decidedly drab. Sally was much more in the part with her flowing blue caftan and matching headband. He wondered where she had obtained it.

The arrival of Tim and Jacques brought an end to his musings. The latter acknowledged their presence with a casual wave as he took his place in the circle.

Being noticed by the leader felt good—yet if Ewan and Sally had anticipated a discussion group for their benefit, they were quickly disillusioned. At a signal from Tim, the musicians began to finger a cool, unstructured melody, improvising as they played. It was music suited to meditating. Sitting cross-legged with their backs erect, palms on their knees, and eyes closed, the members of the group, as if on cue, started to sway their bodies gently in time to the music.

Then one of the girls began to sing in a clear, lilting voice:

The Rock, the Mother of our dawn;
Gifts the sea from which we're born;
Waters of Her womb;
We are coming soon.
We are coming soon.

Spirit of free-born open skies;
Breath of life within us cries;
Wind-song of the heart;
We are coming soon.
We are coming soon.

To Her return through love and death;
Universal peace, your breath;
Fearless feel your way;
We are coming soon.
We are coming soon.

The group took up the dreamy chant, "*We are coming soon. We are coming soon . . .*"

Ewan, feeling very detached from the group experience, glanced at Sally. She returned a weak, slightly apologetic smile. They had not spoken about the previous night's activities, as neither had felt able to broach the subject. In any event, both were unsure as to exactly what had occurred. Instead, in the interest of peace and by mutual silent consent, they had let the matter go, but not without a certain degree of unvoiced awkwardness. To avoid that difficulty, Sally closed her eyes and sought to go with the music. Ewan lounged on one elbow, gazing unfocused into the distance, pondering the words of the song.

The notion of the Rock as the universal Mother was novel to him. It was also unsettling, for his relationship with his own mother had always been fraught with tension and conflict. He recalled the numerous occasions when she had sent him, an only child, to stay with others while shadowy men slipped in temporarily to take his place in her affections. Then, just as suddenly, they vanished and she welcomed him back with open arms, showering him with overweening matriarchal adoration as if to assuage her conscience by making up for lost time. He wasn't sure which had been the hardest—the separation or the smothering. If the Rock was Mother, he hoped fervently that it was not like his own.

"Do not fight it. Explore it. Unite with it. All is one."

The earnest voice belonged to Tim. At once the chanting intensified, and a powerful emotional force swept through the company like a sudden breeze. Psyche conjoined with psyche in mystic ecstasy; it was the most tangible spiritual experience Ewan had ever encountered, and its sheer intensity jolted him.

One by one the members of the group rose to their feet and began to drift around in a detached, free-form dance, flowing with the hypnotic ebb and rise of the music, arm brushing arm, bodies weaving in harmony, beatific smiles on their faces.

Ewan and Sally simply sat and watched from the outside. Neither was yet ready for such an abandonment of themselves.

Then, unexpectedly, the tempo changed and the easy rhythm gave way to a strident rock beat. The spell was broken, and the dancers, released from their trance, broke into sudden, energetic movement. Another party was under way.

The pulsating music was a signal to the whole community. Within moments, people streamed onto the walkways, bustling and chattering with the buzz of life. *It just as easily could have been a market day,* Ewan thought. All around them music blared from doorways and windows in a tuneful cacophony.

Jacques came across to where Ewan and Sally sat. He laughed at their bemused expressions.

"Welcome to Vanity Fair," he said, adding, "Forgot to tell you. It's one of our carnival days. We have lots of them. Come and enjoy the scene. It's all part of the experience."

Ewan looked around him. Some members of the group were still spaced out, but most were gradually dispersing to join the crush of people moving toward the center of the floating village.

"I'm not really sure how to—or whether I want to," he answered slowly. "I was expecting something a bit different, to be honest. You know, a discussion of some kind. It threw me a bit when you began to meditate. I couldn't get into it, anyway."

"Truth lies beyond discussion," Jacques replied enigmatically. "You have to feel it, experience it."

"Is that what you mean by this 'tuned in' business?" Sally asked. "I mean, just what are you people into? Come on, Ewan's right. We're new to all this—so why don't you tell us what you really believe?"

"Hey, philosophy time," Tim drawled as he sauntered across. "Tell it like it is, Jacques!"

Jacques sat down and assumed the posture of a teacher. "Okay. Here goes, then. We all agree we live in an uptight world, right? Everyone's got their hang-ups. Mostly it's to do with the Rock. We all know it stops us exploring any further, so it's become the symbol of repression—political, psychological, aesthetic, you name it. The Rock dictates everything we do and think, even our hatred of it. We're trapped, every one of us."

He paused to let the point sink in.

"We need a way out, some expression of the human spirit which is true freedom. That's what 'tuning in' is all about."

"So how do you do it?" Sally insisted. "I mean, we know all this stuff about the Rock. What's new?"

"An existential cosmic leap," Jacques replied.

"Why don't we take them to see Frannie's demo?" Tim suggested. "That will help them see what we're getting at."

"Good idea," Jacques agreed.

Ewan and Sally looked at each other, shrugged, nodded, and said, "Fine." Two minutes later, accompanied by Tim and Jacques and following the drift of the crowd, they passed under a psychedelically decorated arch embroidered with the name, *Vanity Fair*. It led into a square that contained a large number of stalls and stages and positively bustled with people.

"Have a look at this," Jacques invited, indicating a small improvised stage to their left upon which stood a girl and a fellow. A small crowd had gathered for a performance which evidently was about to begin. "That's Frannie. Her guy's name is Will."

The latter had positioned himself at center stage, standing with arms and legs outstretched. Frannie, wearing a white straitjacket, began to march jerkily up and down before him, her features fixed impassively ahead as though she were an automaton. Two parallel white lines painted on the stage floor dictated her path. Yet every so often she turned abruptly and tried to cross one of the lines in order to reach the back of the stage, where there stood a jug of water on a table. On each occasion Will barred her way and forced her back between her parallel white lines.

The girl's frustration soon became evident, and she began to give vent to it by struggling with her straitjacket and crying out at the top of her voice, "I hate you! I hate you!"

Then she stopped and looked upward, as though something had caught her eye. Slowly, a light of realization dawned on her face. With a sudden shrug, she shook off the straitjacket and, giving a cry of delight, began to flap her arms and mimic a bird flying.

On seeing this, Will collapsed to the ground. She leapt over him unhindered and reached the table. Theatrically, she raised the glass of water in a toast and drank deeply, all to the hearty applause of the onlookers.

"The existential moment," explained Jacques, "is when you abandon yourself to your feelings and choose by some self-determined act to break free from the boundaries set by the Rock. That's when you authenticate your being and prove yourself to be truly human."

"That's tuning in," Tim added. "After that, there's no limit to the reaches of your spirit. What you previously thought was reality turns out to be just a tiny part of an infinite cosmic consciousness. You wonder how you ever lived in such a shrunken world before."

"I don't understand," Sally interposed.

"The Rock is finished," Jacques answered promptly. "We're on the threshold of a new age—an age without violence or alienation. A time when love will unite us all. We'll no longer fear the Rock—we'll transcend it in our spirits."

"That sounds really great," Sally interjected enthusiastically. "I've often felt uptight, detached, and—and frightened of the Rock. I mean, we've been reared to think that way, haven't we?"

"But the Rock kills people," Ewan protested. "You can't just reinterpret it in psychic terms. I mean, it's a harsh reality that won't go away just because we pretend it has!"

"Didn't you listen to Mary's song?" Jacques asked. " 'Love and death.' Death isn't the end. Death is joining the one cosmos. It's the final fusion of our spirits with the cosmic Mother, and the Rock is part of that. Sure, the Rock spells death, but that's the noble tragedy that births new life."

"So there's nothing to fear about death?" Sally nodded. "Or about love?"

Tim smiled appreciatively at her. "I think you're getting there, sister," he said.

"So where does my experience fit in with all this?" Ewan demanded. He could not hide the resentment in his voice. Sally was embracing the new creed all too easily. Had she embraced Tim, too, he wondered?

Jacques intervened. "You are a very special person, Ewan. Few people have spontaneous experiences like yours. No wonder you set out on a quest. I mean, you've discovered single-handedly that the Rock doesn't have to be an enemy. In fact, it attracts you now. All you want to do is communicate with it somehow. That's great, man!"

"So you're saying that what I had was some type of cosmic, mystical experience, and you've all had similar?" Ewan said slowly. He warmed to Jacques' evident sincerity and affirmation.

"The difference is, you got there without drugs, or music, or—or anything," Jacques said enthusiastically. "That's incredible. You have fantastic vibes, Ewan!"

"What do you think, Tim?" Ewan asked.

"You should join us, both of you," he answered promptly. "You'll be a natural guru, man. Go with it. We need you guys."

It was a generous invitation, and instantly Ewan felt ashamed for questioning Tim's motives. He looked around him. The warm sensuality and psychic energy of these people, coupled with their laid-back creative lifestyle, had a lot going for it. Sally obviously felt at home here, and Ewan could sense that in the last few minutes she had radically revised her opinion as to the significance of his experience. Perhaps he had been wrong, too. Ignorantly, he had thought of people living on the Rock, or of maybe finding a way through it to a better world. He saw now that this had been a crude, materialistic view. The cosmos pounded with life! Eternal Spirit was everywhere for the having—all you had to do was take the leap. Accidentally or fortuitously, he had already done so.

His sense of relief was sudden and overwhelming, so much so that it brought tears to his eyes. The terrible tension of the past few days was broken. No further need to strive and to search. Just embrace the universe and abandon yourself to Love.

"It . . . it's j—just too much," he stammered. "Amazing. Fantastic, like you say. Yes, I—we want in." He flung his arms around all three, and they embraced warmly. People nearby sensed the occasion, and they joined in and engulfed Ewan and Sally with empathetic hugs of acceptance.

"Great, man," Tim replied. "Great."

Ewan had resolved his quest—at least, for the moment—and became a monistic, romantic, existentialist guru with arcane undertones, and with a sigh of relief Sally settled down to have a good time.

THEY SPENT THE REST OF THE DAY drifting in a happy haze around Vanity Fair, discovering something of the vibrant creativity of the community. These people turned almost everything into an art form, from food and clothing to exotic paintings and sculptures. They soon discovered, too, that happenings—spontaneous, creative events—were commonplace.

Some of these were fun, like the group caricature of the sea crashing against the Rock. As many people as possible were bundled together in a tube of blue paper; they rolled across the floor against a row of spectators until everyone fell over in a helpless sprawl of intermingled bodies. The apparent point of the exercise was lost in the considerable groping fun that people had untangling themselves from one another.

There was no end to the soapbox teachers, either.

"Fear alienates us," one cried. "Fear of giving ourselves, fear of nature. We've been taught to hate what we fear. So we have wars and violence. But what we really need is love—love to embrace and to be embraced by the cosmos. Release, through love, the spark of deity within each of us, and we become part of the universal godhood."

He was urged on by a zealous female entourage, who patently displayed an avid commitment to be generous with love.

That night there was a party in one of the larger cabins. Ewan and Sally drifted by at mid-evening. By now she had dressed Ewan in more appropriate gear for their new scene. In headband, psychedelic smock, beads, and sandals, he felt quite the part.

An atmosphere of heady sensuality filled the room, and the sweet smell of cannabis drifted with the smoke. A couple on the stage were engaged in an erotic dance-drama. They were dressed in costumes consisting of little more than black leather straps that accentuated their figures. The message was unambiguous.

As the music drifted through the night and the drinks and drugs moved round, what few inhibitions existed soon began to fade, and the carousing got under way.

A girl sidled up to Ewan. He recognized her as the Mary who had sung that morning. Now, in this sensual atmosphere, he recalled that the ambivalent implications of her song hadn't escaped him at the time. He looked in vain for Sally through the smoke, but she was nowhere to be seen.

Ewan succumbed without protest. He and Sally never spoke about it, or about what had happened to her that night, either. Infidelity was to become a part of their accepted lifestyle—a lifestyle that was to last for several months as they settled in to become full members of the community and to explore the heady realms of transcendental consciousness.

They met many fascinating people, for the philosophy attracted a large and diverse following. This was, as they said, where the action was.

Cyril, with effete urbanity exuding from every pore, was a sculptor who regularly produced masterpieces. Sally struck up a friendship with him.

When she accused him one day of vanity, he laughed.

"Life is vain. She preens herself even in death," he replied. "Look at the garish fungus that grows on dead wood, if you doubt my assertion. All is vanity, so why should I not be so, too?"

Ewan discovered that the arcane was never far from this community. It was considered a virtue to explore the boundaries of acceptability and to push them back farther. Sex and drugs were commonly used to promote consciousness-raising experiences, as were yoga and meditation, along with various food and health regimens. Some took it all a stage further and engaged in conscious efforts to manipulate spiritual power. They spoke of out-of-the-body experiences and of "spirit guides" who shared the secrets of the cosmos with them.

He too became a dabbler in such matters yet was never fully persuaded. Though Ewan readily acknowledged the reality of occult experiences and was party to many psychic phenomena, something in the back of his consciousness still hung onto the simple purity and spontaneity of that night when the light had fallen from the Rock. That fateful event remained a unique experience always quite distinct from his other weird and wonderful trips.

With a decided emphasis on the primacy of *eros* and *thanatos*—love and death—within the community, it was no surprise to discover that sexual themes and the exploration of violence were commonplace.

David, who lived three cabins down from Jacques, painted pictures of the Rock. He also painted naked women. Usually he combined both subjects, so that the Rock appeared as a woman lying stretched out across the sea and yet still retained its own familiar identity. He was a highly accomplished artist, and Ewan marveled at his technique. "Earth mother, earth goddess," David explained. On occasion, he painted dying figures clinging to his earth-woman. "Death is the ultimate sexual experience."

Sexual death was also the theme of a fringe group Ewan found distinctly not to his taste but whom, to his surprise, Sally quite liked. They were the true pornographers of the group—those who used their talents to explore sadomasochistic fantasies to the full with unbridled, lascivious imagination. She posed for some of their work, and soon was in constant demand by painters and sculptors because of her attractive face and figure, along with her willingness to assume any role required of her.

It was the one thing that disturbed Ewan. In other respects he had become a full-blown hedonist, indulging freely in all the vices from which he previously had abstained, reinterpreting them as expressions of love and freedom. Almost nothing was beyond the pale now. All fed his ravenous desire for mystical experience and his new belief that indulging the senses was the means by which to obtain it.

The Haunter changed, too. He still turned up regularly in Ewan's dreams; but instead of being the threatening figure who previously had terrorized his sleep, he became something of a welcome friend. Ewan's drug trips often featured this now-benign being watching over him and filling his mind with a cornucopia of delights. Like a cosmic conjurer, the Haunter apparently was capable of producing virtually anything to order within Ewan's imagination, saturating him with vivid colors and inspiring him with soaring flights of fantasy. Ewan often painted what he saw, and as a result he produced work of quite startling brilliance.

Ewan became, as predicted, something of a guru for the others. Coached by Jacques and Tim, he interpreted his experience as a cosmic revelation in accord with the philosophy of the commune. They all needed to see the light. It came to some from out of the blue, he taught, but you also could seek it transcendentally through meditation, drugs, and sex. Many were happy to sit at his feet and to drink in his words.

"Love and do as you please. There are no other absolutes. Shed your lesser rules and inhibitions. Let love alone be your guide in every situation, for by doing so you embrace the cosmic soul and enter perfect harmony." For such thoughts, his willing audiences applauded him.

As for his sense of longing—the yearning that had hurt like the pain of an unreachable love—he consigned it to the catacombs of his soul. Sensuality replaced searching. Present fulfillment negated hope. The arcane obliterated mystery. And the universal Mother smothered his need for a father.

Life might have continued indefinitely in this fashion for Ewan and Sally—if not for one fateful day when the commune received two visits.

❖8❖

AS UNEXPECTED AS A GUST OF WIND, as determined as a falling stone, certain days come that change the course of human destiny. Yet who can say why this day or that one? Thus Ewan awoke on an otherwise undistinguished Thursday in March with the quite irrational premonition that this would be for him one such day.

Pondering this notion during his waking moments, he glanced at Sally's slumbering form beside him and smiled. He was glad it was she and not one of the number of women he had known over the past months. Not that his conscience troubled him. He had, he thought quite properly, moved beyond the outmoded concept of fidelity, taking to its logical conclusion the idea that if love imposed no bonds—and they never had entered the bond of marriage, had they?—then both were free to do what they wanted. Indeed, he had freed himself from almost all restraints as his former mores dissolved in the slinky miasma of sexual permissiveness.

For all that, though, Sally remained special. "What is it about her?" he mused half aloud, yet not so loud as to awaken her. "Has it just to do with taste, like a natural preference for cod rather than mackerel? Put it down to chemistry, then. That explains it all—and it's the reason I'm not homosexual and accounts for why I don't fancy every girl I meet. Simple."

Now he scratched his head.

"On the other hand, supposing it's love? But love is undifferentiated in our society. Everything's love. What's special about this one? Loyalty? Familiarity? Makes us sound like a couple of old sweaters—worn but comfortable. Is that why we always come back to each other?" He dismissed the thought as unworthy. Sally wouldn't appreciate the comparison.

Suddenly, Ewan had the sneaking suspicion that he was missing some vital piece from the jigsaw of his life. This wasn't the first time he'd felt so. He laughed at the irony of it all and swung out of bed, disturbing Sally in the process.

"I love you, darling," she grunted sleepily. He hoped she knew whom she was addressing.

He rummaged about for the necessary items to brew some coffee, got it started, and wandered into his studio. They lived on the communal raft nowadays, finding it much more convenient and closer to the action—as well as more spacious—than *Seaspray*.

Quizzically, head to one side, he contemplated his latest work.

Like all his best paintings these days, it focused on the shimmering green light that had launched him on his quest. But, true to his current philosophy, he had thoroughly reinterpreted the phenomenon as a cosmic revelation of the universal life force into which he and others had tuned. Sometimes he depicted it by filling the canvas with an explosion of vivid, vibrant color. On other occasions a noble hero bore the light in the finest tradition of romantic idealism. In Earth Mother mode it shone forth from a voluptuous goddess.

This latest work, which Sally considered his finest, depicted a coffin floating on an ethereal sea meant to represent the realm of mystic consciousness. Within the coffin lay a broken eggshell, idealizing death, white against the red silk lining. From deep within the shell glowed the green light, shining like a beckoning beacon, drawing the onlooker farther and farther in until, mesmerized, one fell endlessly into the universe of eternal birth, there to be reincarnated through every act of love.

Ewan liked the more or less finished result. Yet, even as he studied it, an odd feeling of detachment came over him. Was this really the truth?

He gave a start as Sally, bathed in the sleepy, warm aura of a woman just risen from bed, joined him. "Brilliant," she said, peering through bleary eyelids.

He smiled and put his arm around her.

"Yup. I guess it is," he said.

She shot him a curious look.

"What's up, Ewan?" she asked.

"Oh, I don't know." He laughed lightly, somewhat embarrassed. "Been thinking, that's all. About us. About everything. Just one of those moods really."

He loosened his arm from her, and she recognized his familiar need for space.

"I mean, where do we go from here, Sally? We've tuned in, turned on, taken more trips than a pleasure boat, let it all hang out, done our thing—and a few things that weren't our thing. So now what? Is that it?"

She regarded him cautiously.

"You're not thinking of moving on again are you? Oh, come on, Ewan! Come on! What's got into you?"

"I don't know," he exclaimed. "I honestly don't know."

"Nor do I," she snapped. She scowled furiously and stomped off to the kitchen.

EWAN WANDERED AIMLESSLY around the commune. Unable to account for the way he felt, he responded indifferently to the greetings of his many friends and acquaintances. Their more suggestive invitations he ignored completely. By midday he was sitting alone with his back to a bollard, gazing forlornly out to sea. Life seemed pointless. Suddenly he was overwhelmed by the infantile nature of the surrounding culture. Such silly ideas—carefully cultured unreality dressed up as a vast, cosmic consciousness. Was it all just a way of justifying free sex? Where does the truth lie?

A boat drew near to the commune. Ewan glanced at it idly and returned to his thoughts.

The next moment, however, his attention was broken by the deeply disturbing sound of women screeching and screaming. The noise came from the approaching boat. He leapt to his feet and stared out at the boat as others came running from their business, equally disturbed, to join him on the quay side. In less than a minute, a sizable crowd had gathered, agog to know what was happening.

The craft, a moderate-size yacht painted jet black, came to within about three lengths of the village raft and then swung broadside to reveal some twenty-five women standing on the deck in a row facing the community. All of them were screaming shrilly at the top of their voices—not in pain, Ewan quickly realized, but out of hatred, a hatred that was almost tangible in its impact. There were no men visible on board.

Having attracted their considerable audience by such a simple device, the women, almost all of whom wore dungarees and had their hair cropped, began to raise a huge canvas. It depicted vividly a woman being crucified. The object was shocking and horrific in the extreme.

"That's what men do!" screamed one of the women. "Hate! Hate! Hate!"

The crowd watched this spectacle in stunned silence as the women continued the chant.

There was another flurry of activity on the boat as the women began to raise a huge second canvas. Ewan was horrified—it depicted a man whose body grew out of the Rock and who clearly represented it. He was being tortured at the hands of several wild-looking crones.

"Revenge! Revenge!" chanted the women. "We want vengeance!"

Ewan prided himself on his tolerance, living as he did in this laid-back, free-thinking community. His initial thought was to assume an urbane, man-of-the-world attitude toward what he was witnessing. But something deep within him revolted. Was it the image of crucifixion? The overt blasphemy? He had never considered himself religious, nor had religion in the slightest way ever consciously come within his orbit. He'd thought himself indifferent to blasphemy—yet this image disturbed him deeply. It might mean something to people he had never met, he reasoned.

As for feminism, he was an avid supporter. It was, in any case, part of the status quo in a community which by definition flouted traditional roles. And it was perfectly consistent with romanticist philosophy for women to express their views in such a manner.

So why the problem? Even the extreme violence of the tableau should not have shocked him. He had accepted, after all, the ravings of the pornographers as the harmless dissipation of sublimated sexual distortions. This was only the obverse case, vividly put.

Yet Ewan knew that the cause of his revulsion lay beyond all this. Strangely detached from everyone around him, Ewan began to see through—beyond—the boat with its hideous pictures and raving women. The garish facade seemed torn away like paper, and suddenly he was engulfed in a blinding cloud of noxious, slimy evil. Gobs of filth spattered his mind. The stench of excrement overpowered his senses. His skin ran with pus, and he felt himself sinking helplessly into a vast, open sewer.

With a violent heave of his stomach, Ewan turned aside hastily and at once became gut-wrenchingly sick. Gasping and retching, he cursed the weakness of his flesh.

Sally found him some twenty minutes later.

"Ewan! I've been looking for you. Where have you been?" she demanded. She quickly noticed his shattered condition. "What on earth's the matter with you? Is it something you ate?"

He shook his head and wiped his mouth. "Sorry. No, nothing physical," he croaked. "But metaphorically, yes. That blasted spectacle. It turned me over."

"Oh, that!" She waved a dismissive hand. "You mean the radical feminists. Apparently they put on a tableau like this every so often. One of their most shocking yet, Tim says. It's their way of provoking a violent reaction to stir up interest in their cause."

"Well, they gave me a violent reaction, that's all I can say," Ewan retorted. "Women's rights are one thing—making me sick is another! I genuinely found it disgusting. Didn't you?"

To Ewan's incredulous exasperation, Sally didn't answer at once.

"Well, didn't you?" he demanded.

"In a way, I suppose. But you must admit they have a point which can't be denied. Anyway, they've as much right to self-expression as we have. I think they have a worthy cause."

"You're not going to join them, for goodness' sake?"

"No. But I did have a good talk with some of them when they disembarked. I wanted to know why the man was growing out of the Rock."

"And?"

"And, though they believe in the Earth Mother like the rest of us, they refuse to include the Rock. To them it's an enemy—*the* Enemy. They feel the Rock is the icon of all male arrogance and harshness. They hate it. That's why they showed the man growing out of it."

"They certainly know how to express it forcefully."

"You can hardly blame them. Most of them seem to have suffered at the hands of men at some time during their lives," Sally replied. "By the way, you missed the excitement that followed. They've smashed the sadomasochists' shack. Quite a nasty fight broke out."

"Well, I'm not sorry, really," Ewan answered. "Never was very keen on that stuff. Even though I grant its legitimacy," he added quickly, lest she should think for a moment he entertained any notion of censorship. "You didn't mind it, though. Strange that."

Sally glanced away sharply.

"So now what?" she said, abruptly changing the subject. "What's next in your crazy life, Ewan?"

He heaved a sigh. "Oh, I don't know. Something will turn up, I expect. Sorry I'm not much company today. I'll be all right later. Just need to be alone at the moment."

She gave him a brief, taut smile, and without further comment, turned and walked swiftly away.

Having no desire for food, he skipped lunch and wandered to the far end of the commune's raft, where things were quiet and he could be undisturbed. The light was as ghastly as ever, but a certain gray serenity lay over the ocean. It would help to clear the pollution that filled his mind.

What had he seen? Was his vision of disgusting pollution really a disclosure of the truth about this culture of which he was now not only an acolyte but also a mentor? Corruption overlaid with a fading patina of pleasure-justifying slogans and buzzwords? If so, hell was imminent—and Ewan wanted out.

Considering all this while gazing blankly at the lead-gray sea, he failed to notice a small craft drawing alongside.

"Ahoy, there," cried the occupant. "Make this line fast, will you?"

Ewan jumped out of his reverie. "Oh, sure," he replied half-absentmindedly. "I didn't see you. Sorry. Miles away."

The bewhiskered old sailor wore a battered navy blue cap under which flashed his piercing blue eyes. Those eyes fixed on Ewan as he rose from making fast the mooring. "Who sees anything but at the moment of illumination?" he said cryptically.

Having no riposte at hand, Ewan laughed. Inside, he trembled. The sense of premonition with which he had awakened that morning returned abruptly.

The sailor, apparently unaware of the effect he was having, stuck out his hand. "Baz," he said.

"Oh—er, pleased to met you, Baz. I'm Ewan." He shook the proffered hand.

His new acquaintance eyed him quizzically, "Fancy a drink? You look as though you need to talk."

The invitation came, like the boat, from out of the blue. Ewan was nonplussed: just when he needed to speak to someone outside the commune, this man had come along and somehow perceived his need. Was his destiny in some way tied up with this chance encounter, he wondered?

He suppressed his irrational excitement and gave not a hint of what was running through his mind. "Sure," he replied easily. "Why not?"

Ewan boarded the small vessel, and, descending the steps into the forward cabin, he recognized that Baz was a painter like himself.

"Must do something about the mess one day," his host muttered as they clambered among a tangle of easels and canvases.

Ewan laughed. "I'm an artist myself. Don't worry. My place is just as untidy."

"I thought you were," Baz replied with a quick glance. "Anyway, through here. This is the galley." He produced a bottle of wine from a pile of papers and soon had two glasses poured.

"Can I see some of your work?" Ewan asked. A mouthful of quite excellent vintage had suitably tantalized his palate.

"Hmm. Through here I keep a small gallery—from galley to gallery! The journey of life." Baz grinned at his guest.

The moment Ewan entered the gallery, he knew he was in the presence of a master. He stared with fascination at the man's work, drinking in the stunning luminosity and confident sweeps of color that characterized his paintings. Baz seemed to have captured the essence of those rare, transcendent moments, when the sun broke through the uniformly ghastly skies of their existence and brought all the colors to life. His seascapes were buoyant with life. Portraits of men, women, and—uncommon in Ewan's experience—children arrested vividly the mood of the moment. The face of one little girl positively glowed with life.

"You like my work?" Baz observed.

"Like it? It's astonishing," Ewan replied, genuinely awed. "I truly have never seen the like before."

He moved to stand before a stunning impression of the Rock lying low on the horizon, bathed in light. Marveling at the rich russet hues, for the first time Ewan perceived that the Rock could be truly beautiful.

"How do you do it?" he asked.

The old man smiled. "I try to capture the moment of bright light," he said. "I have less interest in the facts than in the fleeting illusion or impression a scene makes on me. It may sound like a contradiction, but that's the reality for me."

Ewan moved on to study other equally brilliant canvases.

On the far wall, he came to a small curtain fitted with a draw cord of the kind used for unveiling plaques. Curious, he pulled the cord. What he saw almost knocked him off his feet. Flabbergasted and unnerved, he stared in openmouthed incomprehension—for what the curtain revealed was a painting depicting with luminous vitality, a night scene lit by a shimmering green orb falling from the Rock toward a boat.

He had come face to face with his destiny.

"I thought so," said the old man quietly from behind him.

After a long interval, Ewan turned. "Where . . . how . . . ?"

"You've seen it before, haven't you?" said Baz, eyeing him keenly. "Here, come and sit down."

In a daze, Ewan obeyed and eased himself into a chair. All the longing that had first impelled him to his quest revived from the dormant depths of his being, like the awakened desire for a long-lost loved one once you've heard the person is alive after all. When Ewan found his voice, he almost choked out the words.

"You . . . you must have had the same experience. How else could you have painted it? I—I've been looking for months to find someone else, and now . . . you . . ."

Baz smiled benignly. "Always the same," he said.

"You mean, there are others? You've met others with the same experience?"

"I've lived a long time. Traveled far. Yes, I have encountered many."

"Well, where are they all? What did they do? Where did they go? How come you're here?"

Baz held up his hand and chuckled. "Hold on, my young friend! I'll tell you." He settled back and gazed at the picture, but his bright eyes saw far beyond the canvas.

"It happened many years ago, when I was your age, or possibly even younger. One night I was drifting close to the Rock, perhaps closer than I should. Curiosity maybe. Suddenly, I saw this light, high on the Rock. I couldn't believe what I was seeing. I shouted and hollered, hoping for a reply. But none came. I heard only the dying echo of my own voice." Baz sighed. "Then the light fell. Like a graceful flare it was. I hove about, trying to estimate where it would land. I was too late, of course. Everyone is. It plunged into the sea. So near, but so far."

A wistfulness tinged his voice at that moment, and Ewan nodded sympathetically.

"The experience changed my life, I can tell you," Baz continued. "From then on I was fascinated with the idea of the illuminated moment capturing the essence of life. I began to paint with new insight."

"But didn't you feel a great yearning in your heart," Ewan interrupted, "a desire to find the source of that light?"

"Oh, yes. That too. I began to search for a place to land on the Rock. I wanted to track down whoever, whatever, had cast the light toward me."

"Did you find it?" Ewan leaned forward eagerly now. His knuckles grew white as he gripped the arms of the chair.

"It took a long time, but, yes, I did find a landing place," Baz replied.

Ewan was half out of his seat with excitement. "What happened? Did you land?"

Baz lifted his arms expressively and allowed them to fall to his knees.

"Alas, no. I lost my nerve at the last moment," he said. "The sea wasn't right, somehow. I'm afraid I've never been ashore. I left it, and the moment passed."

Ewan looked at him incredulously. "But how could you? I mean, such overwhelming desire as I feel—you must have felt it, too. Just like that, after such a long search, you backed off?"

The old man hesitated, then looked Ewan squarely and openly in the face. "I am old enough to be honest with you," he said quietly. "Something . . . *someone* turned me back."

"The Haunter?"

"You've met him too, have you?" Baz's eyes darkened. "Of course, you have. Everyone does who searches for the light. Well, you may consider me foolish, but I preferred peace." He sighed. "I've had it, too. The Haunter never troubled me again once I decided not to land. So I got on with my painting. With modest success, I may add. I owe my whole style to that moment when I saw the light."

"What about the others?" Ewan demanded. "What has happened to them?"

"I don't meet many others. Mostly, if I see them once, it's the last time. Maybe they land on the Rock and stay there. Perhaps they find people. Maybe they die. I don't know."

Ewan was on his feet now and began pacing the cabin agitatedly. "You've got to tell me where I can land," he demanded. "I must have my chance! Whatever fate or destiny there is has brought us together today. I mustn't let the moment go."

"Oh, it's not that difficult," Baz replied. "He who seeks shall find. In fact, you are not far away now. But I warn you—it's treacherous. And you may expect trouble from you-know-who."

"Stuff the Haunter!" Ewan replied energetically. "What do I look for? I mean, where is the landing?"

"There's an inlet, and a place where the Rock shelves into the sea. It's the only place I know like it. With care you can land there. But be careful—they say you can get washed ashore and never get off again. People perish, so the rumors have it. Not an easy place. Just a mile or two up the coast. But you have to go dangerously close to the Rock to find it. Most people stand too far off, that's why they never see it."

"I'll start tomorrow." Ewan's eyes blazed. "This is what I've been waiting for." He grasped Baz's hands. "I can't thank you enough."

"Don't mention it. I wish you luck," he replied. "Too late for me, I think. Missed my chance. But you're young. Maybe you'll make it."

Ewan tried to persuade the old man to come with him, but Baz was adamant that his time had passed, and no amount of cajoling would alter the fact. Eventually, Ewan conceded. And, reluctantly, he took his leave.

"Thank you again," he said. "I'll never forget what I owe to you."

The old man's eyes became watery. "Don't know why I even called by," he said. "I don't find this lot much to my taste these days. Perhaps Fate decreed that I should meet you. Strange world. Well, good-bye, my friend. And good luck."

SALLY WAS FAR FROM ENTHUSIASTIC when Ewan told her of his meeting with Baz.

"You're just reacting to those feminists," she said coldly. "I know they upset you, but they've moved on now anyway. Why let it get to you like this? A good night's sleep and you'll feel better."

"No, it isn't that," he protested. "Sure, I didn't like their aggression. That's just not my style. But it's more than that. I suddenly saw that we're living in a gilded coffin here. Everything's bright on the outside but putrid on the inside. We wanted to break with hypocrisy, Sally, but we've become hypocrites ourselves."

"I honestly haven't a clue as to what you're talking about," Sally remarked haughtily.

"Can't you see? We call it love, but it's really lust. All we're doing is using a noble word to justify our behaving like animals because we can't *be* like animals. We are something more than that, Sally! That's why we have to con ourselves when we want to give in to our lower nature."

Sally stared at him incredulously.

"What on earth has got into you, Ewan Jones? You've never spoken like this before."

"Well, I'm going to from now on!"

"In which case we'd better get off here before they throw us off!" she shouted angrily.

"Good. Because that's what I want!" he retorted with equal venom. "We never should have stayed here in the first place."

He heaved a sigh and held up his hand in peace. "Sorry, this isn't going to get us anywhere." He paused. "I just don't want to make the same mistake as Baz. He missed it, you know? Bottled out at the last moment."

He reached out to Sally and held her close, but she remained taut.

"I've got to go. I know it's hard, but I want you with me. Really. I love you."

He felt her soften.

"I honestly thought you'd found what you were looking for here," she said quietly.

"So did I," he replied. "But once I saw Baz's painting, I knew I hadn't. This isn't it, Sally. Really, it isn't."

"So you want to find the place he told you about?"

Ewan nodded. "Come with me, Sal," he begged. "I know you're not sure. But let's at least take a look together. It's not that far, and if it's too dangerous we can always come back here."

Reluctantly, and after much persuading, she finally agreed to accompany him—just so that he could lay this thing to rest, she assured herself—but on the firm condition that she didn't have to go ashore with him.

That night Ewan slept badly. The Haunter came back with a vengeance. Ewan's skin crawled in the presence of the sinister shadow that seemed to brood over him. And there was violence this time. He felt red-hot claws tearing into his flesh. His ensuing shout woke Sally.

"Sorry," he groaned.

"I'll be glad when tomorrow's over!" she said.

In spite of the bad night, Ewan felt a new surge of energy the following morning. They slipped their moorings and left the commune unobtrusively in the early light, and soon *Sea-spray* was sailing close to the wind as Ewan looked for telltale signs that would indicate the inlet.

He found it mid-morning when he spied what appeared to be a rough, vertical fissure in the Rock. Ten minutes' sailing brought them close enough to see that this was indeed a cunningly concealed channel. If they hadn't been looking for it, they would have missed it.

Ewan was almost beside himself with excitement.

"There it is, Sally. We've found it!" he cried.

Bringing the helm around and reducing their sails to a minimum, he carefully eased *Seaspray* off the open sea and into the channel. All around them the Rock rose in sheer russet cliffs. For the first time Ewan felt a twinge of trepidation as they passed beneath the awesome heights. He had never experienced anything like this before.

Sally stood at the prow, her face a mask of grim concentration as she checked the depth and kept a sharp lookout for underwater rocks.

Ewan spotted the sloping shelf before she did.

"There it is, Sally," he cried. "Look!"

A tongue of rock ran down smoothly into the sea just a few cable-lengths ahead. At the top of its slope it leveled off somewhere out of sight. What lay beyond was anyone's guess.

"So there *is* a way onto the Rock," Ewan breathed. "I knew it!"

Sally was not enthusiastic.

"Just you keep an eye on the boat," she urged. "It's dangerous here. The currents are very confusing, and the water's not very deep. I can see the bottom. How can anyone possibly land here?"

Ewan ignored her and eased their craft closer. Soon they were within a cable-length of the shelf. Ewan eyed it steadily. A tremendous sense of exhilaration gripped him. This was what he had been searching for these past months. It was what his longing had been all about. He could land here and explore for the first time the inner reaches of the Rock—and discover whoever it was who'd thrown the shining orb in his direction!

"We can't go any closer," Sally warned. "There just isn't the clearance."

"We'll drop anchor and take the dinghy, then," Ewan retorted.

"I don't want to. It looks too risky. Come on, Ewan, let's pull away a bit. This current's too chancy."

He cast his eye up the long, sloping shelf of sea-washed rock. They couldn't go back now. He thought of the wistfulness on Baz's face. Had the old painter reached this far? At least there was no sign of the Haunter.

Ignoring Sally's concerns, he pushed the tiller hard toward the shelf. When they were almost alongside it, in what he hoped was a fairly deep bit of water, he dropped anchor.

"I want you to come with me," he said to Sally.

"I told you I'd only come this far," she retorted. "I'm not going ashore."

"But look, it's so near. It would be a shame not to be able to say you landed."

"I don't care. I'm not going with you."

Ewan huffed with exasperation and tried again to persuade her, but it was no good. Sally was adamant.

"Well, at least come with me in the dinghy," he pleaded. "Otherwise I don't see how I can get ashore by myself. I'll have to wade a bit, anyway. There's no way I can beach the boat on that rock. You'll just have to get me as close as possible and wait until I return."

Nautical logic finally persuaded Sally. She agreed to row him as far as the shelf, but only on the condition that he kept his reconnaissance brief. Ewan assured her that would be sufficient. He would need to organize himself if he were to go further. That could come later.

They launched the dinghy.

What caused the following episode neither could say, for it took both of them completely by surprise. The water was slightly choppy but not hazardous. Sally had maneuvered the dinghy so that a few more strokes of the oars would bring them almost aground on the shelf. In fact, Ewan was ready to jump. Then, out of the blue, a freak wave of enormous proportions caught the boat and flung it onto the Rock, tipping both Ewan and Sally onto the ground and soaking them to the skin. Before they could recover, another wave followed, washing the pair and the dinghy even further up the shelf. Then, just as suddenly and unpredictably, the sea returned to calm.

Gathering their wits, they lay sprawled next to each other.

"We're on the Rock," said Ewan, awestruck.

"We're on the Rock," Sally repeated glumly.

9

FOR SEVERAL MINUTES EWAN AND SALLY LAY on the shelf of rock gazing blankly at one another, unsure what to do next.

Sally felt shocked and angry at the capricious manner in which she had been dumped against her will onto the Rock. Her first instinct was to rant and rave at Ewan for getting her into such a ridiculous predicament. But she thought better of it and managed to bring her feelings under control by breathing slowly and deeply. She realized she was quite frightened.

Ewan, elated by the fluke landing, should have leapt to his feet at once and begun eagerly to explore his new surroundings. After all, he had spent months searching and longing in the hope of precisely such a moment as this, and now he had arrived. Unfortunately, however, like many a dreamer, he discovered his nerve to be less strong in the moment of truth than he had fondly imagined it to be. He was as frightened as Sally.

With extreme caution, he looked around. It was probably safe enough to risk standing, he decided. He told Sally so.

Her sardonic expression made it clear his reassurances hadn't impressed her. Nevertheless, she accepted his hand and stood up with him.

Their first impression was one of nausea. Accustomed as they were to a lifetime at sea, where the gentle roll of their boat felt as solid beneath their feet as the ground would to a land-dweller, the stability of the Rock registered in their minds as a disagreeably heaving geological monster. This *terra firma* seemed more like an earthquake, and their first attempts at standing up resulted in their giddily stumbling about and falling over. In all, it took some twenty minutes before they had adjusted sufficiently to remain gingerly on their feet.

Their gross physical sensations had temporarily overshadowed other, less tangible, feelings. With the stabilizing of their sense of balance, they each became distinctly aware of just how eerie this place was. Severed from all contact with familiar people and places, they were in forbidden territory—a land of taboo where, presumably, nameless horrors awaited the feckless, let alone the presumptuous, trespasser. The terrifying, impassive silence warned of powers wishing not to be disturbed on pain of having loosed upon them the Dreads and Wraiths, those pitiless ghouls that devoured the souls of lesser men. You could die here, or worse. Foreboding fell over them like a shroud, cloaking their hearts with wordless portents of doom.

"Let's get off here, Ewan," Sally said quickly. "I don't like this place."

Ewan clutched her tightly in his arms, unsure whether he was seeking to protect her or to comfort himself with her presence. Was this what he had journeyed so far to find? He had battled against all the odds—seduction, threats, confusion, doubt—and he had steadfastly overcome them all in his relentless pursuit of the truth. Drawn by that strange, inexorable longing, kept restless by its sweet ache, and now excited by the nearness of discovery, he had arrived at the place of destiny only to be swamped by dismay. They were unwelcome here. No visitors. The doors were closed and the dogs might be loosed. There was nothing to do but go home.

Just twenty meters away their catamaran bobbed on the relative safety of the sea. The dinghy lay beside them. It would be easy to say they had done it—they had stood on the Rock. Memory and imagination could slowly nurture the experience until it evolved into the adventure of a lifetime. *Oh, yes, Sally and I well remember the day. Years ago now, of course, but nothing since quite compares to it. A rare experience indeed—*

horrifying, but you get used to it. Amazing feeling. It changed our lives, of course. You must try it, if you ever get the chance.

"Like the fish that got away," he said to himself. "You'd be lying, Ewan Jones."

Pride fought off fear and gained a reprieve.

"Let's at least go a little further," he murmured in Sally's ear.

"I don't know why I bother," she sighed. He could feel her trembling. "Ewan, don't you understand? I'm scared. This place is weird!"

"I know. I know." He tried to be as soothing as he knew how. "I feel a bit shaky, too. But it's just because we've never experienced anything like this before. We'll soon get used to it, you'll see."

Sally heaved another sigh. "I suppose it was too much to ask, mere mortal woman that I am! OK, then, have it your way. But I'm not going very far." Then, in a last, desperate bid for sanity, she pointed out, "Don't forget we haven't brought any provisions. We'd be stupid to go any distance without food and water."

Much to her relief, Ewan agreed.

"Why don't we just climb to the top of this slope and see what's there?" he suggested. "At least that will give us some idea of the lay of the land. It'll help us plan what to do next."

Progress up the steep and somewhat slippery slope wasn't all that easy due to their lack of experience in walking on land. It wasn't long before they realized they could do better on their hands and knees; that way, at least they wouldn't fall over.

Their sense of awe grew the further up the slope they scrambled. Sally glanced longingly back at their boat nestling against the shelf. They were a good thirty meters above its deck, and it looked disconcertingly small. She had never felt so far away from home.

Ewan, grim-faced and silent, continued his inner struggle against the repressive atmosphere of the Rock, and, by sheer willpower, he fought to reconjure his sense of longing. At the moment, however, he was having difficulty believing that the whole affair was anything more than a passing whim, a flippant fantasy he had been fool enough to take too seriously.

One factor kept him going: He was curious. Something about the Rock fascinated him. He had always taken for granted its bland, brown ugliness. And he'd never paid much attention to its surface, even when attempting to paint on the cliff face. But now at close quarters, he saw that it possessed a subtly veined and marbled texture of many varied colors. This observation in itself was of no great significance, except that in his present mood it was sufficient to convince him his initial perceptions of the Rock might not have been the whole truth. It was worth persevering, he presumed, just in case there was more here than at first had met the eye. Moreover, however great the risks, Ewan needed the satisfaction of knowing he had made a thorough job of his exploration.

Fortified and keened by this observation, he became dimly aware of another factor, one almost too bizarre for his mind to handle: There was something unmistakably palpable about the Rock. Physically, it was unyielding, as expected; yet it radiated a kind of power that he sensed was qualitatively distinct from the oppressive atmosphere all around. Was it his imagination, or did his fingers tingle to the touch?

"Nearly there," he exhorted. "Are you all right, Sally?"

She nodded bleakly. He waited while she caught up with him. Beads of sweat had formed on her forehead, and in spite of her exertion, Sally was as pale as a sheet. Ewan could see she was near the breaking point.

They breasted the slope together. A small plateau of jumbled, heavily weathered, barren rock lay before them. Ewan gazed at the scene with eyes full of wonder and excitement. This was his first glimpse of the new world he had so longed to find.

However, his hope-filled gaze turned rapidly into an expression of dismay and incomprehension. Not more than a hundred meters from where he and Sally lay, a concave wall of sheer, smooth cliff stretched upward as far as the eye could see, until its crest was lost somewhere in the ever-present clouds. It was obvious at once that it was quite unscalable, presenting an impassable barrier to would-be explorers.

The realization hit him hard. He swore quietly.

Sally broke into a hysterical laugh. Fiercely and wildly bright-eyed, she turned her sweat-streaked face to his. "It's a dead end," she gasped, breathing heavily. "All this high-blown stuff about lights and quests, all the hassle, all the sleepless nights, and this is what it comes to. You've been conned, my darling—well and truly conned!"

She rolled onto her back and gazed up at the sky.

"There's nothing here. Nowhere to go. The whole thing's a joke. Oh, joy! Oh, bliss!" she shrieked at the top of her voice.

Ewan felt sorely tempted to hit her. Torn between anger and disappointment, he didn't need Sally hysterically rubbing salt into his wound.

"Have you quite finished?" he snapped.

"Oh, darling, I am sorry," she replied, wiping the sweat from her face and into her hair. "But you must admit it is rather ironic. I mean, here we are, terrified out of our wits, expecting to meet goodness knows what, and lo and behold, there's nothing here at all! Come on, Ewan. The Rock is just behaving true to form."

Ewan could hardly gainsay her words. He stared glumly at the blank cliff. In spite of the trepidation he had felt, he was desperately disappointed now. Though he had known his courage might have failed him once—and certainly he would have had a battle on his hands in persuading Sally to join him on a trip into the hinterland of the Rock—at least he would have had a choice. But the scene before him dashed any such hopes. The tale could never grow. *We landed. We clambered up the slope. We could go no further. That's all there is to it.* He would have to rationalize his longing through his art after all. There was no further reality. Life on the Rock? Hah! If there were, you certainly couldn't reach it from here.

"I guess you're right," he sighed. "Still, it was worth a try, I suppose. At least now we know for certain." He hung his head. "Come on, let's go back and get drunk."

Sally put her hand on his arm. Her wild look had turned to one of sympathy.

"Oh, Ewan, I really am sorry for your sake. You know that. I can't help how I feel, because I really was afraid to go on. But I know how much you'd set your heart on this. You must feel cheated."

He shrugged. "There's no need to apologize. It's just the way things are. I'm grateful you came with me this far."

She smiled modestly. "Look, we don't have to rush back. Why don't you take a look around? I know it's not much, but—well, it might help. Go on. I'll stay here and wait for you."

He gave her a rueful smile of gratitude and squeezed her hand. Why shouldn't he take a look around the place—maybe pick up some different images, fresh perspectives, novel feelings? He could profitably weave them into his painting. After all, experience-collecting was an artist's stock-in-trade.

In this frame of mind he rose and, somewhat gingerly, began his reconnoiter of the rock-strewn plateau. The boulders were well-weathered and of great antiquity. The timelessness of the place seemed to Ewan to accentuate the puniness and insignificance of his existence. Generations would come and go, but these stones would remain, unchanged and virtually unscathed. He looked back to Sally, hoping for the reassurance of a friendly wave, but she had turned and was sitting at the top of the slope, her arms clutched tightly around her drawn-up knees. She gazed at the security of their craft below. He wouldn't stay long, for her sake, Ewan decided. Anyway, the powerful atmosphere was playing havoc with his emotions, and already he had begun to feel quite exhausted.

In a few minutes he had almost reached the foot of the cliff. Somewhat unconsciously he decided to touch it and then return. Yet just at that moment, something on his right caught his eye. It was no more than a barely perceptible change in the light—a faint, greenish haze over the boulders—but it paralyzed him in his tracks. Then it began to draw him as irresistibly as a magnet would a needle. Wordlessly, he started toward it.

Suddenly the air seemed charged with electricity. The hair on the back of Ewan's neck bristled. Powers beyond his imagination both attracted and repelled him. He was in the presence of the gods, terrified, overwhelmed. The insignificance he had felt among the boulders was nothing compared to this. Here he was, a passing breath, a mere ripple in the ether. To them his death would be no more than incidental.

Barely able to walk, yet unable to resist the power of its draw, he staggered across the rocky terrain toward the source of the haze. His heart pounded wildly; a kaleidoscope of colors danced before his eyes. His head was fit to burst. He knew he must press on.

His destiny lay beyond one final sloping boulder. Gasping and sweating, he scrabbled to its crown and peered over. There, in an open space, was what he had come so far to find.

Tottering to his feet, he called to Sally.

"Come here! Quick!" he cried.

She turned and rose hesitantly.

"What is it? What do you want?" she called.

"I've found a way into the Rock. Come on. Look!"

It was the last thing Sally wanted to do. Reluctantly, she began to traverse the plateau to where Ewan stood gesticulating. With every step her apprehension grew. Something was wrong, terribly wrong—she could feel it.

She had chosen a slightly different route across the terrain than Ewan had taken. Ewan stood before her at ground level. One glance at the fey look on his face told her he must be deranged. Finally, a few steps away from him, she could see past the last boulder and into a hole in the ground—a narrow, cruciform fissure, dark and forbidding.

"This is it, Sally," Ewan gasped. "This is the way in! Look, you can see the green light. It's the same as I saw fall from the Rock!"

Sally stood stock still. Terror gripped her throat. Her chest tightened, and her body hurt all over. There was no green light. Nothing at all—just darkness.

"Come away, Ewan," she pleaded. "This place is evil. Come on, please!"

He stumbled toward her and took her hand.

"Don't you see?" he whispered earnestly. "The light is the same color as the jewel I saw that night. That's the connection. Sally, I don't think the life is on the Rock. It—it's inside it!"

The horrifying realization dawned on her. "No!" she screamed. "No, Ewan—you're not going in there!" Her eyes were wide with terror. "You can't, anyway. It's too small a gap! I'm not going—don't try to make me. You may be crazy, but I'm not!"

She snatched her hand away and backed off, her body tense with fear. She eyed Ewan warily as he took a step toward her.

Then the long-awaited storm broke.

"Don't touch me!" she screamed. "Get away, you stupid madman! I've had enough of your insanity! Do you hear? I've had enough!" She turned and ran, stumbling and sobbing, toward the security of the slope and the sea below.

"Sally! Sally!" Ewan called after her. "Come back! It'll be all right. Don't go!"

But for Sally, enough was enough. She ignored his pleas. Running for her life, she disappeared from his sight down the slope.

All alone, Ewan turned to face the cross-shaped fissure in the Rock.

At precisely that moment, the Haunter appeared.

❖10❖

EWAN WAS FLUNG to the ground, as helpless as a rag doll in a storm. He needed no further explanation for the hostile atmosphere of the place. In that shocking instant it had become all too clear: The Haunter ruled the Rock, and his power was absolute.

"Do not move!" commanded the uncompromising voice. "You may not pass further."

Ewan was pinioned to the ground by a raw, malevolent power that seemed to shrivel his soul to ashes. He struggled to face his adversary. A monstrous black shadow reared between him and the opening in the Rock—a towering eternal emptiness, the utter negation of all things and the antithesis of hope. Despair crushed the ashes of his quest to powder. *Apologize for your impudence, don't argue, retreat slowly, and you may be able to get out of here alive,* he thought. *If he spares your pathetic little life, it will not be for the sake of mercy or pity—he has none—but because you have the sense to cause him no further irritation.*

Ewan lowered his face to the ground and wept.

"I want to go into the Rock," he heard himself say. "You mustn't stop me."

They were ghastly words—and they surprised him. What a fool to challenge the Guardian of the Rock! *You are a dead man now. Why didn't you just go quietly? Are you really willing to die rather than forsake this mysterious longing of yours?* Ewan knew now—finally, absolutely—that he was willing. He bowed his head in anticipation of the fatal blow.

"You are a fool, mortal." The Haunter addressed him with scornful arrogance. "What did you hope for, eh? Tell me about your dreams, while you prepare yourself for the endless nightmare into which soon I shall plunge you."

His head still bowed to the earth, Ewan spoke like an earnest child making a confession. "I dreamed that there was life on—perhaps *in* the Rock. Good life that called me and drew me to itself. Someone, something that wished me well, that would give meaning to my existence and lead me to a better place—some distant shore. That's what I dared to dream."

The Haunter laughed coldly. "Life? Life on this barren rock? Look at it. Look at it, you little fool! When has it ever spelled other than death and despair for you and your like? Are you so deluded by your arrogance that you can't even see the obvious?"

"But the light—" Ewan began.

"The light was no more than a phosphorescence, a pretty trick of nature."

Ewan faltered. He was thrown by the Haunter's use of the past tense, and indeed he no longer could see the light through the shadow. He gulped for air.

"It was—it is the same color as the jewel I saw," he gasped.

"Coincidence," the Haunter sneered. "You pathetic mortals are all the same. You search desperately for coincidences, those chance happenings in a random Universe, to give some sense of meaning to your miserable lives. If the coin spins twice in your favor, you call it luck. If a star falls and a baby is born, you call it destiny. Stupid mortals! When will you ever learn?"

In spite of his utter fear, Ewan edged a little closer to the shadow and the opening that lay beyond. His movement did not pass unnoticed.

"So, you dare to persist in this folly, do you?" the Haunter mocked. "What is it—curiosity? You just have to find out!"

"No, it's not curiosity," Ewan replied. "It's longing. I have searched for months to find this place. Against all the odds and arguments, my deep yearning to discover the source of that light has drawn me here. I can't go back now. Whatever the cost, I must yield to my true desire."

"People long for many things," said the Haunter. "Humans have many hungers. You need food and sex. You had all this in abundance. Why do you wish for something more?"

"You know the answer to that," Ewan replied steadily. "I perceive you have no mortal needs, yet you have hungers, too." Ewan felt he had gained the moral advantage. He was swift to press home his point. "You have spiritual needs, and so do I. It is in my spirit that I yearn to be satisfied."

"Then the comforts I offer will not satisfy you?"

Ewan shook his head.

"Not even Sally?"

It was a vicious riposte. A pang of remorse stabbed Ewan's heart. In the intensity of the situation he had quite forgotten her. Now he felt guilty.

"You love her," the Haunter reminded him. "She loves you also. Isn't that a spiritual matter?"

Before Ewan could reply, the Haunter lunged in. "You will betray that love if you proceed further. Already you are on the point of abandoning her for this foolish whim. She will die at sea without you!"

Ewan had no doubts concerning Sally's seamanship. She often handled the rigging better than he. He saw that the Haunter's veiled threat was more insidious in its intent, designed to stir up fears that would send Ewan racing back to protect her from unknown dangers.

"I wanted her to come with me—to share in the quest," he protested.

"At the cost of her own inner peace?" came the scornful reply. "She was dragged here against her will by your selfish desires. When was she ever given the chance to make a free choice? You possessed her body, and in that pleasure bonding captured her emotions to your will, demanding more and more sacrifice. She followed you against her better judgment, in spite of the pain it caused her. At last, it became too much, even for her. She has fled for her life. And you abandon her to death! Don't talk to me of spiritual desires. You have despised the best you ever had!"

Ewan was nonplussed—the Haunter was right. He glanced over his shoulder toward the brink of the plateau. Sally would be down the slope by now, back in the skiff, waiting, knees drawn fetally to her chest. How long would she wait? Would she come looking for him? Or would the depths of confusion and fear—and her sense of betrayal—drive her from him forever? He lay in an agony of indecision.

"Let me assist you," said the Haunter. Ewan noticed a sudden change in his tone, though it was not for a moment kindly.

With a drawn countenance, Ewan raised his head and nodded weakly. He was aware his strength was rapidly being drained by the intense demands of this spiritual encounter and the sheer horror of the place. He would have to act soon or die of exhaustion.

Through the empty shadow he could see a world coming into focus. The scene resolved to reveal an open-air art gallery lined with the most exquisite paintings. A continuous throng of viewers passed by, their faces rapt with admiration for the artist's genius. And Sally was there, smiling happily.

"It all can be yours," offered the Haunter. "You have considerable talent. The world hasn't yet done you justice. Many still treat your work as infantile, just because you are somewhat of an outsider. I can change all that—turn you into a master of your craft. Let me be your inspiration."

"You!" gasped Ewan. "But I hate you!"

"I don't expect us to be friends," the Haunter replied urbanely. "But we can trade. Return to your people, and I will supply you with the transcendent skill that most of your peers lack."

"Why?"

"It is in my interests," the being answered enigmatically. "Just as it is in your interests. We all trade for our own motives."

Ewan acknowledged this truth readily enough. People were prepared to enter the most unlikely bargains in business, honorable or otherwise, to obtain their requirements. He recalled the time he agreed to do a series of pornographic drawings for a dealer, simply to purchase paint for his serious painting. He had intellectually transmuted the base pecuniary motive into an abstruse experiment in form and figure necessary for the development of his artistic skills.

The temptation now was strong. He could strike the deal. Forget this vain quest of his, sublimate the longing, trade his soul to—

He hesitated. No, he would not trade his soul. It was a sudden, strange thought. Until now, Ewan had hardly ever used, let alone thought about, the term *soul. Spirit* was the current jargon for the nonmaterial, creative, inspirational side of human personality. *Soul* was an altogether more sturdy word—the essential, reflective reality he called "I." Ewan himself—more than the mere sound of his name. Soul was worth holding on to. Don't trade it lightly.

"I've lived long enough without fame," he replied soberly. "I've also managed with my own talent. At least that's honest. Thank you, but if I'm to become famous, I want to do so without outside assistance. No deal."

The anger and irritation of the Haunter were quite palpable; Ewan felt pricked by a thousand pins and needles. With a shock he realized that throughout this discussion he had been edging unconsciously toward the shadow so that its fringes now played menacingly over his prostrate form. In spite of the pain and discomfort he felt, Ewan had no desire to retreat.

The vision of the art gallery vanished. Now, peering through the darkness, and no more than two meters distant, Ewan could see dimly into the crevice. As far as he could make out, the hole was no more than a shallow trench. For a crazy instant he imagined it had been formed by a man falling from a great height and splaying crosswise into the Rock. At the head of the resultant hole appeared a low tunnel wide enough for a person to enter if he used his outstretched arms like flippers to propel himself forward. It was from there that the faint green light emanated.

Ewan saw that once he entered the narrow trench it would be difficult, if not impossible, to get out again. He would have no choice but to commit himself to the tunnel. Indeed, with so little room to maneuver, he realized that it wouldn't be easy to enter in the first place. He would have to stretch out his body, face down, in a cruciform shape to fit into the hole. Only then would he be able to drop into the trench.

He hesitated. Entry into the Rock would require a total, once-and-for-all commitment.

The Haunter must have read his thoughts.

"Mad, isn't it?" he said. "How ignoble! Look at yourself. Already you are sprawled on the ground like a half-dead cat. Why debase yourself further? Whatever happened to the dignity of man you are supposed to believe in? Can you imagine a more vile position than to crawl on your belly and abandon yourself to the most despised shape in existence?"

Ewan considered the point. He could hardly fail to see how debasing his position was at this moment. If Sally were to return, all she would see was a groveling, tear-stained, and exhausted man—hardly someone to be proud of! Yet the Haunter had made a curious mistake by using the word *abandon.* The word strangely seemed to possess a certain attraction to Ewan.

He paused. "I am prepared to grant you one last chance," said the Haunter. "If you are willing, I will permit you to return to your people as the Seer of the Rock."

Ewan blinked with surprise. "What on earth do you mean?" he asked.

"Based upon your experience of 'illumination,' you already have a reputation as a guru. Unfortunately for you, there are many such teachers and so little distinction between one another. The world soon grows weary of familiar ideas. It needs fresh inspiration. You can provide it. Have you not visited the Rock? Have you not tasted the effects of light and darkness? Who better to resolve the eternal conflict by teaching people to live in balanced harmony with both? With me as your mentor, you could herald a whole new age of unity for the human race."

This new offer presented a heady attraction for Ewan—especially now, in his enervated state. The gurus he knew were too well-fed; their lives had been an easy indulgence in the surrounding pleasures provided by equally sleek acolytes. How shallow they seemed! By contrast, he had trodden the path of true enlightenment. Single-minded searching, pain, loneliness, encounters with ultimate forces—surely this all was the making of a true philosopher-priest.

As for light and darkness in harmony, wasn't that the nature of life, anyway? Day and night, life and death, good and evil—why should these be in opposition? A whole world of possibilities could open up, granting a new perception of reality. If it was true.

Ewan had his doubts. Lying prostrate on the ground, all but engulfed by the Haunter's presence, he marveled that he could think at all. But he dared to.

Monism and the notion of harmony between supposed opposites assumed there was nothing outside a closed universe. There was no "other"—no God, except the projection of people's selves as part of nature. It was a big assumption to make.

Why was the Haunter so intent in keeping Ewan out? Suppose the "other" existed and lived inside the Rock? An even more terrifying thought assailed him. What if the Rock itself was somehow part of the "other"? That might account for the feelings of dread he was experiencing—far more so, possibly, than the presence of the Haunter.

In an illuminating flash, as stark as a bolt of lightning, it dawned on Ewan that there was nothing at all transcendent or otherworldly about his adversary. Every inducement, every enticement and threat he offered was no more than what Ewan could find in any society on earth. To be called Seer of the Rock would mean remaining part of the same old order, however esoteric the dressing. But he wanted more. There was something more here, and it was clear he was being prevented from obtaining it.

Ewan had no need to say anything further to the Haunter. The die was cast. Wordlessly, he began to crawl through the towering shadow toward the crevice.

"You'll die!" screeched the Haunter. "You'll die! I shall kill you!"

Ewan struggled on through the blackness. A stench of hot metal stung his nostrils. His ears buzzed and he could scarcely breathe. Something buffeted his head. The struggle had become primeval.

Ewan gained ground in spite of his failing strength until suddenly, unexpectedly, he was *through the shadow.* He involuntarily let out a dry laugh. He had conquered his fear and now by a miracle of endurance, was lying alongside the crevice. The green light shone clearly from within. It was now or never.

Almost faint with exhaustion, he took a deep breath and began to shuffle sideways to position himself above it.

The shape was exactly his size. There could be no negotiation; it meant lying face down with arms outstretched, or nothing. Utter abandonment—death. Ewan eased himself over the hole. With his toes on the lower edge, hands on either side of the longer rift, supporting himself on his arms, he gazed down into the shallow tunnel beneath.

It would have to be done in one go, a commitment from which there could be no return, no second chance. He began to edge his hands out toward the arms of the crevice until his body formed a perfect crucifix; only his toes and fingertips held him back. One moment of relaxation and he would be in. Ewan took a last, deep breath.

Suddenly Ewan's body was racked with pain. It came as a shock, unexpected. Talons bit deeply into his arms, fierce and merciless in their grip. A huge beak seized him by the neck. A grotesque vulture of hideous proportions had pounced from seemingly nowhere and, with a furious thrashing of wings, sought to tear its prey to pieces. Ewan would have screamed if he could, but the beak had all but choked off his air supply.

The sickening talons gouged his arms as, relentlessly, the creature dragged him from the brink. Vainly, Ewan scrabbled for purchase. The vulture's wings beat the air. Ewan began to faint.

"I'm dying!" he gasped. "Let me go."

"I warned you," rasped the voice of the Haunter from the vulture's throat. "Don't say I didn't warn you!"

❖ 11 ❖

EWAN CHOKED AND STRUGGLED in the vulture's remorseless grip. With eyes bulging and sinews strained to the limit, he fought to enter the sanctuary of the Rock. Finally, in a burst of manic energy, he threw off the creature and scrabbled for the entrance. But the bird pounced on him again in a furious flurry of feathers, fiercer than ever this time.

The pain Ewan could bear. It was the fear of defeat, of losing all he longed for, that was the real horror. He cried out in distress, "Help! Someone help me!"

For a moment Ewan thought it was his imagination, but soon there was no doubt about it. Suddenly the ground began to move. Squirming above the crevice like a speared fish, bound in the vulture's cruel claws, Ewan could see before him that the cross was enlarging. Brilliant, green light streamed from the fissure and flooded his vision, blotting out all else. His pain became insignificant as the glorious luminosity swamped and saturated his entire being. Within moments he felt himself drawn steadily down into the Rock by a confident, determined power, greater than that possessed by the vulture. Somewhere, far in the back of his mind, he heard a faint shriek of defeated rage. The talons loosened their grip, and Ewan sank gratefully into the light.

A pleasing shiver of anticipation ran up his spine as the walls of the Rock closed around him. Then, with a sob of relief, he rested, sprawled cruciately, face downward on the floor of the crevice. He had made it. Ewan Jones was in.

He lay still for he didn't know how long. He only knew he had to recuperate from the ordeal. He pondered what had happened. Slowly he let the awareness of his surroundings sink in. Ahead stretched the low tunnel bathed in soft green light. A wry smile creased his face. He knew everything was going to be all right.

Gone was the dread—that awe-inducing magic that had made the Rock so threatening and "other-ish" from the outside. Here, now, he felt warm and secure, like being back in the womb, he imagined. Indeed, this perception made him wonder if perhaps he had embarked on a journey involving some kind of rebirth, though he had no idea as to where or to what it would lead. Yet this idea, he decided, would enable him to face the one-way journey ahead with anticipation rather than apprehension.

It was only then, having reassured himself he had made the right decision, that Ewan fully realized the secret truth that lay three-quarters buried at the back of his mind. At once he began to thrill with all the excitement of a child who discovers that his best dream, his most hoped for secret wish, is actually true after all! There and then Ewan discovered that the Rock was, in a manner beyond his comprehension, categorically and indisputably *alive!*

Of course, he had thought before how there had to be life on the Rock. How else could the light have been cast in his direction with such unerring accuracy? Had he been questioned, he would have said he was looking for people. How modestly we speak when we fear that our true hope might not be realized and, in consequence, we are made to look foolish!

So Ewan had acted. But now he was without doubt—he knew that his unvoiced and scarcely believable intuition had been the truth. The life was neither on nor in the Rock—it belonged to its very nature. He could feel it, sense it all around him like a vast, warm ocean. This was no petty local deity or animist spirit to be placated by offerings as imagined by primitives. Ewan was in the presence of an Infinity free of all such needs and desires—and he marveled.

"Who are you?" Ewan whispered in an awestruck voice.

He heard no audible sound, but he could not mistake the rich, sonorous voice that replied. It spoke into the very depths of his being, seeming at a stroke to satisfy all his longings, answer every need, and fill the eternal, aching void as nothing else ever could or would:

My roots reach down beyond the depths of time;
My heights surpass the pinnacles of space;
Infinity I hold within my arms.
Eternal love, unshakable: I am.

There was no arrogance in the tone. It was a simple statement of fact. Ewan knew then that the Rock had no need to justify its existence or to defend its cause. Such complaints are mortal, even among the gods. The Rock was beyond them all. It made Ewan feel suddenly very small and highly privileged that the Rock, unthreatened and having no need of him, should have drawn him into this embrace.

"May I go forward?" he asked in childlike simplicity.

"You have a lengthy journey ahead of you," the Rock replied.

"Will we talk like this all the time?"

"As much as you wish, and as much as you need. You will see."

"What is my destination?"

"That you also will see."

"Well, here goes," said Ewan, and with that he began to belly forward along the narrow tunnel.

For a man who had known only the open seas, he felt little fear in this constricted place. Perhaps it was the vibrant sense of personality all around him. Or the light. Or the relative ease with which he moved, for the tunnel was well-cut and had none of the rubble one might have expected to find on the floor. Ewan concluded that the flow of many waters had washed and smoothed it clean.

The tunnel was far from straight, however, and within a short time he gave up trying to work out any sense of direction, except to say he didn't think he was going in circles. Humming happily to himself, he pressed on.

Gradually, he became aware of a change in the light. The greenish glow of the Rock began to give way to a reddish hue. At the same time his consciousness of the Rock's personality diminished rapidly. Ewan hesitated, and his former confidence began to waver. He was trapped in a tunnel deep underground. Suddenly, he felt very alone and frightened.

"Hello?" he called anxiously. "Are you still there?"

He received no reply. Cautiously, he edged forward.

"Hello?"

"Good day to you, sir," boomed a voice from nowhere.

"Who are you?" cried Ewan in alarm.

"Oh, really! Tsk! I should have thought you'd have recognized me at once," the voice replied. "Most people do."

"Well I don't," Ewan answered curtly. He was less sure of his reply after a moment's reflection. "Anyway, I can't see you."

"Easily remedied, dear boy."

Immediately Ewan saw standing not twenty paces in front of him the spectral figure of an urbane, middle-aged man dressed in a flamboyant, cream-colored painter's smock, complete with a large blue bow and a floppy, black beret worn with casual refinement. The whole demeanor of the man was one of extreme dandification, right down to the elegant, silver-strapped walking cane with which he posed. His face looked strangely familiar. With a shock Ewan quickly recognized it as his own, though aged by a considerable number of years. He peered at the image with irresistible fascination.

"That's better," said the man with evident satisfaction. "Ewan Proudman at your service."

"I'm not sure I require your service," Ewan said. The first inklings of what was happening began to dawn on him.

"Ha! You can hardly do without me, old bean. After all, it is I who have kept your life going—and, I may say modestly, with more than a modicum of success," Proudman replied.

Ewan found the manner of his purported *alter ego* profoundly irritating. Never having considered himself vain in any significant measure, this apparition (if that's what it was) seemed to be an unnecessary intrusion into his life. And it had appeared just at the time when he thought he had made the final breakthrough for which he had sought so long. He said this in no uncertain terms. "I've never met you before in my life. Now clear out of my way!"

"Tut, tut!" replied Proudman, quite unperturbed by this display of annoyance. "Let me remind you of Sellinge and the Mayfest."

"That was years ago," Ewan protested, piqued and knowing precisely to what Proudman referred. "Anyway, I was simply a better artist than Sellinge. I deserved to win the contest, and I thought I could."

Proudman clapped his hands together. "Precisely! And that's why you entered the competition."

"I wasn't going to," Ewan protested, spotting the trap into which he was about to fall. "My friends encouraged me. You remember them—Scotty, Teresa, and Margo."

"Oh, I remember them all right," Proudman replied knowingly. "I remember how they did it, too. Told you you were the best. Why should you take the back seat and let your rival win? But you wouldn't have heeded them and taken up the gauntlet without my help, would you?"

The trap sprung shut. Ewan admitted it. "But I was good, wasn't I?" He smiled at the memory.

"Of course you were, dear boy." Proudman answered expansively. "Quite the best work for a long time. They all said so. You had the beginnings of a great career."

"I couldn't believe it when Sellinge won," said Ewan.

"A foolish mistake on their part, dear boy. No need to take it to heart," Proudman said understandingly.

"I could easily be the best in my field," Ewan responded quickly. "Just a few breaks, that's all I need, and I could do it. I've got the talent."

"You could do with an agent," Proudman suggested. "I think we could supply someone suitable. A few exhibitions, a bit of publicity, and you'd have it made."

The artist's self-doubt in Ewan suddenly reasserted itself. "Are you really sure I could do it?" he asked. "I mean, do you honestly think so?"

Proudman turned his head to one side and placed the crook of his finger to his mouth. He gazed at Ewan from the corner of his eye; Ewan felt an air of embarrassment well up inside him.

"There is a slight problem, old boy."

"What is it?" Ewan asked anxiously.

"I hardly like to mention it. Not for me to say, of course, and all that. But really, do you think it's appropriate for an artist of your caliber to be in here? I mean, groveling on your belly in this awful place. It is rather, how shall I say, unbecoming."

"It's where I am, and I can't turn round," Ewan explained.

"There is a way out," Proudman replied.

"Oh?"

"Yes. Just a little farther along you'll find a shaft. I will escort you if you wish. What is more, you will be able to stand upright and walk like a man, instead of behaving as though you were a worm!"

Ewan suddenly found himself thrust onto the horns of a dilemma. If he stayed in the Rock he would sacrifice all opportunity for fame and glory—of that he had no doubt. Proudman would desert him. How would he, could he, survive as an artist? *The meek shall inherit the earth,* he remembered hearing once. Ruefully, he recalled the punch line. *They get dirt—that's all!*

On the other hand, if he decided to follow Proudman out of the Rock, it would mark the end of the road as far as his quest was concerned. There would be no way back. He would lose forever what destiny awaited him here. Yet now the spirit of the Rock seemed very distant. Perhaps he had imagined the voice? Overwrought emotions could play tricks with the mind. Wish fulfillment could be a powerful deception. The walls of this tunnel might be no more than lifeless, red rock suffused with a natural phosphorescence.

He decided to follow Proudman.

"Thank goodness!" Proudman exclaimed. "For one awful moment I thought I had lost you forever. A wise choice, old boy, if I may say so. Now follow me. Let us remove ourselves from this ghastly place without further ado."

Ewan scrambled forward in pursuit of Proudman's retreating specter. Before long they came upon a tunnel leading off to the right. Proudman waited until Ewan was almost at the juncture before turning off himself. The new tunnel was large enough for Ewan to stand up. With a sigh of relief, he finally stretched himself to full height.

"Better, eh?" chuckled Proudman.

"I guess so," Ewan replied. "How far is it now?"

"As long or short as you wish to make it," he replied enigmatically. "It really depends on how much you are prepared to pay, and how quickly."

"You never mentioned anything about cost," Ewan protested.

Proudman began to walk more rapidly, and Ewan had to hasten to keep at his heels.

"Well, you can hardly expect something for nothing, can you, old boy? You are not the only one out there with a reputation to sustain."

"So what will it cost? I haven't got much money, if that's what you mean."

"Pity that. Always helps if you have. But no, that's not the real cost. Lack of pecuniary wherewithal need be no hindrance."

"What, then?" Ewan persisted.

Proudman stopped and turned on him, emitting a heavy sigh of exasperation. "Isn't it obvious?" He spoke as though he were addressing a particularly dull pupil. "You'll have to learn to be selective in the company you keep. You're far too gregarious. Don't mix with lesser beings. Ingratiate yourself with the famous. Flatter them."

"What else?" asked Ewan dubiously.

"Don't be so self-critical. Develop a healthy blindness to your own flaws. Talk a lot about experimentation and breaking new ground when questioned about an apparent lack of style or technique. Never be negative. Assume that you are always right. Others may fail, but not you. Cultivate a reputation as an authority on the inadequacies of others' work. Use your critical faculties as a weapon of war and climb to the top on the bodies of the slain!"

"Anything else?" Ewan inquired glumly.

Proudman's pace became brisk and efficient.

"Get yourself some decent clothes," he called back. "And a better boat. Advertise yourself. Never be seen weak or down-at-the-heel. Work on your image. Hire a publicity expert."

Ewan stopped. A vast pit seemed to yawn before him, and he was walking straight into it. With a knowing expression on his face, he stopped.

"I think I would prefer to do without you, Ewan Proudman," he said, and with that he turned and ran full-pelt back the way he had come. Proudman made no attempt to follow him.

"Rock, Rock, where are you?" Ewan panted. "Get me out of here."

At once, and to his relief, he found himself back on his stomach, crawling in the glow of the green light.

"I am glad you decided to come back," he heard the comforting voice say.

Ewan smiled to himself. "So am I," he said. "So am I."

❖12❖

THE CLINK OF THE COIN WAS UNMISTAKABLE, and it provoked in Ewan an immediate reaction.

"That's mine!" he cried. "Leave it alone!"

It had been a while since the incident with Proudman, and during the ensuing hours—though it might have been days or weeks for all he knew—Ewan had discussed the matter at length with the Rock. The novelty of this latter experience fascinated him.

At first, the thought of having to sustain an endless conversation with the presumably tireless Rock seemed daunting. But Ewan quickly learned his host was content mostly to be a benign, supportive presence in the background of his consciousness. Companionship was the word that best described it, he thought. It reminded him of his best times with Sally.

Ewan initiated these conversations, but on occasion the Rock intruded his thoughts with a subtle, but definitely "outside" idea, transcendently pictorial or poetic in form. These usually were designed to pull Ewan back to the subject of pride, for his own questions and speculations were apt to range haphazardly from subjects such as the meaning of life, to the origins of the Haunter to the spatial dimensions of the Rock. The Rock seemed determined to keep Ewan to the matter in hand.

Ewan did acknowledge ruefully that his relative lack of ambition had been a form of inverted snobbery all too easily exposed once confronted by Proudman. Secretly, he had admired himself and his own talents, all the while cherishing the perverse pleasure of denying the world access to his brilliance until everyone should come, cap in hand, humbly beseeching him to forgive them for their blindness and failure to give honor to whom honor was due. It was a sobering lesson.

"He made a mistake with all that talk about money and fine clothes, though," Ewan laughed. "That sort of thing has never appealed to me. As long as I have enough to live on, I'm happy. And as for clothes—well, just look at me!"

"Money is not the only thing people covet," the Rock answered.

"No, I suppose not," said Ewan somewhat uncertainly. "I guess there are folks who are greedy for fame. Or they want someone else's property. Or they even desire to possess another person for themselves."

"You have not yet understood," replied the Rock.

Ewan, thinking the Rock had misread his lack of conviction, hastened to assure him that he recognized perfectly the all-encompassing power of greed. Obviously, money was only a small part of it. The dangers were everywhere. He would be on the lookout for any trace of covetousness in his own life and do his best to guard against it in the future.

"You have not yet understood," the Rock repeated.

The conversation petered out at this point, and Ewan crawled on in silence.

Not long afterward, a certain coldness began to permeate his bones. The walls of the tunnel were changing color again, the pale green glow now giving way to a metallic, silvery black. He shivered in the harsh, brittle light and suddenly felt alone. Uneasy in his spirit, he stopped. It was then he heard the sound of the coin.

He spotted it almost at once, glinting hypnotically on the floor of the tunnel just a few meters ahead. The sight galvanized him into action: unable to restrain his feelings, he scrambled toward it. To his consternation, however, the coin—as though possessed of its own perverse intelligence—rose onto its edge and began at once to roll steadily away from him. Ewan crawled faster, disregarding the discomfort to his knees, for the tunnel had by now become distinctly rough in texture. Soon the little silver disc was almost within his grasp. Panting, he stretched out his fingers to claw it to himself. Life itself seemed to depend upon this moment.

But the coin responded by rolling just a little faster. Ewan's fingers closed on thin air. He let out an involuntary howl of frustration that echoed hollowly off the tunnel walls. Redoubling his efforts, he chased after his elusive prize. Again and again he reached for it, but each time it slipped from his fingers. To make matters worse, the tantalizing coin had begun steadily increasing in size as he pursued it. His desire for it drove him to fever pitch.

"I must have it. It belongs to me," he gasped, increasing his efforts yet more. "It's mine!"

Spittle drooled down his flushed face. His eyes bulged from their sockets. Gulping air in hoarse gasps, with his trousers ripped and his knees raw, he scrabbled along to the limits of his endurance. But the coin gave him no respite. All the while it grew in size, yet it remained steadily beyond his grasp.

The tunnel was growing larger. To Ewan's relief, he found he could rise off his hands and knees and adopt a crouching posture. Before long the gallery was high enough for him to run upright, and his hopes of catching the coin renewed his vigor.

Just then, he spotted a large crowd of people gathered not fifty meters ahead of him. Panic welled up inside him. His coin was rolling straight toward them.

"Don't touch that!" he shouted. "It belongs to me. Nobody must touch it!"

The coin passed into the ranks of the crowd and was momentarily out of sight.

"Thieves! Leave it alone!" he cried. He rushed blindly into the bemused crowd, most of whom appeared entirely uninterested in the object and faintly surprised at his zeal.

Carelessly and impatiently he barged against the bodies, roughly pushing them aside, thinking of nothing other than laying his hands on the coin. His foot caught a little girl in the face. It didn't seem to matter. He trampled on a baby boy and swore because the nuisance hampered his pace. The crowd, he noted, consisted of an inordinately large proportion of children, and they had a particularly irritating habit of getting in the way. Heedless of the pain and distress he was causing, however, he charged through.

The coin had grown to gigantic proportions; it was now the size of his foot in diameter. Somehow it seemed unhampered by the crowd, and it continued to roll too fast for him to reach it. At times the people slowed him down so much he almost lost sight of the coin altogether. Driven by desperation, he lashed out in all directions, heedless of whom he struck and leaving a trail of devastation behind him. But Ewan had no time for the bleeding, bruised faces and broken bones he had caused. At any cost, he had to possess his coin. Nothing else mattered—his obsession was absolute!

At last he broke free of the distraught melee of protesting, crying people. Now there was only the sound of his thudding feet and panting lungs to break the silence—that, and the irresistible whir and tinkle of the coin.

Ewan gasped with pleasure. He realized that, freed of all these impediments, he at last was catching up with the coin. He spurred himself forward in one final, earnest effort. In a few moments, he had caught up with it. Sobbing with joy, he stretched forth his hand, his taut fingers closing greedily.

He was so intent on the task that he had not noticed a sudden change in the terrain. The rock floor had given way to an iron grating underfoot. Even as his fingers were closing around the coin, it lost momentum and pivoted precariously on one of the bars. Ewan's fingers snapped thin air. Then, before he could make a second grab, the coin teetered over and dropped neatly through the grill. Horrified, and with a cry of desperation, Ewan threw himself forward and plunged his hand through the grating.

To his overwhelming delight he felt his fingers close around the object of his desire.

"Got it!" he gasped. "I've got it!"

For a few minutes he lay on his stomach, gasping to regain his breath. His sense of satisfaction was immense. He had obtained what was his by right. No one could steal it now. The coin was his alone. The fulfillment of all his desires tingled between his fingers, and a warm glow of satisfaction spread up his arm, carrying with it the promise of endless bliss.

He glanced backward cautiously to ensure nobody was waiting to pounce on him and steal his treasure. He rose to his hands and knees and pulled at the coin—or, at least, he tried to. In a sudden, stark, and terrifying instant, Ewan discovered he could retract neither the coin nor his hand from the grating.

The old "how to catch a monkey with a jar and some peanuts" syndrome, he thought bitterly. If he wanted his hand released he would have to let go of the coin—but that was the one thing he would not do. The first inkling that he might be in bondage to the object of his desire began to force itself into Ewan's mind.

He tugged in vain to free his prize but succeeded only in skinning his wrist on the unyielding bars. The problem, as he realized at once, was the thickness of his own hand. No matter how much he twisted and turned it, it was simply too wide to pass through the bars while clenched. Carefully, he attempted to purse his fingers to taper his hand. That only made his hold on the coin precarious, and he scrabbled quickly to regain his purchase lest it fall into the darkness below.

Frustrated, he lay on the grating, pondering his dilemma. "If only I had got there that much sooner. It's those people's fault. Why were they in the way? They were trying to stop me from obtaining my desire. Wanted it for themselves, I shouldn't wonder. Selfish thieves! I should have been harder on them. What a fool being so softhearted!"

He heaved a great sigh.

The coin was proving to be heavy—heavier than he had expected. A satisfied smirk gashed his face. It must be worth more than he had previously imagined—a small fortune in silver, no less. He gripped it even more tightly. His wrist ached, and he had to ease up a little, but not too much. Conscious now that he was sweating profusely, he could feel the coin slip slightly between his greasy fingers. Feverishly, in spite of the cramp, he gripped it tightly again.

Ewan's face was set in a rictus of concentration. The pain made him sweat even more, and it increased the difficulty of holding onto the coin. Bursting with frustration, he pounded his forehead on the grating and banged his toes and free arm in a childish tantrum. It achieved little more than a slight release of tension and left him gasping like an exhausted fish. It was only then he noticed the full purpose of the grating. Deep below his prostrate form glowed a faint red light. It was no bigger than a cigarette butt burning in the darkness, but was bright enough to reflect off the walls of what he surmised to be a borehole of inestimable, dizzying depth. Suddenly, Ewan felt very insecure and sick with vertigo.

Worse still, something shifted beneath him, making a dull, grating sound. Heaving himself onto his hands and knees but remaining careful to keep a tight grip on his coin, Ewan surveyed his predicament. He was about halfway across the grating, which traversed a space three times his body length. With a shock he discovered that the bars which kept him from plunging into the pit were beginning to move. They were slowly drawing apart in the middle, like two intermeshed combs. Already the tips of the adjacent bars were visible. It was clear he had little time to regain the safety of solid rock before he fell into the abyss below.

In vain he looked around for a means to get clear and at the same time to pull the coin with him. It appeared impossible. The bars behind and in front of him were parting more rapidly than those beneath him. The only way of escape was to release his hold on the coin and flee for the safety of the tunnel ahead or behind him. But that was precisely what he would not do.

Unexpectedly, he heard the familiar voice of the Rock. "What use is it to gain everything and lose yourself, Ewan?"

The logic was unimpeachable—the reality, otherwise.

"But it's mine," he protested. "I found it. I worked for it. I chased it. And I caught it!" He was unable to mask the triumph in his voice.

The Rock repeated the question: "What use is it to gain everything and lose yourself?"

He stared down at the coin glinting in the dull light on the other side of the bars. It was so big, so weighty, and so precious.

"I own you."

With a start, Ewan realized the coin had spoken.

"You serve me," the coin added.

"No, I own you," Ewan protested.

"Think again," said the coin scornfully. "You can't release me, so you will perish with me. Oh, I know I shall perish. I always do—but I can be recycled. You, I take with me once and for all." It mocked him with a bitter, ironic laugh.

Ewan was in mortal conflict with his desires. Torn by his passion to heed the Rock and, at the same time, by his all-consuming covetousness for the coin, he cried out in despair. The grating continued to part remorselessly.

Ewan made up his mind. He would release the coin—he had to. It was the only sensible course of action, after all. The trouble was he had no power to part his fingers when it came to doing this; his fingers had gone numb. Back on his knees, he reached through the grating with his other hand in an attempt to pry his fingers open.

He began with the little one, forcing it back. Such was the pressure required that he feared he would break the bone in the process. He tried the next one, but his fingers seemed to be spring-loaded: as fast as he broke the grip of one to start on another, the first one sprang shut again. In desperation, Ewan attempted to wedge one finger above the other, to prevent this from happening. The excruciating pain was unbearable, and he cried aloud.

"I want to let go!" he gasped.

Suddenly, his mind was filled with the faces and bodies of all those he had trampled underfoot in his desire to catch the coin. He saw their hurt, broken forms. Their confused faces spoke eloquently of their pained souls, wondering what they had done to deserve such callous treatment at his hands.

"I'm sorry," he cried. "Sorry to you all. It was madness that drove me. Forgive me! Somebody help me, please!"

The grating by now was nearly parted. By painfully twisting his hand with the other, he had almost broken the grip. But time was running out.

"You'll never do it," mocked the coin.

Panting with effort and feeling every moment the increasing terror of the abyss below, Ewan suddenly saw the issue for what it was—not simply a conflict of desires, but a matter of ownership. He saw vividly and literally that all people are owned by what they set their hearts on. He had wanted to fulfill his sense of longing. That had brought him thus far into the Rock. Now another craving, of a different, ruthless, destructive nature, had possessed him. His longing for the Rock had been affirming. This one was deadly.

"I want you, Rock. I want life!" he cried.

"There can be no other besides me," the Rock cautioned.

"I know—I don't care. Set me free and possess me!"

At once, his fingers opened as though a hidden key had released the lock. The coin fell spinning and glittering into the pit. Ewan did not wait to hear it hit bottom—if a bottom was there—but scrambled desperately across the almost-parted bars to the safety of solid rock. Struggling clear, he clutched at the ground, sobbing with relief and kissing it with gratitude. And in this position he passed into a peaceful slumber.

He awoke sometime later, wonderfully refreshed and bathed in the comforting green light that told him he was again in communication with the Rock. He noted to his surprise that the tunnel had returned to its former size and was just large enough for him to crawl through. Behind him lay a small hole in the floor, no more than a hand's span in diameter. A small pang of regret seized him for a moment as he gazed upon it.

The Rock seemed to sense his mood.

"Ah, yes, Ewan, you have lost something. More than you will ever know. But you have saved yourself. That is what matters."

❖13❖

EWAN HEAVED A SIGH of exasperation. In spite of the Rock's assurances that he had made the right choice, he was feeling thoroughly peeved over the whole business. He had entered the Rock to find life. The last thing he had expected was to have every undesirable aspect of his character dragged to the surface in such a cavalier and uncompromising fashion. This could continue for weeks—or longer!

He also felt guilty about Sally. She would have waited for him, cold and lonely, until nightfall. Once her anger had died down, she would have been racked with guilt herself. Maybe she ventured up the slope to check whether he was there. Perhaps she even reached the opening and called his name—if the Haunter had let her, that is. In the end, however, filled with sadness and regret, she would have taken the dinghy and returned to *Seaspray*. Sooner or later she would depart altogether and find her way back to the commune.

Ewan was desperately sorry to lose her in such traumatic circumstances. He hoped that somehow things would turn out right. But there was nothing he could do about it now.

The combination of his exasperation and guilt made him blurt out his complaint.

"I'd very much like to know what's going on around here, if you don't mind," he demanded. "I mean, if you're the Eternal Rock, why do you keep disappearing from my consciousness? It's like trying to keep a candle alight in a storm-force gale!" He laughed hollowly. "All I wanted was to get to know you. That's why I came here in the first place. I wanted to find life. It wasn't easy, you know. And it still isn't."

"You don't like the truth about yourself?" the Rock queried.

"I don't like the way it's being done, if that's what you mean," he answered irritably. "Look, I accept that there are things about me that need changing. But why can't we just discuss the matter like—like reasonable adults? Why treat me as a child?"

"Perhaps it is because you are a child," the Rock suggested.

"Huh!"

"You make the mistake of thinking discussion can change behavior," the Rock continued, blithely ignoring Ewan's skepticism. "Conduct is a matter of the will, not the intellect—of decision, not debate. You have to make real choices to effect real changes in your character."

Ewan spread his hands in a mock gesture of acceptance.

"OK. Supposing I buy that? It still doesn't explain why you keep leaving me to the mercy of these stupid quasi-personalities, or whatever they are."

"Ewan, you need to understand that I have not once left you since you arrived here," the Rock replied. "How could I, since I surround you and support you on all sides? Your entire life—your breath, the fact that you need neither food nor water, even the light around you—all are dependent upon me. If I truly withdrew, you would simply cease to exist."

"So, what is happening?" Ewan demanded, somewhat less confidently. He wavered before the unimpeachable logic of his situation. He felt perhaps he was speaking out of turn.

There was an unmistakable tinge of sorrow in the Rock's voice. "You say you want to be with me, but there are parts of your personality that wish anything but that. When they predominate, they draw you away from me—but not me from you. I myself will never leave you. Of that you may be certain. But I cannot yet say the same of you."

The Rock's words sobered him considerably.

"What must I do, then?" Ewan asked meekly.

"Fight and win," answered the Rock. "Understand that it is our very proximity that provokes those undesirable aspects of your inner self to come out of hiding and to create such havoc. Your true desires will have to battle against those warring factions within you until you have conquered them. You must determine to become a man of undivided affections if we are to have an uninterrupted friendship, Ewan."

"What if I don't succeed?" Ewan replied. "Why don't you help me?"

"My help is closer than you will ever know," the Rock replied enigmatically. "Yet I cannot compel love. You will triumph, if that is what you truly wish." Then he added, "If not, I fear you will find yourself within all-too-easy reach of your past."

Ewan considered the matter for a moment. He recalled his conflict with the Haunter and shuddered.

"I wouldn't want to go through that again," he said, shaking his head.

"Oh, you would never be troubled by him again. Have no fear of that! Indeed, he could make life extremely pleasant for you," the Rock answered. Then he added meaningfully, "The real problems come at the end of life, when you reap what you have sown."

"I don't want to leave here." Ewan spoke as sincerely as he knew how.

"Are you sure?"

He opened his mouth to protest, but already the Rock seemed distant again.

"Blast!"

He struck the ground in frustration, bruising his knuckles in the process. The light in the tunnel faded to a wan yellow. It matched his mood. Wondering just what he had let himself in for, he crawled on in sullen, resentful silence.

"LET'S HAVE some fun!"

Ewan started at the unexpected sound of the perky little voice. Then he gasped with horror as something living scampered up his back and over his head. A small figure somersaulted to the ground and spun around to face him. In appearance, the creature was as impish as his tone of voice, dressed in red, candy-striped trousers and a short blue jacket, neatly topped off with a pointed red hat from under which poked equally pointed ears.

"Who are you?" Ewan yelled, bristling with shock.

"Lust," came the pert reply. "Just call me Lust."

"You frightened the life out of me. Stupid fool! What's the big idea?" Ewan demanded. "Anyway, sex is the last thing on my mind at the moment."

"Who said anything about sex? Whatever made you think of that?" Lust rejoined unperturbed. "Come on. I want us to have some fun together."

"What sort of fun?" Ewan eyed him suspiciously.

"Toys, of course. Don't you like toys? Come on, everybody does."

"I'm a bit old for toys, don't you think?" Ewan replied dryly.

"Not for these, you're not!" The imp spread his palms. "Look, it's only for a laugh."

Ewan tried to make contact with the Rock, but he could sense nothing of its presence. Life seemed suddenly to have lost its sparkle. His mundane existence in this drab tunnel bored him to distraction. Anything for a bit of excitement, any harmless diversion to break the tedium of his toil! With a sigh of resignation, he agreed to follow the imp.

Lust skipped along the tunnel until they came to what looked like a large box, painted bright green. It turned out to be a portable cabin. On the door was a picture of a rainbow springing out of an egg. *Toy room*, it read underneath.

The imp pranced through the door and into the room while Ewan, being of considerably larger size, did his best to squeeze through the entrance without becoming stuck.

Once inside, he found himself in a dark room barely large enough in which to crouch. It was furnished with no more than a small baize-covered table and a chair. The imp sprang into the chair at once and bade Ewan join him on the other side of the table, where he was obliged to sit cross-legged on the floor. On the table Ewan noted a pack of cards, a small orb of gold attached to a fine chain also of gold, and a crystal ball from which emanated a pale light that lit the room. He glanced around the cabin. Everything else was in darkness.

"Strange toy room," he said with some sarcasm.

Lust laughed. Ewan observed the imp's face—thick-lipped, sallow-skinned, and deeply creased by age, with heavy bags under large, shrewd eyes that were accentuated by the pale light. By no stretch of the imagination was the imp attractive physically, yet Ewan could not deny a curious and compelling attraction to the creature's personality. Lust, he sensed, had the power to meet an unarticulated, deeply-felt need within him.

"Children have too many useless toys," said the imp. "You only need a few, as long as they're the right ones. And these are the right ones." He gave Ewan an emphatic glance from under his lowered brows.

Ewan picked up the gold orb and toyed with it. To his surprise, the moment he held it experimentally by the chain, it swung to one side of its own accord, defying gravity, as though drawn by an invisible, magnetic force.

"Oh, ho!" laughed the imp, clapping his hands with glee. "Plenty of energy in you, Ewan, my boy! I can see this will be a lot of fun."

He began to deal out the deck of cards face down, spreading them competently in an arc on the baize.

"These cards are marked with a mixture of letters, numbers, and symbols," he explained. "Here, give me the pendulum and I'll show you how we play."

Ewan handed it over, his curiosity aroused.

"Let's start with names, shall we? I'll find yours and you can find mine," Lust suggested. He held the pendulum over the cards. Ewan watched it swing and then suddenly remain poised above one of them. The imp turned over the card to uncover the letter E. He repeated the process three more times until he had spelled out Ewan's name. Ewan was unimpressed, and said so, accusing the imp of cheating.

"You try it, then," offered his tutor.

To Ewan's amazement, the pendulum worked for him—to his considerable satisfaction, he had to admit. He successfully spelled out the word LUST.

"I told you you'd be good," said the imp enthusiastically. "Let's play again."

This time he proposed to spell out a piece of information he didn't already know. "Think of something, say, an object, and I'll see if I can get it right."

Ewan thought of an apple. The imp successfully spelled it out with the pendulum.

"How does it work?" Ewan asked.

"Easy. Mind over matter—or, I should say, spirit over matter. It's your psychic energy tuning into the cosmic forces that release the power and give you knowledge you wouldn't otherwise have. Not just anyone can do it. But you seem rather good," he added. "Here, try again, while I think of something."

Ewan took the pendulum. It swung over the cards five times in succession and produced LASYL. "What on earth's that?" he exclaimed.

The imp looked bemused for a moment. "I was thinking of your lover," he explained, giving Ewan a quizzical look.

Light dawned on Ewan's face. "Why yes, of course," he laughed. "It's quite right. I just got the cards in the wrong order. It must be because I'm new at the game." He reshuffled the cards to spell the name correctly. "There you are. Sally," he exclaimed triumphantly. "She's my lover."

So engrossed did Ewan become in the game that he lost count entirely of how many times they played. He became increasingly proficient, to the point that he seemed to be working in perfect harmony with the pendulum, using no conscious effort at all.

"You know, there's a lot one could do with this technique," he said. "I mean, you could diagnose diseases and the correct treatments for them without ever having to study medicine in any depth, for example. Or you could find out what's going on in another part of the world. Just think how useful it could be for business if you knew what would sell and when." His face brightened. "Hey, come to think of it, if knowledge is power—and they say it is—then you could have power over almost everyone else. Absolute power." He did not find the thought at all daunting.

The imp eyed him curiously.

"Not quite absolute power—or, at least, not necessarily so," he chirped. "There is such a thing as Destiny, you know, and not everyone can control it to their own ends."

"Explain."

"Let's play the game again, only a bit differently this time. We'll try to work out your destiny—past, present, and future."

Ewan agreed and picked up the pendulum. It hovered over a card which the imp promptly reversed to reveal a picture of entwined lovers.

"You and Sally. Your past," he explained.

He repeated the action. This time the card showed a turret from which blazed a fire.

"The present," said Lust. "You are undergoing violence and destruction of some kind."

Ewan nodded thoughtfully. What was being destroyed, he wondered? His relationship with Sally? His old life? Himself? He felt his chest tighten at the last thought. What would his future hold? He waited tensely for the third card.

It seemed to take forever for the imp to turn the card indicated by the pendulum. When at last he did so, he gave it a brief glance and then looked at Ewan with large, solemn eyes. "Oh, dear," he said. "Look."

The card showed the Grim Reaper. Death.

"That can't be right," Ewan snapped. "Shuffle the pack again. Let's have another go."

The imp shrugged his shoulders and obeyed. Again the card came up as Death.

Three times Ewan tried the experiment—each time with the same result. He felt exasperated.

"This is impossible. It can't be right," he exclaimed agitatedly. "What can I do?"

"Why not play another game?" suggested Lust.

"Don't be ridiculous!"

"I'm not. Why don't you simply change your destiny?"

"But I can't. We've just tried that, and it doesn't work. Surely destiny is fixed, anyway?"

He slumped his head between his hands and battled with his feelings of despair. "I don't want to die. There's so much I want to see and do. And I want to develop this power that I've got. What's the use, though, if I'm just going to die?"

"You don't have to," Lust explained patiently. "You can change your future by drawing on those same cosmic powers that helped you in the first place. It requires a bit more commitment, but you can do it."

Ewan grasped at the offer like a drowning man seizing a straw. He looked the imp straight in the eye and leaned forward earnestly.

"Where? How? Show me."

"Look next to you. Place your hand on the crystal ball and you'll see for yourself. Don't be scared. All these toys work properly, you know."

Ewan obeyed. At once he felt a surge of something akin to a mild electric current tingling up his arm. He closed his eyes and breathed deeply, satisfyingly.

"That's right. Focus," instructed the imp. "Focus your spirit."

Ewan began to see a vision. He was floating out of his body as though on a thin, white thread. For a while he seemed to drift through a mist, but then it cleared to reveal he was soaring high over a city built on water. Drifting down, he floated unseen along the crowded, narrow streets. With the certain childish satisfaction of the voyeur, he slipped noiselessly through windows to observe people at their toilet and lovers wrapped in passion. He listened to families trapped in their petty conflicts. He also saw secret crimes committed and many a political intrigue and covert business deal executed.

"Knowledge is power," he breathed. "And power means control over my destiny."

It dawned on him that the whole problem of government was lack of real power through lack of real knowledge. In which case, the solution lay in dramatically increasing the amount and reliability of available information. What better way of doing so than by an esoteric occult method whereby nobody even knew it was going on?

Ewan could see his future role clearly. He would not be the public figurehead in society but rather the real power behind the throne. As the trusted adviser—the one in the know, whose word was authoritative—he would become quite invincible. He wanted that very dearly. Here at last was the way out of ignominy, powerlessness, and mediocrity. Here was the way to cheat even death itself!

"Yes, yes!" he cried in an orgiastic act of self-affirmation.

His eyes blazed with the possibilities. Nothing would be beyond his reach—nothing at all. He landed in one of the streets and began at once to stride invisibly and purposefully this way and that. He was the master of his destiny. Each path he trod was a personal conquest. All these people would be his subjects. Life itself was under his feet!

In the midst of his orgy of self-realization, he had wandered blindly down one street after another without any sense of direction. Suddenly, he became aware that he had left the crowds behind and was descending a silent path banked on both sides by tall, dark-green hedges. This led him to a wooden jetty that stretched into a vast blue sea whose far shores, if they existed, were lost in a pale, opaque mist.

Then with a jolt, he saw standing before him the spectral figure of the Grim Reaper.

"No! No!" Ewan cried. "Not now. I want to live! I must be in control. Don't take it all away from me," he pleaded. "You mustn't! You can't!"

The skeletal mask of death stared at him, silent and impassive. Panic gripped Ewan by the throat. He coughed and spluttered until tears streamed down his fevered cheeks. Driven now by his lust for life and power, he fell to his knees and cried out.

"What must I do to be spared?" he yelled. "I'll do anything—I'll pay any price."

"A life for a life," boomed a voice.

It came not from the Grim Reaper but from the sky above. Ewan gazed upward to see that a small, white cloud had unexpectedly materialized and now hovered above where he knelt. Awestruck, he watched as red streaks and smudges bled hazily through the white and evolved into the mask of a stern, male face.

"Who are you?" Ewan gasped.

"I am the Force beyond all forces and the Power beyond all powers," the voice tolled. "A life for a life. That is the rule."

"What do you mean?" asked Ewan in consternation.

"You cannot have the power you seek without cost. You can avoid your own death, but someone must die in your place."

Ewan glanced again at the specter of death standing before him.

"All right," he gulped. "Yes, all right. Who must it be? Anyone I suppose. I don't mind. Just give me what I want."

Under normal circumstances, the ease with which he had offered a random life for his own would have appalled Ewan. But now the lust for life, knowledge, and power had completely overwhelmed his conscience. He would sell his very soul to the will of this strange figure in the sky if that would give him what he desired.

"Are you sure you wish to become a disciple?" demanded the hollow voice.

"Yes, yes, anything. I told you," Ewan replied impatiently.

"Very well. This is the life you must sacrifice."

At once, Ewan saw lying before him the familiar figure of Sally. She wore a gray shroud and her face was very pale, though he could see that she still lived. Next to her lay a large, ornamented ceremonial knife.

"Now, do what you have to do," commanded the voice.

·14·

EWAN STARED aghast at the prostrate figure before him.

"But—but this is Sally. I can't kill her," he stammered. "Anyone else, but not her!"

The blood-outlined face gazed down with all the impassivity of a trader who knows he has his customer hooked and needs only to wait while he comes to terms with the high price demanded for the goods.

Lust churned in Ewan's stomach. The splendid array of glittering prizes stretched before him—indisputable life, fame voiced in awe by gawking admirers, the intoxicating promise of unlimited power. It would take only one, simple thrust of the dagger. She wouldn't feel it—wouldn't suffer. She was asleep already, probably drugged. Maybe she's ill? Yes, that's it. She's dying anyway. This would be a mercy for her, a painless relief from needless suffering.

He stretched out his hand and grasped the knife. It felt heavy, horrible to the touch, like a loathsome reptile.

He hesitated.

"You can do it, Ewan."

Ewan started. It was the voice of the imp.

"Her sacrifice will not be wasted, you know. Her life force will become part of the cosmic power. She will live on through you."

For one wry moment, Ewan thought Sally would hardly have approved of this notion. But it was too late—he was over the brink. Lust's gravitational pull dragged him inexorably to his fate. Gripping the dagger, he raised it above Sally's still form and took a deep breath.

At that very moment, a sudden fluttering of wings blocked his vision. A white dove had appeared out of nowhere and now hovered between Sally's body and the deadly blade, as though it were riding a thermal high over a mountain range. Its presence made it impossible for Ewan to strike.

"Get out of the way!" he shouted. He took an irritated swipe at the bird, but it deftly avoided his intended blow and continued to flutter above the prostrate girl.

A madness of uncontrollable urgency took possession of Ewan. "Get away!" he screeched. The dove's intrusion became the focus of all his passion and desire to pay any price to satisfy the lust within him. He slashed the air wildly with murder in his eyes.

The inevitable happened. For all the bird's aerial agility, it was impossible to protect the girl and at the same time to avoid Ewan's vicious onslaught. One of the blows caught the dove on the wing and it fell crippled to the ground. With a snarl of rage Ewan leapt upon it. Grasping the creature by the throat, he began to slash and hack its body in a blind fury, splattering himself with blood and feathers in the process.

"That will teach you to get in my way! Nothing is going to stop me," he cried through gritted teeth.

At last his rage was spent. Besmeared with blood and sweat, he knelt prostrate with his head turned to one side amid the carnage. Slowly, he opened his eyes. He sought to summon the energy needed to fulfill his interrupted intention.

He got the shock of his life.

With a scream of sheer horror, he saw lying beside him a human face ripped and shredded almost beyond recognition but unmistakably his own. Recoiling with revulsion, he saw his entire body lying hacked to pieces on the ground. Ewan Jones had killed himself. Devastated, he staggered to his feet staring wildly at the incriminating, blood-stained knife in his hand.

"Oh!" he cried. "Oh my. What have I done?"

He flung the knife away and turned to where Sally lay. Next to her stood the imp. In his hand he held another dagger.

"Don't worry, Ewan. I'll do it," he piped. "I'll do it. It's all a game, really."

Reality hit Ewan with the chilling jolt of a bucket of cold water. "Oh, no, you won't," he snarled.

In three swift strides he was in front of the imp. Without hesitation he swung his foot and kicked the creature in the midriff as hard as he could, sending him hurtling through the air and straight into the form of the Grim Reaper, who still presided impassively over the scene.

The imp emitted a terrible scream. For a moment he stuck like a fly to the Reaper's black shroud. Then he slowly dissolved into nothingness as though eaten away by acid.

Ewan turned his face upward to confront the scowling visage in the cloud.

"You are a liar," he called. "It's all a dirty, warped lie. What kind of so-called Power or Force are you that demands innocent sacrifice for the gratification of lust? I won't pay your evil price—ever! The deal's not worth it."

With that he turned to confront the Grim Reaper. "As for you, you don't frighten me anymore," he said quietly. "I've nothing to lose really."

Stepping across Sally's prostrate arm, he walked steadily toward the waiting figure.

To his amazement, he walked straight through the Grim Reaper, feeling no more than a brush of cobwebs against his skin. Quite unharmed, he found himself standing at the end of the jetty overlooking the sea. He glanced over his shoulder and smiled. The specter had disappeared, as had Sally, the cloud, and his own corpse. The street was completely empty.

Turning again to face the sea, he found himself instead back inside the tunnel surrounded by the familiar green glow of the Rock's presence.

"You have won a significant victory," commended the Rock. "Well done, Ewan Jones! You are beginning to heed the truth."

"THAT REALLY WAS BAD NEWS," said a relieved Ewan a while later. "I just never knew lust could be like that. I would have killed her, you know. Sally, I mean. Horrible." He shuddered in disgust.

"The best emotions can be the worst when directed to the wrong ends," the Rock answered.

"You won't ever put me in that position, will you?" Ewan asked anxiously.

"I never drive—I only invite," said the Rock. "That is the difference."

"Oh, that's all right, then. I'm glad."

He started forward on his journey with renewed confidence. The green aura indicated the Rock's presence with him. It was a pleasant relief after the last episode.

"What did you mean about the best emotions being the worst?" he asked suddenly. "Isn't lust always wrong? I mean, to you, at least?"

Something like a chuckle emanated from the Rock.

"No, far from it. The power to lust is given to you humans as a blessing, not a curse. Would it help if I use the word *passion*? It has fewer evil connotations for you. In which case, surely you recognize that without lust, or passion, you could not paint? Nor could you love."

"I don't think I really know what love is," Ewan replied sadly. He came to a halt. "Oh, I love Sally, I suppose, but . . .

well, passion as you call it—I don't know. More what I usually call lust, really."

The Rock waited for him to continue.

"I was thinking about Sally before that last episode." He hesitated. "I know I did the right thing in coming here, but I do feel guilty about deserting her. Do you know if she is all right?"

"For the moment, yes. You need not fear the worst."

Ewan felt relieved.

"Will I ever feel a passionate love for you?" he asked abruptly.

It was an awkward thought, and he felt even more awkward expressing it. He was aware that the Rock exuded a certain masculinity and that gave him, as a heterosexual, difficulty with the idea of loving the Rock. Yet, for reasons he couldn't fathom, he did not think a homosexual would find it any easier. The Rock seemed at the same time both to affirm and to challenge his masculinity. Ewan suspected it would do the same for a woman with respect to her femininity. *Maybe,* Ewan thought, *I don't understand either term properly.*

The Rock seemed to sense his thoughts and answered in a sympathetic tone.

"People grow to love me with a passion greater than that felt for all others," he replied. "But it is a pathway of discovery, not an overnight experience. Some lack the capacity to love fully when they start out. Others misinterpret their love for me in terms of quasisexual satisfaction because they have not learned to distinguish their loves. That is what you fear."

Ewan leaned back against the wall, crossed his legs, and folded his arms. This was going to take time.

"You'll have to explain what you mean," he said. "I thought love was love, and that's all there was to it."

"It is a common mistake but easily remedied," the Rock replied. "Consider for a moment. There is a love enjoyed by members of a family. It is deeply loyal and capable of riding out all kinds of adversity, yet it contains no sexual element. If it did, it would be the perverting of familial love by what you call lust."

Ewan nodded thoughtfully. This much was clear. "Go on," he said.

"You have another kind of love for your friends. It is not born of blood ties, nor of sexual passion, but of the free choice to cherish someone whose personality and interests somehow find an affinity with your own."

"Is that it?"

"There is one other love, and it is the highest of all. I mean sacrificial love. This is the act of the will, the heroic love that may lead a person even to lay down his life for another."

Ewan was silent for a while. "That last kind is outside my experience," he said candidly. "I really am a very selfish person at heart. As far as I can see, I only love those who love me first. That's a shocking thing to have to admit, isn't it?"

"There is hope for you," said the Rock kindly.

"Will you teach me?"

"Better than anyone else," came the reply.

The conversation ended as Ewan pondered the matter. It was hard to put into words or logical order the complexity of thoughts and emotions running through his mind. The intense yearning that had driven him against all odds to find his way into the Rock was largely satisfied. He knew he was in the right place, undergoing the journey of his life. But there was still so much he didn't understand. He felt restless.

He scratched his head in perplexity.

Life was far from static inside the Rock—that much was plain. The possibilities for growth and adventure excited and challenged him. Maybe that was just it. He had tasted, and it had whetted his appetite. A door had opened to reveal an infinity of opportunities yet unsatisfied. Frustrating.

He frowned.

There was the matter of the fierce temptations that assailed him. He wondered how many more there were to come. In his previous existence—he considered it realistic to think in such terms—Ewan had always thought himself a reasonably pleasant person. He was forced now to recognize the awful truth of human corruption within himself. Would this limit his progress, he wondered? He determined that he must win through.

With a slight sigh, he pressed on with his journey through the tunnel. There was bright light ahead. He hastened hopefully toward it. Perhaps this was the end of his trek?

To his amazement he entered an art gallery. Furthermore, he recognized most of the works. They had been painted by people of his acquaintance. He perused them appreciatively: good stuff. He prided himself on respecting the work of his peers. Many were by his arch rival, Sellinge, and even these Ewan grudgingly acknowledged to be quite accomplished pieces.

His appreciation began to diminish, however, the further he crawled along the art gallery. Not that the works themselves depreciated in quality. It was something else that bothered him—at first as no more than a niggling anxiety, but then a doubt, and finally an outright irritation. So far, he had not come across even one work of his own. Sellinge was everywhere, but Ewan Jones apparently was unknown.

Suddenly there was the man himself, in a cameo surrounded by his admirers, holding the award for the Mayfest in his hand. A large smile wreathed his modest face. It was the last picture in the gallery. Ewan, feeling unknown and unwanted, an outsider on the fringes of someone else's party, studied the scene with growing envy.

His eye grew more jaundiced the longer he stared. They should have feted him—he was the better artist! Malice rose from the recesses of his mind.

How I hate that man! he thought. *I wish he had never been born. Why did he have to live at the same time as I? I'm doomed to be forever in his shadow. If only I could be rid of him!*

The more he considered the matter, the more his sense of injustice and outrage grew. Repeatedly in his mind he relived every encounter between them. How similar their artistic themes were—but Sellinge had surely plagiarized Ewan's ideas! They were the same age and moved in the same circles. There just wasn't room for both of them. He found himself scheming to dispose of his rival.

He ruled out murder, as he was still smarting from his recent ordeal with the imp. But there were other ways. He would prove his rival's works were fake, derivative, superficial. Expose them for what they were. A ruinous scandal would put an end to the competition once and for all. He gloated over the thought of the Mayfest award being publicly withdrawn. If that wasn't successful, he determined he would paint manifestly better works instead. "I'll show them. I'll produce such masterpieces that they will consign Sellinge to the shadows forever!"

Pride, covetousness, and lust, those viruses of the soul, lurked nearby. He could sense their presence almost tangibly.

The Rock was present, too, and it was he who spoke.

"Ewan, I am about to grant you two visions. One of the future and one of the past. Learn from them, or you will leave me quickly."

On the screen of his mind, Ewan saw himself. He was standing before a large canvas, dressed in his artist's smock with brush poised and about to paint the first definitive stroke. But the brush never reached the canvas. Ewan saw himself turn away. He could read his own thoughts in the vision: Sellinge and the Mayfest. Distracted from work, he was running over the wretched affair yet again.

A whole morning passed. The afternoon was no better.

At length, Ewan's patience gave out. "Get on and paint, man, you can't stand there all day!" he shouted to the vision. But it made no difference. By the end of the day the canvas was as blank as at its beginning. The next day was the same. And the next.

Ewan gazed in wonder. In a surprisingly short time he appeared as an old man. His face was bitter, twisted, and cynical. Still he stood before the blank canvas. Still no brush had caressed its surface even once.

It took no wisdom for Ewan to see why. Like parasites, envy and malice had sucked dry his creative juices and wholly absorbed his time and energy. Before long he would die. And there would be nothing to show for his wasted years.

"All right," he muttered to the Rock. "Point made. But I still feel jealous of him."

The Rock's response was the promised second vision.

This time, Ewan saw Sellinge. The occasion was the prestigious Mayfest, and there Sellinge was, irritatingly modest and looking genuinely pleased, receiving accolades for his work to the applause of all present. Ewan scowled.

In the vision he watched his rival return to his boat. His gaze followed him into the cabin, where Sellinge promptly slumped into a chair, buried his face in his hands, and began to cry. Wonderingly, Ewan watched as he rose and walked across to a portrait that hung on the cabin wall.

"I wish you could have been there to see it, Dad," Ewan heard him say. "I really do."

Ewan felt embarrassed that he had intruded upon such a personal scene. He wanted to turn away and leave the man with his private anguish.

Sellinge was addressing the portrait again. "I owe it all to you. You inspired me and encouraged me. You sacrificed for me."

The vision shifted, and Ewan saw a young lad whom he presumed was Sellinge. His father stood beside him encouraging his drawing. Scene after scene flashed by. The boy grew and always the father was there, helping, guiding, directing. Father and son were obviously very close. Ewan felt his envy rising again. He didn't even know who his own father was. No wonder Sellinge had done so well.

"If I had been given that kind of encouragement, I could have been as good," he muttered to himself. "No, better. I would have worked harder."

Just then the scene changed. Sellinge, still a young man, stood alone. Grief devastated his face. In front of him lay the all-too-familiar sight of a drowned man's remains. His father had been washed overboard—another victim of the cruel sea.

Ewan sought to empathize with the appalling loss. He hadn't really missed what he'd never had. But Sellinge had been so close to his father. The light of his life was extinguished, and darkness draped every horizon.

Ewan watched the man approach a canvas. It was blank. Blank for a long time. "Just like my canvas," Ewan thought. "He's eaten up with grief. He'll never paint again."

It was then he recalled that this was a vision of the past. Sellinge had painted again, and very successfully.

He saw the artist reach for his brush. His face was full of emotion. Slowly he dipped it into the paint. Even as the tip touched the canvas, Ewan could see the pain etched on the man's face. Every stroke was excruciating. Agony, exhaustion, perplexity—Ewan saw it all. He tried to keep pace with the artist's passion, to match his creative heartbeat, but he was out of his league, and he knew it.

This man, from the profundity of his pain, would transcend the pinnacles of glory. What he painted was simple but beautiful in the extreme: a curled brown leaf, the last remnant of winter's rage, distorted and dead, slowly rotting—yet by its death nourishing the growth of a solitary, slender, green spring shoot. It was the artist's eloquent testimony to hope and meaning in a hostile world.

Ewan felt like a wrung-out rag when the work was completed. Just observing the process had drained him beyond measure. He was no match. Suddenly, he felt ashamed. He had hated his rival without cause. What right had he to judge this noble man? How had he ever dared to consider himself the better artist?

In a flash he saw that it was people like Sellinge who created the environment for the lesser men and women. If it had not been for the presence and inspiration of this great man, Ewan would not have attained even his own mediocre standards. Envy, cowed by shame, died a silent death and parted from him like a sigh in the wind.

"I have never seen it like that before." He shook his head in wonder as he addressed the Rock.

"You viewed your rival only from the outside. You desired his talent but had no idea of the price involved." It was a patent statement of fact.

"I understand that now—and I'm sorry. I'm humbled, too. As an artist I'm supposed to possess insight. My envy blinded me to reality." Ewan paused. He asked, "Is there always a price? I mean, can there be no greatness without pain?" He ventured more boldly. "Do you feel pain—as the Rock?"

Immediately, Ewan's world began to fall apart. The walls of the tunnel shook violently, then shattered into a thousand flying fragments that were immediately sucked into a vortex of blinding light. Ewan hovered unsupported in a dark void, alone, deep in a starless space. Nothing else existed except the spinning, shimmering helix that hung before him—a world within a world that needed no other. He had never felt more acutely the transitoriness of life nor his total ignorance of its real meaning.

"Learn now from the dawn of wisdom." The voice echoed through the void.

Ewan observed as from the helix a billion stars were flung in glittering showers until the heavens blazed bright with their diamond fire. Worlds followed by the trillion, some large, some small, of many and varied hues. Then tumbled one of no great size but which was encased in an aura of blue as though special beyond all the others. To this Ewan was drawn.

Gazing in wonder he saw rise from the sea a vast annulus of land, a circle of burnished rock ablaze with inner fire. Then, within the sea thus enclosed, there arose many islands, but they were dull and gray.

Though he had never before imagined its full shape, Ewan at once recognized the ring of land to be the selfsame Rock of his acquaintance. People appeared upon its heights and roamed freely over its easy, nurturing contours for many happy years. This was their home.

Then, to Ewan's horror, a flash of lightning struck some of those people, and a cloud of thick darkness fell across the Rock. Within the cloud there arose wars and violence between the tribes and families. Soon there was not space enough to contain their conflicts and their angry demands. People set sail from the Rock and journeyed to the gray islands. Before long the Rock was deserted, and a sullen cloud hung endlessly over the enclosed sea.

Theirs was a self-imposed imprisonment on the islands, and the people again grew restless. They did not know they had taken their curse with them. Some set sail again. Ewan hoped they would return to the Rock to find help, but when they reached its encircling shores they swore and cursed and hurled stones against its cliffs. They accused it of every crime they had done themselves, then vowed its destruction as their only hope of freedom.

The sea grew rough, and it cast many to their doom. But this only increased their rage against the Rock; they blamed it, not the sea, for their deaths. No offering of peace was ever made.

Suddenly Ewan felt sucked down into the very heart of the Rock, where throbbed an emotion of fearsome power. He knew it to be a passion beyond all others, a zealous love that burned as a raging, unquenchable fire, more awesome than hell itself. Desire beyond desire, an eternal love had roused to win back the rebel hearts of men. Subterranean forces boiled and welled until the pressure grew to bursting point, and Ewan let out a long wail of empathetic anguish.

White-hot lava rose from the very heart of the Rock. Like searing life blood, it carved an agonizing path toward the surface until at last it burst through in a tumultuous crashing wave of molten fire and billowing smoke. Love wounded, wept and bled and died.

There remained just one sign when the cataclysm was over. Ewan recognized the cross-shaped fissure—the access into the Rock. Then it began to rain. Water streamed down the hills and gullies. A waterfall cascaded from the heights and poured through the cross in to the very heart of the Rock, where it cooled and soothed and healed. Love lived again, and the way was open for all to enter.

There was nothing Ewan could say. Silent tears rolled down his cheeks. All his life he had been mistaken about the Rock. He saw now that it blocked only the path to self-destruction. He had hated it in ignorance. The Rock had responded with love, a sacrificial love that had forged a path through pain to win him back.

"Rock, I thank you," he said at length. "I still understand so little, but this much I now know—you really do love and care for me." He took a deep breath. It was a profound risk, but the words came out. "Yes, I am beginning to love you in return."

15

THE PERIOD THAT FOLLOWED WAS ONE of superlative happiness for Ewan.

He entered what he imagined must be the nearest thing to a state of bliss. Time ceased to register as a sequence of events and became the fullness of the event itself—an everlasting moment of pure, inexpressible joy. In fellowship with the Rock, he felt he had discovered the true meaning of eternal love.

It would be pointless to record what he and the Rock talked about, or to measure how long this phase lasted. Records can only relate history like the wake left by a boat. Love's intimacy is better described as an ever-widening ripple, radiating from a vibrant center where two souls join as one. Suffice it to say that Ewan's joy was unsurpassed and that he had never felt more alive or in touch with ultimate reality than now.

This being the case, the unexpected manifestation of Sally appeared as an abrupt and unwelcome intrusion upon his present disposition. His immediate response was to wish her away, as is the wont of intimate friends who do not wish a third party to disturb them—particularly when the latter is a former flame! It seemed to Ewan that the love he had felt for Sally in the past was crass and base compared to the transcendent beauty of his present experience.

However, for all his high-mindedness, it was not that simple. Sally beckoned with her seductive eyes. The old feelings suddenly overwhelmed Ewan. In spite of his newly discovered noble instincts and aspirations, he succumbed greedily. It was good—yet not enough. Like a man long deprived of food who is suddenly let loose in the cupboard, his appetite overwhelmed him. He needed her again. To his delight she was compliant—and generous to a fault.

Soon he felt another willing body alongside them. His arms enfolded her too. Next, another one appeared on the scene, then another, until he was veritably engulfed.

His appetite burst all bounds and proprieties. He was in a hedonist's golden paradise. He had become the universal stud in the eternal harem.

His relationship with the Rock, once so vibrant, remained no more than a faded, sepia memory.

"Lust after one woman and you lust after all," he dimly recalled from somewhere. It meant nothing.

IN SPITE OF HIS PRODIGIOUS PROWESS, Ewan grew tired. He had sated his appetite, too, and he now wanted no more than to relax and savor the afterglow of his spent passions.

Yet there was to be no rest. Greed, even lacking appetite, relentlessly drove him on—desire against desire, one compelling need above all other needs drowning his protests and forcing him between ever-narrowing walls, all the while replacing options with obsession.

He felt less urgency this time, and his lust was satisfied the sooner. There was no afterglow of pleasure, either. When he was finished, he gazed at them with a jaundiced eye. Who were these women? Some he recognized from his past, but many were strangers to him. Sally cropped up occasionally, but he hardly recognized her and seemed to desire her no more than any of the others. It dawned on him that he didn't really know her at all, nor she him—and that went for all the rest, too.

Nor did he love them—though, it being the way of man, he murmured appropriate words of endearment at the right time. "A delusion to trigger desire," he thought. "A game played with everyone believing it while they played, until the cold light of day told them otherwise."

He had used the words a lot, but now he saw that "I love you" had meant "I enjoy you"—like, "I love ice cream." Not a very noble sentiment.

The walls of his existence pressed closer. Under the remorseless demands of greed, the physical acts continued interminably, but his heart was in it less and less. So jaded was his appetite that he had to rack his brains for stimulating images. All tenderness and lover's skill departed from him, and he became violent and perverted, degrading and degraded.

"I have become an addict," he thought. "I can't live without this." Panic gripped him. "There's something wrong with the drug. It's not strong enough. I need more—much more!"

He plunged frantically back into the fray.

Willingly the lovers came, hour after hour, day after day. And still the glutted glutton took his fill as though his very existence depended upon it. But the walls were now exceedingly high, and they cast a deep shadow over his soul. A sinister, black mist seeped from the ground. He began to hate his paramours and their endless demands. What little humanity he once felt for them had long since passed. All that mattered now was satisfying his need. Mechanically, he took their living bodies and human souls and wasted them.

A moment later the reality hit him.

With a shock he discovered that the woman he was using had ceased to be flesh and blood at all and had turned instead into a mechanical automaton. Her body and limbs had degenerated into no more than servo-driven pieces of metal. Her face was a steel mask. He gawked at the scene around him. The once erotic theater now resembled a macabre scrap-metal yard filled with tangled, clanking, clanging rods and tubes. Seized with panic, he looked with horror at his own body: he was rapidly deteriorating, too! Already his hands and arms had been reduced to metal levers. Before long he would be a machine like all the rest.

In desperation, he flung himself from the metal figure of his present paramour and stumbled away. The black mist swirled about his feet. Time seemed to speed up. He stared aghast as the jerking humanoid machines, dried-out and worn with age, one by one screeched and groaned to a halt. In the sudden silence, he watched as the corrosive mist ate into their tangled limbs, until finally they crumbled into small piles of meaningless dust. With a sob he turned away.

The fear of death once again gripped him in its cruel claw. Beholding his own decay into mere mechanism, he shuddered with horror and let out a long, terrible cry of anguish. It emerged harsh and metallic, unhuman, echoing desolately from the bleak, imprisoning walls of his dying existence.

"What have I done? What has happened to me?" he cried hoarsely. "I was a man. I behaved like an animal! Must I die a machine? How shall I escape this hell? Oh God, help me!"

Overwhelmed with despair, he sank to his knees like a latter-day penitent.

Where had it all started? The first taste unchecked? Was sex just an appetite demanding satisfaction? Was it love, or the fulfillment of love? Should he then never, ever, in any circumstance, have used a woman for his self-gratification? Ought he only to have indulged in sex as the consummation of a mutually shared and committed love within a marital relationship? Greed could never have grown untrammeled in such a setting!

"I'm sorry, sorry to you all!" he blurted out.

There was no pity in return, nor could there be. No abandonment exceeds that of the man who has eaten himself hollow. Bitter of spirit and utterly alone, Ewan sank into the mist and lay down to die there, in the rusty, dusty mechanist graveyard.

SOMETHING CAUGHT around his foot. It stung slightly as though he had touched an electrically charged wire.

With a faint effort he tried to move his metallized leg clear, but the thing remained attached. He glanced down at it, lifted his leg from the swirling mist, and saw that a thin, silver thread had curled around his ankle. Again, he tried to shake himself free, but the moment he did so it tightened abruptly.

In the next instant, he felt a sharp tug. Before he could do anything to stop it, the tendril began to drag him helplessly across the ground.

Even those dying of despair sometimes put up a last fight. Ewan was no exception. He seized the thread with both hands and pulled. Something akin to an electric shock jolted his body, and the wire leapt from his hands. It then coiled about him with a swift, silvery hiss, and in moments it had him trussed on the ground like a chicken ready for the oven.

The wire dragged him inexorably deeper into the mist. Faintly, he perceived a narrowing corridor between two high walls. He could only assume that this was the last stage of the journey, that it was to end in his total and no doubt painful destruction.

"How else should I go?" he groaned to himself. "I entered into bondage—in bondage I must die."

The darkness deepened, and he lost sight of the walls. All perceptions ceased except the remorseless pull of the thread. He could not even feel the surface of the ground underneath him and, for all he knew, might have been drifting through space.

"Is this hell?" he wondered. "Will I be dragged forever through a lonely, silent void until at last I go insane? Will it be my own madness that will torture me for eternity?"

Suddenly, he felt the thread loosen around his legs and ankles. But this brought on new fears. Was he now to be cast adrift altogether? That would be an even worse hell—an unconstrained madhouse with an inmate of one!

He moved his legs experimentally. To his amazement, his feet touched solid ground. Clanking as though dressed in a suit of armor, he began walking through the darkness, following the insistent tug of the thread that still bound his wrists. Metal legs or not, this was better than the void. A glimmer of hope lifted his spirits.

On and on he paced through the night. As he journeyed he became aware that life—real, flesh-and-blood life—was slowly but surely returning to his limbs. The clanking ceased, and he marveled at the contrast between his former mechanical progress and the living roll of a normal human gait. If previously he had taken this for granted, now he treasured it as never before. Humanity was not for squandering, that was for sure!

The silver thread was exceedingly slender, but as far as Ewan could tell, it was absolutely unbreakable. With a wry grin he thought he now knew how a fish felt when it was being reeled in on a fishing line.

So who was on the other end? And where?

He looked around as the line drew him steadily onward. The darkness had eased, and his spirits rose further. Before long he could perceive the high walls that had previously enclosed his path. They were much further apart now and commensurately lower.

Within a few minutes the mist passed away completely to reveal a dove-gray sky. The walls had vanished altogether, and he was ascending an easy path that led to a low ridge in an otherwise featureless landscape. A growing sense of anticipation sped his pace so that the thread no longer had to tug but simply adjusted to match his mood.

It was obvious to Ewan by now that he was not destined for death. In fact, it had become clear that the insistent thread which first had dragged him away when he was unable to help himself had rescued him precisely from that state. Now, as it led him gently by the hand, Ewan had more than an inkling as to who lay behind his salvation.

"Rock! You didn't let me go. You wouldn't let me go!" he exclaimed aloud.

Fellowship beckoned—love, joy, and peace streamed from an inexhaustible well! Exalted in spirits, Ewan broke into a run. The thread adjusted its pace accordingly.

Panting, he reached the brow of the hill and gazed on a vista of jumbled hills and valleys on the other side. His path swept down to the foot of a tall cliff face, and from where he stood Ewan spied the dark smudge of an opening. The silver thread ran straight toward it. There was a way back into the Rock.

Ewan whooped with delight.

"As fast as you like!" he cried to the thread. "I can see it all now, Rock. Your love is real. It's unbreakable. It will follow me anywhere and keep drawing me irresistibly to yourself. Well, I'm coming—and by my own free choice!"

With that he broke into a sprint and raced down the hill toward the welcoming mouth of the cave. The thread moved at exactly his speed so that he was in no danger of tripping. Within two minutes he had reached the base of the cliff. There he stopped to regain his breath before entering the cave.

Possessing himself like an actor about to go on stage, his face wreathed in smiles, Ewan stepped toward the entrance. It was good to be back. He would say so to the Rock.

Suddenly, a vivid tongue of flame shot from the cave's mouth.

Ewan halted in his tracks. Dismay clouded his features. Had he been duped? Surely the last and cruellest torture for those doomed to damnation was that the very thread in which they hoped should prove an illusion designed to heighten the agony?

He gazed into the fire that now blazed in the cave's entrance. The thread ran limply into its midst. No longer did it pull him forward. Ewan realized that it would be quite possible for him to untie his hands and walk away free.

The thought revived his hopes. This was not the way of torturers, he reasoned. They quickly crushed any illusion of freedom with pitiless violence. Choice was not a word found in their vocabulary.

But it was found in the language of love. Indeed, it was a key word central to the whole notion. It dawned on Ewan that love might jealously rescue him from destruction; and it might lead him to a place of safety. But it would not force him back into fellowship. Nor would blind enthusiasm be sufficient. There was a choice to be made and a price to be paid. He would have to walk through the fire if he wanted to be back inside the Rock.

He sat for a long while and pondered the matter. Was it sex that had all but killed him? Surely not. Sex was a good and natural thing, a wonderful gift to be enjoyed. He had been mistaken in thinking that one love canceled another. A man and a woman should love each other, and family, and friends—and the Rock, too.

Perhaps the last love should condition and suffuse all the others. In which case, there would be no contradiction between the four loves—and "I love you" said in a context of eros would not negate the "I love you" addressed to the Rock. This had another implication, however: The passionate loyalty that characterized the Rock's love would surely have to *infuse* the other loves, notably the sexual.

Ewan whistled in amazement at the novel thought—he, remaining faithful to one woman. It was certainly different!

It was precisely this challenge to faithfulness that enabled him to revise his view of sex. Until now, consciously or not, he had behaved greedily. The hunger had demanded satisfaction, and he had responded accordingly. Yet now, for the first time in his life, he fully understood that sexual love was for giving, not for taking. He was being invited to do nothing less than make one woman happy for the rest of her life.

Maybe he really could rise to the challenge.

"I'll do it," he said quietly. "I've nothing to lose and everything to gain."

With that, he stood to his feet and walked steadfastly into the flames.

❖16❖

FIRE IS to living creatures at once the most fascinating and most fearsome of the four elements. The air they freely and gratefully breathe. The earth they trample underfoot and eat of its produce; water they drink and largely consist of the same. But fire is alien. Living beings cannot assimilate fire; it will always burn them if they try. If fire is not mastered, it will destroy without mercy.

With this in the back of Ewan's mind, it was no easy matter for him to surrender himself to the searing flames that blazed from the cave's mouth. As good as he had reason to presume the outcome to be, the primeval fear shared by all flesh and blood still made him sweat and tremble as he contemplated his fate.

"I am given a choice between death and death," he mused resignedly. "Perhaps that is the meaning of life—to opt either for death by degradation or for death for a higher design. Either way, it's a painful path to have to walk!"

He heaved a sigh and gritted his teeth. This was going to be exceedingly painful.

And with that, he plunged into the flames.

But the anticipated pain never came. His first bold, self-abandoning step into the fire brought no searing agony of blistered flesh, no acrid smell of burning hair, no scream of unendurable pain portending death. Instead, Ewan found to his surprise that he was walking unscathed through a swirling kaleidoscope of bright, ever-changing colors so vivid they blotted out all other perceptions. He gazed about him in wonder. Somehow the thin, silver thread was in his hand again. He clutched it tightly and began to follow its course as his sole guide and comfort through an otherwise totally disorienting and unexpected experience.

He had taken only a few paces when he heard a woman's voice. Like the oracle of some guardian spirit, she seemed to address her clear, mellow tones not to this one passing stranger in particular but to all who chose to pass this way.

"I am Wisdom," she said. "Through me lie the paths of life, though I am not to be found easily. Seek me as you would for silver—search as for the treasures of the deep—for in my counsel is the salvation of the foolish. I am a tree of life to those who find me, and my reward is finer than gold."

She was in Ewan's sight an apparition in the heart of the whirling colors. At first glance she was slender and silver-haloed, a willowy Wisdom of ageless, shining beauty, gray-eyed, serene, and still. A second glance revealed her differently: She was old and gnarled, clothed rustically like a homely oak, and her keen eyes gleamed restlessly from beneath her discerning brows as she searched and knew the hearts of men. The first image one might seek with admiration; the second one would approach with awe. But there would be no rejection in either case. Wisdom smiled in both her forms, and to all who asked she offered sense without reproof.

"Listen, listen now to my words, for I am from the beginning and shall remain beyond the ending of all temporal matters. Turn aside from the path of those fools who seek their own gain. For here is a great folly that I have observed: a man desires what he does not have, so he desires the harder until he tastes a little; then not content he wants it all; and greed thus unleashed turns and devours its bloated slave!"

Her words registered with Ewan. In a dreamlike trance, he began making his way toward her, climbing multicolored steps of fire.

"Be greedy to give, if you want to be wise." The tones rang out with bell-like clarity. "In giving is receiving, in dying is living. This is the eternal wisdom of the Rock."

Ewan pondered the words well as he clambered the stairs toward Wisdom. He felt the tingle of the silver thread as it ran through his fingers. He recalled how the Rock had poured out his love in fiery, passionate self-sacrifice. It was surely his love that had forged the indestructible cord by which the Rock drew willingly to himself the hearts of men and women. In giving all, he received all—and that without regrets of any kind.

Ewan sensed that his entire perspective on life was being redrawn. Where previously he had seen himself as the center of his existence, demanding rightful satisfaction for all his desires, now he perceived that the satisfaction of others must come first. That was the unquestionable heart of the Rock.

As though in response to this change in his outlook, the dizzying colors began to make sense to Ewan. By the time he had ascended the staircase and reached the lady Wisdom, the kaleidoscope had resolved into steady patterns of incredible intricacy and harmony. It was as though a lens had focused his previously fuzzy conceptions into a needle-sharp filigree of intelligible meaning, quite beyond what he had thought possible.

Wisdom spoke no words to him but smiled and laid a hand of benediction upon his brow. A deep, soothing peace suffused his mind. He need no longer be a child of his times, tossed to and fro by the foibles and fancies of the dilettante and the desperate alike. It was a blessed release. Some things, he realized, simply were *right*—in fact, they were truly true! Always and absolutely.

He departed her presence with a newfound confidence and moral resolution, marveling at the clarity of the world around him and wondering why he had never seen it before.

It wasn't long before the beautiful patterns all around him gave way to a familiar green glow. Ewan was safely back in the Rock.

"Ah, there you are," said his host.

"Did you think you had lost me?" Ewan answered.

"No, you are too loved for that," the Rock replied.

"Well, I nearly lost myself." Ewan spoke with the seriousness of a child. "It has been a terrible experience, but I feel much better now. Purified and, er—clarified, if you know what I mean."

The Rock chuckled, a deep and throaty sound that echoed down the tunnel. "I see you have met with Wisdom and learned her lore. It is good, is it not?"

Ewan nodded. "It was the thread of your love which led me from the place of the dead to the pathway of life," he said. "I'm very grateful to you, because I don't think I could have found the way back by myself."

"Doubtless you could not," the Rock assured him. "But your heart is much healthier, and you are making excellent progress. It will not be long now before you arrive at your destination. I have not told you before, but you may now know that it is called The Haven of Souls."

Ewan blinked with surprise. His experiences had so occupied him that he had given very little thought to his eventual destination. Indeed, he had scarcely considered if there were one, let alone what it was like or who was there.

"What is The Haven of Souls?" he asked.

"You will soon see," the Rock replied, evidently in a good-natured mood and enjoying playing with Ewan a little. "Suffice it to say that you will not be alone. You will meet many others like yourself. And, of course, you will always have my presence. There is nothing to fear."

"Will that be the end of my journey, then?" Ewan asked, with a hint of wistfulness in his voice. Much as he might appreciate meeting fellow pilgrims, he had no desire to surrender the splendid exclusivity of his relationship with the Rock.

"It will be more like the beginning," was the enigmatic reply.

"Is it far?"

"For you, just two steps—but big ones," answered the Rock.

"You're talking in riddles," Ewan protested. "And I thought I had just gained Wisdom!"

"She is not for the getting or the possessing, but for the continual asking," the Rock answered. "But that is by the by. One of the riddles is about to be unraveled, if I am not very much mistaken!"

With that his presence seemed to diminish and Ewan, with a slight sigh of exasperation, waited in the gloom for his next fate.

It was not long in coming. Suddenly, a deep, hollow roar echoed down the tunnel.

Ewan knew of lions only from pictures. He had never encountered one face to face, let alone in an enclosed place. But a lion it was, and there was no mistaking it.

The creature in question came bounding toward him at great speed, then stopped abruptly and eyed him warily. Ewan checked his instinct to flee and somehow stood his ground before the ferocious beast. It was obviously angry; he could sense the primeval fury smoldering in the beast's slit yellow eyes. Ewan knew at once it was an issue of territory. The lion commanded the way ahead, and Ewan was a trespasser. One of them would have to give way. Ewan braced himself for a fight in which neither would give any quarter.

Slowly the lion crouched into position, his eyes never wavering from his prey, his jaws slavering onto his great mane, his rippling sinews tightening in preparation for the strike. Ewan responded by assuming an alert, guarded stance, poising his frame like that of a martial-arts fighter. He waited.

However ready one may be for an attack, the actual moment is never without its element of surprise and panic before the adrenaline surges to convert into defensive action. Thus, any illusions Ewan possessed concerning his ability to ward off his adversary were instantaneously dashed to the ground as, suddenly, with a throaty snarl of rage, the lion sprang. The animal's sheer, overwhelming weight smashed Ewan helplessly to the floor.

At once the beast was upon him, and Ewan struggled frantically to avoid the snarling jaws and fierce claws that sought his flesh. He expected to be ripped to shreds at the next instant, but somehow—by good fortune or sheer desperation—he managed to twist himself onto the lion's back and to seize his mane.

It was an all-too-brief respite. The big cat twisted and rolled over, crushing Ewan under his weight so that he thought his ribs had burst. He gasped agonizingly for breath, coughing and spluttering in the acrid stench that reeked from the animal's hide. He pulled hard on the mane. This was sufficient to free him, and he staggered to his feet. In the next instant, however, a startling blow from the lion's powerful back leg slammed him against the tunnel wall. Half-stunned, but in time to avoid being torn to shreds, he dived beneath the lion's belly and delivered a well-aimed kick in the process.

With a snarl of rage mixed with pain, the animal leapt clear, but as it did so its hind paws clawed and tore great gashes into Ewan's flesh. He shrieked with the awful pain. In an instant, the hot, putrid blast of the creature's breath was on his face. Desperately, Ewan kicked and punched, writhing and twisting to avoid the terrible jaws that sought his life.

Such an unequal fight could not last long. Weakened by his wounds and exhausted from the struggle, Ewan staggered back against the tunnel wall and buckled at the knees. Sensing victory, the lion coiled for the death blow.

"Who are you?" Ewan gasped. "Why have you come here?"

"I am your hatred of your father," growled the lion.

"I never knew my father," Ewan protested in amazement. "How could I hate him?"

"But you do," the lion snarled in reply. "You hate him, whoever he was. He failed you. He deserted your mother. He denied you what you saw other children enjoying."

"That's true," Ewan acknowledged.

"Your father never took you on his knee. He didn't teach you to walk or tell you stories. You never held his hand. You had no role model, no guide, no correction, no man you could be proud of and say, 'That's my dad.' He rejected you. He is the biggest traitor in your world. Isn't he?" The lion spat out the words.

"Yes! Yes! That's right. He made me illegitimate and left me an orphan," Ewan cried. "Yes, I have every right to hate him. He deserves to suffer and die. I do hate him! I really do hate him! With all my heart I loathe the very thought of him!" he screamed. "I want him dead!"

"Now you know why I am here," the lion growled.

"But why are you attacking me?" Ewan demanded bitterly. "It's my father you should destroy. He's the culprit, not me."

"I am here because that is my nature," the lion answered. "I cannot be otherwise. I must destroy all who use me to destroy others."

With that the beast snarled loudly and crouched again for the kill.

"No! No! There has to be another way," Ewan cried in desperation. "What must I do? Give me wisdom. Teach me! Teach me now."

Through the red haze of panic he heard the calm, mellow voice of lady Wisdom. "Forgive your father, Ewan."

The words were simple but devastating.

"I can't," he wailed. "He has hurt me too much. He hurt my mother, too."

"Forgive him," she insisted.

"It's not fair," he cried.

"It is merciful—and wise," she answered.

The lion's patience was at an end. With a roar he leapt for Ewan's throat.

"All right, I forgive him. Whoever you are, Dad, I forgive you!" he yelled in desperation.

Ewan twisted instinctively to avoid the gnashing teeth, and by some superhuman effort he managed to leap astride the lion's back. Gasping for breath he curled his arms about its neck and squeezed hard. Strength beyond his own surged through his body.

Harder and harder he pulled while the great beast thrashed and struggled for release. Then Ewan knew he was winning. "I do really forgive you Father," he sobbed. "From my heart. You were wrong, unjust, uncaring—but I choose to be merciful. I choose to let you go."

There was a sudden, sharp crack, like the snap of a stick. At once the lion's body fell limp to the ground. The creature was dead.

With tears pouring down his face, clothes torn and flesh bleeding, Ewan staggered from the kill and promptly fainted with exhaustion.

❖17❖

EWAN'S FIRST SENSATION as he regained consciousness was of cold water dripping onto his face. He shook his head and tried to wipe his eyes, but for some inexplicable reason he was unable to do so.

He lay very still and waited while his head cleared. It was too soon to open his eyes, he decided. Experimentally, he tried to sense the rest of his body: he was lying on his back, wasn't in any pain, and, as far as he could tell, had all his vital organs in place. He couldn't move his limbs, but it was comforting to know he still had limbs to be moved.

Dimly, he recalled his terrible ordeal with the lion. A tremor ran through his body at the memory. It seemed a long time ago now. He had fought, and won—then darkness had fallen.

Slowly, the thudding pulse in his head receded, and to Ewan's relief the irritating drip of water also ceased. He decided to risk opening his eyes.

To his amazement he was confronted by the sprinkler of a miniature silver watering can held not more than a handsbreadth away from his nose. He blinked in astonishment and shook his head to clear the water from his eyes.

"Ah, there you are. Good."

The voice, male and coolly smooth, came from behind Ewan's head. He had to twist and strain his neck in an effort to see who it was standing over and behind him. From his awkward position he could make out the upside-down features of a solemn, gray-faced old man. It was he who held the watering can, delicately poised between an elegant finger and thumb.

Ewan lowered his gaze to his own torso. The reason for the immobility of his limbs at once became apparent. He was lying on a stone slab, and broad leather straps tightly pinioned his arms and legs to it by means of inset steel rings. That fact aside, he appeared to be in good shape otherwise—his clothes were intact, and there was no sign of any injuries.

It all was rather too much to take in, however, and for a few moments Ewan lay in contemplative silence, his eyes fixed abstractedly on the silver watering can.

"Where am I?" he asked suddenly. "Why am I tied down like this? And who on earth are you?"

Unhurried, the figure moved to Ewan's side so as to be seen without causing the bound man to twist his head. The figure in question was tall and thin, and his somewhat angular frame was clad in a long, black university gown. On his head he wore a mortarboard from which protruded wisps of scraggly gray hair. He gazed down at Ewan through a pair of silver-framed, half-moon spectacles perched on the end of his protuberant nose.

"Allow me to introduce myself," he said politely. "I am Pedagogus Pedanticus—your tutor."

"Who?" said Ewan, incredulous.

The man sighed in slight exasperation and repeated his name.

"But—what happened? I mean, the lion? How did I get here?" Ewan gabbled.

"Tut, tut," said Pedanticus, shaking his head. "What is all this frivolous talk of lions, boy? There are no such things. Where do you get such foolish ideas? I can see there is much to be remedied here, and not a moment too soon."

Ewan opened his mouth in protest, but the man held up a palm and continued:

"Imagination is illusion—fantasy is folly. Children's amusements are not for grown men, and it is high time you grew up."

"The lion was very real to me—it still is," Ewan objected.

"So it would have seemed in your disturbed state," Pedanticus answered.

"What on earth do you mean by that? You surely don't think I've gone mad, do you?" Ewan demanded. "Hey," he said suspiciously, "that's not the reason I'm strapped down, is it?" He glanced around at the plain white cell, relieved to see the walls were not padded.

"The term *mad* is so ill-defined and unhelpful that we prefer not to use it. Let us say rather that you have been suffering from a temporary mental aberration coupled with emotional stress—and that is all," Pedanticus replied soothingly. "It is nothing to fear. Such afflictions can strike almost anyone. Fortunately, the effects are seldom more than transitory. As for the safety harness, try not to think about it and you will hardly be aware of its existence."

"But I felt the pain—I wrestled with the lion," Ewan protested.

"Self-induced hypnosis," the professor replied promptly. "A common enough phenomenon. Disturbing, to be sure, but nothing to worry about. You are perfectly safe now."

Ewan tugged doubtfully at his bonds.

"I'm not sure I want to be safe," he said. "I liked it when I was talking with the Rock."

"Goodness gracious! This is worse than I'd first thought," cried Pedanticus. "You believe you have been talking to a rock? *Deludum majorum*, no less! We must work with extreme diligence to return you to normality, my boy."

"I thought I was very normal."

"That is the trouble with delusion—it deludes," said Pedanticus smugly. "I must instruct your reason, for I perceive you to be an intelligent subject capable of the necessary education.

Given time, by means of such an approach it should be possible to restore your rationality so that you may resume your proper place in society."

Not waiting for a reply, the tutor began pacing back and forth across the room, resting one hand on the lapel of his gown and waggling an emphatic forefinger. He was poised to launch into a lecture.

"We commence with ourselves and our awareness of our own existence. In spite of occasional challenges from radical skeptics, our self-awareness is the most certain of all possible starting points. We then verify our existence and the validity of our senses by communication with others of like species. Slowly, painstakingly, we construct a rational framework of ideas built from measurable and observable data, and it is this which provides us with the basis for society and progress. So far, so good, hmm?"

He turned on his heel and approached Ewan with a light in his eye. It was then Ewan observed a ball and chain attached to Pedanticus's right foot. This drew the professor's attention to it and in consequence extracted from him a look suggesting that such matters were not to be referred to in polite, let alone sophisticated, company.

"It is nothing," said Pedanticus indifferently. "I could have it removed, of course, but it so scarcely interferes with my life that it is not worth the bother. There are more weighty matters to be concerned with, if you will pardon the pun, and speaking of which I suggest we redirect our attention to these rather than distracting ourselves with impertinent observations concerning my person."

"Sorry," mumbled Ewan. He set his gaze steadfastly on the ceiling. "Do continue, please."

"Very well. Problems concerning progress arise because of the regrettable human penchant for irrationality. It is all based upon fear, of course—fear of deprivation, of constraint, of domination, even of death. Our dreams are an expression of wish fulfillment, a nonrational longing which seeks to quell this fear. It is a process that eases the burden caused by the unfortunate mortality of our existence. But—and this is the point, my boy—it must never be allowed to become the basis for our existence. If it does, then madness ensues."

"But supposing those dreams—those illusions, as you call them—are the dim reflections or even the signposts to something or someone who is actually there?" interjected Ewan.

"Impossible to know," Pedanticus said curtly. "By definition unprovable."

"So you give no credit to my experience, simply because your particular measuring apparatus is incapable of assessing it," Ewan remarked scornfully. "Suppose I come across others who have had the same experiences?"

"Mass delusion. Mere racial and cultural archetypes reinforced by mutual reassurances to one another," Pedanticus replied with equal scorn. "There are always fairies at the bottom of the garden and wicked witches in the woods. Why? Because one generation passes the myth to another, *ad infinitum.*"

"But why should these, and others like them, be the common archetypes?" Ewan demanded. "You dismiss their reflecting any objective reality on the grounds that you don't consider them capable of scientific investigation. So you relegate all our dreams and longings, our images and aspirations, to nothing more than folklore. Really! For a tutor you don't seem to think very deeply."

"I'll ignore your insult, for the moment," Pedanticus said testily. "Frankly, I'm not prepared to waste the effort on vanities. My own theory is that the communality of the archetypes is due to a generic electrochemical process in the human brain. I expect the evidence to be forthcoming in the not-too-distant future. For the present, given the state of current research, orthodoxy dictates that they merely reflect and express our unconscious longings for security and meaning in an otherwise meaningless universe."

Ewan tussled at his bonds in frustration.

"So you assume that it all has to do with our search for meaning," he said. "Suppose someone were searching for us? Suppose they were trying to make contact?"

"Sheer nonsense—unless you mean intelligent life-forms from other planets, which I take it you do not," the tutor said with an urbane air. "There is nothing out there—no God, no spiritual reality."

"Where is your evidence?" screamed Ewan. "You just will not look!"

"Now that's enough, young man," Pedanticus said sternly. "Are you really so arrogant as to challenge the findings of every serious scholar on the planet? Have you no respect at all for the accrued wisdom of mankind?"

"Not when it is intellectually dishonest and downright lazy," Ewan answered hotly.

"I fear you will obtain no advancement or preferment if you continue with these obscurantist, not to say, fundamentalist notions," Pedanticus warned. With some affectation, he assumed a more relaxed, intimate posture. "Listen, my boy, I was like you once. I questioned the status quo. I searched for a spiritual reality, for someone—or something—out there. But I discovered it to be a foolish venture, a sideline to true intellectual pursuits. Believe me, if you follow this current you will miss the mainstream of human progress."

"You mean the orthodoxy of rationalism," said Ewan. "The closed system of cause and effect. The world that allows for no intervention."

"Precisely."

"I thought that way once upon a time," Ewan said. "I believed along with everybody else that there was no life in the Rock. I took it that all human experiences had to be either verifiable or discarded as nonsense. My painting was creative and emotive but always undergirded by cold rationalism. Then one night I saw a shining jewel fall from the Rock. It wasn't an illusion. I wasn't drunk, high, or particularly depressed. It happened to me during a perfectly normal evening. But from that time onward I was possessed by an unquenchable longing to find the source of that light. I set out on a quest to do so. Everyone, including the girl I loved, told me I was looking for never-never land. But I found it. I found my way into the Rock—and he's alive—more alive than you or I!"

"This is all very subjective—" Pedanticus began to protest.

"No more than your own observations," Ewan cut in. "You cannot say with any ultimate assurance that your perceptions are real. You even had to dismiss the radical skeptics who deny that we can know anything. On what basis do you do that? How can you know that what you are seeing is real? Surely your own relativistic philosophy seriously undermines the possibility of your being sure about anything. Let's face it, your 'scientific proof' is no more than a current orthodoxy which will be scorned out of court in fifty years' time."

"It works," Pedanticus said lamely.

"So does my perception of the living Rock!" Ewan's words were stout. "Frankly, it answers a lot more questions than what I used to believe ever did. I use the word *believe* advisedly, for I see now that it takes just as much faith to believe there is no life in the Rock as it does to believe there is. Your protests about objectivity are a cop-out. It boils down to a matter of having the courage and the will to explore my option seriously."

"Even if I were to grant you that, I would have to question the worth of your experience," said Pedanticus. "History surely has to do with the human race growing out of those useless superstitions which have hindered progress and kept us in the dark ages for so long. Religion is the constant enemy of progress. Read the history books—the more we shake off its shackles, the more we discover. Look at the improvements in education and health. Consider the wealth of our scientific and technical achievements. If we were to accept your alternative, we would end up with a world consisting of nothing more than visionaries sitting on ash heaps!"

"Even if that were true, it certainly would be no worse than your world of frenetic activists who haven't a clue as to what it's all for," Ewan retorted. "Or are you going to fall back on some myth like blind evolution to justify your pragmatic existence? What's your meaning, your purpose, your origin? Survival of the fittest, genetic determinism, or sheer luck?"

"Evolution is an established observation," Pedanticus attempted defensively.

"Nonsense, it's a circular argument. Assume no Creation, interpret the evidence on that premise, and conclude evolution, not Creation!"

Ewan struggled at his bonds again. They were loosening. "You accept it just because you are afraid to explore the alternatives. I have found a genuine reason for my existence. As I understand it—and I'm still learning—my relationship with the Rock gives me the solid base for a truly purposeful exploration and development of the world for the benefit of mankind."

One hand came free from his bonds. He sat up and tugged at the other strap.

"Obscurantist, fundamentalist, regressive, dreamer—religious cripple!" Pedanticus cried.

"Your kind are always the same. When all else fails you can do no more than settle for smear words to cover up your lazy dishonesty," Ewan yelled. "It's pathetic!"

He pulled at the last strap binding his legs and was free. In one leap he was off the stone slab and standing before Pedanticus. Indignant, he seized the lapels of the man's gown.

"I will respect true learning and honor honest teachers," he said. "Doubtless your credentials are admirable and you have seniority. But you have proved unworthy of the honor!"

With that he tore the gown from Pedanticus's shoulders.

To Ewan's surprise—and to the intense chagrin of his antagonist—Pedanticus wore underneath his gown no more than a set of sickly yellow combinations, across the front of which was inscribed the word *Sloth*. With a cry of dismay and hunching himself like an actor attempting to conceal his modesty in a bedroom farce, Pedanticus clutched the ball and chain to himself and huddled in a corner.

"At last I am free to think," Ewan declared with satisfaction.

He strode from the room and back into the tunnel, leaving the hapless Sloth, alias Pedagogus Pedanticus, to his scientific cesspool.

"Well done," said the familiar voice of the Rock a few moments later. "Most impressive."

Ewan laughed. "I've come a long way, haven't I? Imagine, I thought I had arrived as soon as I entered the cross and got free from the Haunter."

"Ah well, it would have been too much for you to have coped with all that at once. Few humans know just how much they are in need of freeing when first they encounter me," the Rock replied.

"So am I really free now?" Ewan asked anxiously.

"Indeed you are," the Rock boomed bountifully. "Free now to really start growing."

"So what happens now? Do I simply continue through this tunnel?"

The Rock responded with a long, resonant laugh that echoed and reechoed down the tunnel. Ewan began to laugh also.

It dawned on him then that the dimensions of the tunnel were such that he could comfortably walk upright. Indeed, he could no longer recall a time when it had been any different, though he was certain it must have been smaller at some point in the past. Slightly bemused, he shook his head and strode confidently forward.

Just then, he noticed a small stream of water trickling along the floor. It gurgled and tinkled as though it were going somewhere exciting. Eagerly, Ewan hastened on, splashing as he went.

Soon he wished he hadn't—for the tunnel floor sloped unexpectedly downward at such a steep angle that he slipped over, landed on his backside with a wet splash, and began at once to slide feet first down the chute. All around him the Rock laughed with such a deep joy that Ewan found himself not only unafraid but joining in the joke.

Faster and faster he slid, by now enveloped in a flood of gushing water, until suddenly he shot from the tunnel's mouth and landed with a violent splash in a small, ornamental pool of clear water. A light fountain sprayed from a slender alabaster vase directly in front of him.

Unhurt but astonished beyond measure, Ewan looked around to find himself in a huge cavern, the mouth of which opened onto a vast, shining sea lit by a sky of the most exquisite blue he could ever imagine.

A fair-haired young man clad in a white robe stood by the edge of the pool. Standing next to him was a little cherub-faced girl. She had curly blonde hair and wore a white dress.

"Welcome to The Haven of Souls," he said. "My name is Mark."

"And my name is Lizzie, but sometimes people call me Elizabeth," the little one announced.

❖18❖

THE SUDDENNESS AND MANNER OF HIS ENTRANCE LEFT Ewan temporarily stunned. Oblivious to his sopping condition, let alone to the presence of his hosts, he simply sat in the pool and gazed in openmouthed wonder at his new surroundings. The contrast between the muted confines of the tunnel and the billowing volumes of incandescent air that now enveloped him left him breathless and totally deprived of speech.

The cavern itself truly was enormous: a vast, airy space, lofty and grand, a craggy cathedral opulent with light as cathedrals should be. On all sides, coruscated columns of rugged, multihued rock soared, embraced, and celebrated the luminous air. While high in the vaulted roof a wide circle of perfect blue announced an opening, in and out of which glittering white doves flew continually.

A brilliant turquoise sea lay shimmering beneath the cloudless sky beyond the mouth of the cave and gently lapped the golden shore. It was the stuff of dreams to Ewan's entranced eye—an eye that, except in flights of imagination, had previously seen nothing but gray seas and drab skies. He could only marvel at the sight. A warm waft of tangy sea air excited his nostrils and stirred his sailor's blood so that all his senses thrilled in unison to the sudden piquancy of life.

He took a deep breath and returned his gaze to his hosts. Still at a loss for words, he sighed, hardly sure whether he wanted to laugh or cry. Had he doubted he would make it to the end? Had he wondered if this distant shore really existed?

Somehow, he thought, the last step of the journey should have been more painful than this. The fact that he had been granted such easy access to this realm of wondrous beauty left him choked with inexpressible gratitude. He knew he did not deserve it.

"I've actually made it! I've reached The Haven of Souls!" he gasped at last.

"You're all wet!" said the little girl.

The young man beside her laughed cheerfully. "Hardly surprising since he's sitting in a pool of water, is it? You do state the obvious sometimes, Lizzie."

"Obviously," she replied with a cheeky grin.

"She's always like this," he explained to the bemused Ewan. "Pretty impressive, all this, eh? Don't worry, everyone is speechless when they first arrive. You'll grow used to it. Though I warn you, this is only the beginning of wonders! I've been here for years, and I still keep marveling at what I see."

Ewan finally found his voice. "I always imagined heaven would be wonderful somehow, but I could never really picture it or feel what it would be like. But this—this is amazing! The color, and the light. It feels so buoyant, so—incredibly alive! And they've even sent an angel and a . . . a cherub to meet me!"

Lizzie tittered into her hands while Mark, smiling, coughed apologetically. "Um, I'm no angel, I'm afraid. And Lizzie here certainly isn't. We're just human beings like you—nothing special, except that we've come through the Rock, too. Nor is this heaven, if by that you mean the place of final bliss." He looked a shade embarrassed. "I'm sorry. I don't mean to disappoint you. If it helps, I made the same mistake myself when I arrived here."

"I didn't," cried Elizabeth. "I always, always knew!" With that she began skipping around in triumphant circles and then darted off toward the center of the cavern.

"She's my kid sister," Mark explained. "You'll like her. She's great fun."

Ewan relaxed a little. "It's all right. I'm not really disappointed. Probably a bit relieved, actually. I suppose I would like a little bit more warning of imminent heaven, if you know what I mean."

Mark nodded knowingly.

Ewan added, "I'm just glad you've put me right so soon. Let's face it, after all I've come through I realize I've been confused about so many things in my life. And, frankly, I can do with all the help I can get." He laughed and shook his head. "I've grown rather used to all my ideas being stood on their head, so it's nothing new! Anyway, I really am grateful there's someone here to meet me."

"Come on," said his host. "Hop out of the pool and we'll show you round. Don't worry, you'll soon dry out. It's never cold here. I've been told to introduce you to a few people just to get you started. After that, you are free to explore and meet people to your heart's content. Oh, and don't be afraid to ask questions. Ignorance isn't bliss at The Haven of Souls!"

As Ewan clambered from the pool, he realized with a start that he was clad in a white robe similar in style to the one worn by his guide. The change from his old seafaring garb had occurred unnoticed, and he marveled at the subtle humor of the Rock in not drawing his attention to the fact. The material was such that the sheen appeared to pick up color from the surroundings. At least, that was Ewan's first impression; then his artist's eye told him this could not be so unless the light behaved differently here.

Mark quickly noticed his puzzlement. "I couldn't figure it out at first, either," he said. "Then I discovered that the color actually changes according to your mood. It's like having the interplay of your emotions turned into light and projected through your clothes. It makes us an incredibly honest society here, because after a while you can almost always read what another person is feeling."

Elizabeth came running up at that moment. "My brother makes everything sound complicated," she said. "What he means is you can shine what you feel through your clothes." She screwed up her face, and Ewan watched as her dress turned to a blue sheen. "I decided to feel cold and sad," she explained. "Most of the time I'm sunny colored, 'cause I'm nearly always happy."

The thought of such instant transparency turned Ewan's expression a shade doubtful.

"Don't worry," Mark reassured him. "We don't sit in judgment on one another here. And besides, all the really nasty stuff's been taken out of you, hasn't it? That's why you are here in the first place."

"True enough," Ewan acknowledged. "I was just thinking that where I come from, clothes are worn as part of an elaborate act. The last thing anyone wants is to be seen for what he really is. People would sooner be physically naked than show their inner nature."

"The same for me," said Mark. "I'm a sculptor, and in my society nudity represented lust, or shame, or vulnerability, even the heroic. But we always struggled with the idea of naked innocence because we had too much to hide. Still, that's all in the past. Time to get on with the future. You're a painter, aren't you?"

Ewan nodded.

Mark shook his head in amusement. "The Rock does some strange things. You're a painter, so he sends you to a sculptor! Why not to some of the other painters? Ah, well, there's always a reason. I hope you don't mind, but the people who live nearest to here are all sculptors."

"Not at all," Ewan said. "Sculptors always remind us two-dimensional workers that life comes in three planes. So lead on!"

"And painters remind us that form is more than just light and shade," answered Mark. "I can see we're going to get on just fine, Ewan."

"Come and look at the pictures," Elizabeth urged, and she took Ewan's hand and tugged him toward the cavern wall. Amused by her ingenuous charm, Ewan followed easily. Children had played very little part in his previous existence, but in Elizabeth's presence he felt truly relaxed. He enjoyed listening as she chattered away while they crossed the broad floor.

In spite of Elizabeth's childlike zeal, there evidently was no hurry. Ewan was content to marvel at the color and texture of the Rock, to observe with wonder the doves flitting in and out of the opening in the roof, and, above all, to drink in the splendor of the light. He wanted to savor every aspect of his new environment, and though tempted to rush immediately toward the beautiful sea, he suppressed the impulse.

When they reached the far wall, Ewan felt like a spectator at a fabulous art gallery where all the pictures were alive and constantly changing in form. The light played on (or from, he couldn't decide which) the rich hues of the Rock in such an ingenious manner that it was possible to perceive on its surface all manner of differing shapes and pictures: Flocks of wild geese streamed above herds of horses in full gallop. Soaring spires shook hands with fluffy white clouds. Ships in full sail carved exultant paths through seas of liquid crystal. Majestic mountains and fertile plains watered by great rivers glowed under golden sunsets. Whatever else The Haven of Souls might be, it had the makings of a visual paradise for Ewan.

Elizabeth ran from one scene to another, squealing with delight. At one point Ewan spied her stroking what looked like a smiling porpoise leaping from the Rock. "Rock, you are so wonderful and clever," he overheard her whisper.

Ewan realized with a jolt that the presence of the Rock was as real here as it ever was in the tunnel. "Thank you for bringing me here," he breathed. He then added with a twinge of conscience, "Sorry I didn't say so earlier. It was just a bit overwhelming."

To his unutterable joy, Ewan felt within him an answering response that assured him all was well. There would be, he was told, no more sudden withdrawals of the Rock's presence as had happened in the tunnel; and the Rock for his part would not feel at all offended if, while Ewan concentrated on matters occupying his other senses, he did not engage in continuous conversation.

"I am here always, and I will be with you forever," he said. "My voice will come to you through a multitude of forms and people, and we shall speak together directly often enough. Enjoy the full music of my world and begin your new life, Ewan."

As the three roamed the broad compass of the cavern Ewan began to ask questions. He found in Mark a willing source of information. Ewan's first concern was about their whereabouts. It amazed him to discover that the Rock was not, as he had thought, an endless, straight barrier stretching across the ocean, but a ring that completely encircled the sea where he formerly had made his living. He remembered then that this was how he had seen the Rock during his vision of the dawning of creation. At the time he had considered it an incidental detail, a surreal distortion of reality designed to accommodate the Rock in his finite thinking. It came as something of a shock to Ewan now to learn that this was actually how things were! Not that he resisted the notion—indeed, he laughed aloud at the irony of it all. No wonder those who searched for a way around the Rock never found one and they always seemed to come back to where they had started!

"You know, my entire map of reality has been rewritten since I first saw that light fall from the Rock," Ewan laughed.

"I cannot believe how ignorant I was. Talk about the blind leading the blind!"

"Half the trouble with people is that they either have no idea at all of their whereabouts, or they live with a completely false idea," Mark noted. "Take that sea where you used to live. It is sometimes called the Sea of Human Endeavor. Why? Because people don't know their geography. Here, from a better perspective, it's known accurately as the Sea of Futility. It's all a vain search for existence and meaning while trying to escape from the Rock. No one realizes the Rock is inescapable, whichever direction you take!"

"I call it the Sea of Silly Billies, 'cause I can't say that other word properly," Elizabeth piped in. "And they are silly Billies anyway, all those people hating the Rock!"

The two men laughed, and Mark hoisted his little sister onto his shoulders. She quickly occupied herself with plaiting his hair.

Mark explained to Ewan that without the limiting presence of the Rock, human beings, given the chance (and no matter how good their intentions) would always mix a fatal cocktail of untempered progress and unmitigated evil. The result would be an intolerable universe, a hell of endless injustice from which there could be no escape.

"Human activities are poisoned, and given no restraints the poison will always prevail," Mark said trenchantly.

Ewan pondered this for a moment. "You mean like the way we discover wonderful creative and technological ideas and then use them to make weapons of war to destroy the very things we have discovered?" Ewan suggested.

"That's one obvious example," Mark agreed.

"The thing we most hated about the Rock was that it wouldn't let us go any further," Ewan observed. "It was its restriction on our freedom that we found so intolerable. We wanted to choose, even if that meant destroying ourselves. I see now that this is an utterly arrogant attitude, and the Rock has every good and right reason to hinder us."

"It's for our own good," Mark said. "The innocent and the guilty need protecting from an evil that is, if they only knew it, greater than either party."

"I found most of that evil within myself," Ewan said soberly.

"Which is why we all need to find our way into the Rock," Mark replied. "It's the only way to purge the evil. Hard, but it must be faced—as we discovered for ourselves."

"You two obviously have your own stories to tell. And I suppose I'll meet a lot of people with different tales. Tell me, are there many ways into the Rock?" Ewan asked.

"Oh no, only one, and that's the way you came in," Elizabeth interjected. She continued to toy absentmindedly with Mark's hair. "You have to go through the cross, 'cause that's the place where the Rock lets out all his love."

Ewan was silent for a moment and recalled the time when the Rock had shown him this. He found it difficult to frame the next question. "Sorry to ask this, but—if there is only one way in, doesn't that make it very difficult for most people to find their way there? It took me quite a long time."

Mark smiled up at Elizabeth, then at Ewan. "Actually, it makes it very easy," he said. "You see, that shape of the cross always matches the true longing which was planted in your heart. So the moment you see it, you know it's the right way. Didn't you feel an irresistible urge to enter the crevice when you got there, in spite of all the obstacles?"

Ewan acknowledged the fact readily enough. But he still wondered at the length of the journey to reach the opening. For some people it could take a lifetime, he surmised.

"It needn't be as long as you might think," Mark explained. "You see, the Sea of Human Endeavor looks bigger than it actually is. Compared to the Sea of Infinite Possibilities"—he held up a hand to restrain the question on the tip of Ewan's tongue—"it is very small indeed. So, there may be only one way into the Rock, but the entrance isn't really very far from anyone. In fact, you probably sailed past it several times without recognizing it, simply because you couldn't see properly at the time."

"That awful light," said Ewan.

"And the Haunter. I'm sure you encountered him."

Ewan shuddered at the memory. "Oh yes."

"I hate him," Elizabeth said intently. "He used to give me nightmares and things. That's why I went into the Rock. He always gives me nice dreams."

Ewan asked Elizabeth how old she was. She said she thought she was probably about six years of age, but that she wasn't very good at remembering things like that. Mark nodded to Ewan at the mention of the number six.

"Wasn't that a bit young to go through the Rock?" Ewan asked her.

"When you get older your journey gets longer," she replied. Her answer made Ewan realize that she possessed a wisdom beyond her tender years.

"Do you understand about the Haunter?" Mark asked. "He's the Guardian, the warder trying to keep everyone a prisoner. The longer he has people, the tighter their bonds become and the greater their deception. Actually, he's the one who inspires most of the hatred against the Rock, because he's a prisoner, too—a prisoner of his own pride. Lizzie spared herself a lot of trouble by entering the Rock early in life."

Now they were approaching the mouth of the cavern, and Ewan could contain himself no longer. The golden strand and the sparkling blue beckoned irresistibly. He quickened his pace. Elizabeth ran ahead, and Ewan broke into a run himself and joined her on the beach.

Ewan had to shade his eyes against the brilliance of the light.

"This is amazing," he exclaimed.

Presently Mark caught up with them.

"Mark," Ewan asked, "you called this the Sea of Infinite Possibilities. What does it mean?"

"Lizzie calls it the Sea of Infant Billies," Mark chuckled. "Seriously, it means what it says. If you think of the other side of the Rock as restraining evil, here you are in the realm of his endless creative goodness. Because you have been purified from evil, you are free to share the Rock's genius to your heart's content and to use your artistic gifts to the full."

"You mean I can paint?" Ewan gasped. He had quite expected—and had accepted—that with the death of his old self, his artistic gifts probably had died as well, or at least would be forbidden expression. That he would be allowed to exercise those gifts in such glorious surroundings was like being told he had just inherited a fortune. He was overjoyed at the prospect.

Mark laughed at his response. "Yes, I can see you really are an artist. I'll look forward to seeing your work once you get started."

"I think I'll paint the sea first. The water is such an amazing color," Ewan marveled. "And that sky—so blue! But I see no sun. Where does the light come from?"

"Like everything else, it comes from the Rock," Mark answered. "Turn around."

Ewan did so. What he saw caused him to sink slowly to his knees in openmouthed awe.

All his life he had known the Rock only as a drab, formless mass. He had expected to see some type of powerful light set high on a dull ridge or pinnacle. He had not anticipated this.

The entire Rock blazed and glowed, burned and scintillated, sparkled and shone like crystal lit from within by living fire. As high as the heavens stretched and as far as the eye could see, there was nothing but pure, splendid, boundless light. Overwhelmed, Ewan prostrated himself before the sight; in trembling worship he truly knew the meaning of holiness.

"Truth. You are, of all truth, the Truth," he breathed.

❖19❖

EWAN HAD NO WAY OF KNOWING how long he remained bowed before the splendor that shone from of the Rock. It was a moment of pure, timeless adoration that transported him far beyond his mortal sense of beginnings or endings and deep into the realms of infinity itself. Yet one simple, instinctively timed and unapologetic touch on the shoulder by Elizabeth was sufficient to return him to his more familiar sphere.

"You will be able to stand up now," she said with a child's matter-of-factness. "Come on, up you get!"

Ewan nodded dumbly and rose unsteadily to his feet. The light was less overwhelming than at first, but still he felt in a complete daze. Mark smiled kindly at his confusion.

"That was just amazing," Ewan gasped. "I can't begin to describe . . . I mean . . . overwhelming . . . glorious . . . I . . ."

Mark held up his hand. "Don't even try," he interposed. "The glory of the Rock is beyond words."

Ewan shook his head in wonder and sighed. "The glory of the Rock," he repeated. "What an understatement! All these years—and I never even imagined the possibility. What a fool I was!"

"Grown-ups sometimes grow up very silly," Elizabeth piped in. "Especially when they only look at things from one side. I think you should look round the back, 'cause sometimes the back is the front, if you know what I mean."

Ewan laughed. "I think I'm only beginning to understand that, Lizzie."

They waited patiently while Ewan regained his breath and composure.

"Feeling all right now?" Mark asked after a suitable interval. "Because if you're all set we can go and meet one or two of my friends in The Sculptor's Gallery."

"My friends as well!" Elizabeth protested.

"Yours as well," Mark agreed. He tousled his sister's hair good-naturedly while she screwed her face up in a cheeky scowl.

As they walked along the beach with Elizabeth swinging playfully from their arms, Mark and Ewan discussed the splendor of the Rock. Ewan kept his eyes to the ground, still unable to cope with the brightness. Yet he wanted to know why he could now remain on his feet and be in control of himself and why Mark and Elizabeth hadn't fallen down in worship along with him. Had they developed an immunity, or what?

Mark, with liberal interjections from his sister, explained that although the Rock possessed such a glory as to overwhelm mere mortals, it was not his way to invoke sheer power in his dealings with them.

"There was much talk of freedom where we came from," he said. "The trouble is, the more people seek freedom by rebelling against the Rock, the deeper they get into bondage. I think we see the proof of that in their endless quest for novelty."

"How do you mean?" Ewan queried.

"Well, they're forever trying to be different, because at the root there is an unspoken suspicion that they're all trapped in the same circle of futility. Novelty disguised as creativity is a pretentious way of avoiding the terrible truth."

"I'll have to think about that one," Ewan said.

"That's the trouble with my brother, he makes it all too complicated," Elizabeth chimed in. She deftly avoided a playful swipe from Mark.

"I think I've learned enough to realize that the Sea of Infinite Possibilities must represent some kind of genuine freedom. But how do we know that the creativity you talk of isn't a cover-up here as well?" Ewan asked.

"You came here willingly," Mark explained. "There were plenty of opportunities to turn back, but you came. No one forced you, and even now nobody forces you. If you want a simple proof that you're still free, it's the very fact that you are able to walk in this light and are not compelled to fall down in worship."

"Even though the power of the light is more than capable of making me do so," Ewan marveled.

"I just call it being loved," said Elizabeth. "It's nice."

By now they had reached the entrance to another cavern where Mark bid them enter. The *clink-clink* sound of many chisels hard at work filled the air.

"The Gallery of Sculptors," Mark announced. "Welcome to our home."

The cavern was a vast honeycomb of vaults and tunnels, a veritable hive of activity. Ladders and scaffolding ran everywhere, accessing different levels for the scores of men and women who busily worked the stone. The floor of the cavern lay strewn with pieces of rock in various stages of shaping.

The sculptors' handiwork first caught Ewan's eye in the intricate carvings and sweeping bas-reliefs that had turned the rough texture of the Rock into a swarming variety of beautiful figures, symbols, and images. What struck him most as an artist was the distinct impression that the sculptures did not so much adorn the Rock as grow out of it. He never before had observed such a harmony between the medium and the worker. It appeared that the Rock had entered a partnership of shared life and imagination with the sculptor, and the fusion had produced creations that mutually honored the material and the maker. Ewan marveled at the concept and its possibilities.

"What is the key to this amazing unity?" he asked Mark.

"Let's find out. There's Alan over there. Let me introduce you."

Alan appeared to be slightly older than Ewan. The sculptor was working painstakingly on the fine detail of a vase. It was shaped like the tilted trumpet of a flower growing straight out of the Rock, and from it gushed a tumescent wave of water. Several figures swam ecstatically on the crest of the wave. The work conveyed a sense of superabundant happiness.

"I call it *Spirit of Joy*," Alan explained.

"It's magnificent," Ewan said appreciatively. So compelling was the illusion of wetness that he could not resist touching the carved water and fully expected to find his fingers moistened in the process.

He noted that the sculpture had neither the arid grace of classicism nor the efficient abstraction of modernity, nor yet the transitoriness of sensualism. It was, he thought, timeless and truly transcendent. Perhaps beauty could be absolute after all. He smiled to himself. That last thought had been classed as a heresy in his former life.

There were other works nearby, evidently also from Alan's hand. Some were finished, some barely commenced. All carried the same quality of transcendent worth, even the one depicting an old man dying while his two sons fought over his inheritance. Ewan had to look long at the man's face before he understood: Despair, anger, fear, and sorrow had etched his features deeply. Yet nothing could take away the underlying calmness of his mien, which suggested he could see beyond the present crisis to better days.

"It's called *Self-Control*," Alan said. "I'm sculpting the nine virtues of the Rock."

"Love, joy, peace, patience, kindness, goodness, faithfulness, gentleness, and self-control," Elizabeth recited.

"May I ask you something?" Ewan inquired. "Where I come from, frankly, we cannot produce anything like this. The medium doesn't cooperate. We seem doomed to swing forever between the ancient classical lines and the modern, but the modern is full of anger and despair and often is no more than an arrogant reaction against the past. You seem to have broken free from both ancient history and the current spirit of the age. What's the secret?"

"I love the Rock," Alan replied simply. "Remember, I have come from your past, too. I was as much an enemy of the Rock as anyone, and my work was very different then. In fact, much as you describe—classical for the conservatives and alienated for the radicals. You see, if you hated the Rock as I did, then all stone became alienated in your hands. It served neither you nor its Creator. So your only options were either to make the medium a slave to your selfish ends or end up surrendering yourself to it in some form of nature worship that denied your own originality. It was only when I learned to love the Rock that I discovered the secret of true harmony in my work."

"So, if I understand it rightly," Ewan said slowly, "the secret lies not in reacting either for or against nature—or ancient and modern—but in relating personally to the One who transcends nature."

Alan smiled and nodded. "I think you've got it," he said.

"I suppose I'll only know for sure when I start painting," Ewan answered.

"Let's talk to some more of our friends," Mark suggested.

Ewan thanked Alan and then followed his guides onward to speak with other sculptors. Each artist expressed the same wonderful liberation he or she had found since encountering the Rock. Ewan wondered if his own medium of paint and canvas would respond in a similar manner. Yet, for now, he was content simply to see what others were doing with their art forms.

Eventually, the light began to fade. For a moment Ewan wondered how this could happen since the light came from the Rock and not from a sun subject to rising and setting.

Mark explained that it was an aspect of the Rock's gracious accommodation to their mortality. They simply were not yet ready for endless glory!

The sculptors were a gregarious crowd and invited Ewan to join them for an evening meal. Though simple, it turned out to be utterly delicious. Ewan had not appreciated how hungry he was until then.

In milling about after the meal he lost contact with Mark and Elizabeth, so he took the opportunity to wander outside and gaze for a while at the sea. The night sky was wonderfully clear, and for the first time ever Ewan saw the stars as they should be seen—not as fitful glimpses through everpresent clouds but as a vast, bejeweled necklace draped across the velvet sky and reflecting off the phosphorescent sea. He breathed a sigh of pure pleasure.

"It's beautiful, isn't it?"

The voice startled him. He turned to see a dark-haired woman whom he surmised to be in her early thirties.

"Oh, yes. Yes, it is," he stammered, caught unawares.

"Sorry, I didn't mean to startle you."

"Oh, that's all right. It's just that I'm new here," he explained.

"What's your name?"

"Ewan. And yours?"

"Penny."

He took a step toward her and peered at her face. "Penny? Not—you don't mean Jason's wife?"

"Yes, that's right." A slight frown creased her brow. "How do you know? Wait a minute. If you recognize me, then—then you must be Ewan Jones!"

"Yes, I am," he answered in amazement. "But you're supposed to be dead. I mean—what happened? Jason has gone completely to pieces since you vanished."

"I'm afraid Jason always was in pieces," she replied sadly. "That was half the trouble."

"Go on," Ewan urged, curious to know more.

"I was as much to blame as he," she said. "I wanted some sort of spiritual experience, I suppose, to help me cope with Jason's moods. The trouble was, I looked for it in the wrong direction and got recruited into the occult. They said I was the right type, you know—a sensitive one. Ha! All I got sensitive to was the Haunter!"

"What happened?"

"I got involved in lots of degrading stuff. You know the sort of thing. I don't want to talk about it. It was just sickening, really. But they do that to drag you deeper and deeper into fear and bondage. At first you are just afraid of the humans. You know, purely physical and psychological intimidation. But it goes further. You begin to lose touch with reality, and then you find your imagination starts going haywire until you're living in a dream world. You sort of float around in the real world, but you feel detached from it. Then the Haunter comes to make you his slave. You try to run away, but you can't escape back into the real world anymore. It's terrifying, and worse still, nobody understands what's really happening to you."

"It was never as bad as that for me," Ewan said. "But he certainly scared me."

"He did more than that to me. He took me over, possessed me," said Penny. "You know, inside me."

"How on earth did you escape?" Ewan asked.

"It wasn't easy. I tried to kill myself."

Seeing Ewan's shocked expression, Penny quickly dismissed it with a chuckle. "Oh, I'm all right now," she said. "In fact, I've never felt more in love with life. But that's what the Haunter does. He makes you despair and then drives you to destruction."

She paused for a moment. Ewan waited in curious wonder.

"My problem was that he wanted me to kill the man I loved. He said Jason was an enemy and that my life would be all right once he was out of the way. I didn't want to do it, but the pressure was so great that I decided the only way out was to commit suicide."

"We all thought the Rock had got you," Ewan said.

Penny laughed ruefully. "Not that time, and not the way you thought. Jason found me overdosed, drugged up to my eyeballs, and somehow pulled me through."

"How did you feel?"

"Angry, frightened, and in even greater despair. So I tried again. This time I sneaked into our small dinghy one night and cast off without an anchor, sail, or oars. I just hoped that if I got away from everyone the Haunter would leave me alone, and either I would drown at sea or die of dehydration and exposure."

"I think I can guess what happened," Ewan said.

"Yes," she laughed. "By some miracle I got washed onto the Rock, and here I am, alive and free."

"What about Jason? Is there no hope for him?"

"That's the sad thing," she replied. "I've tried to make contact with him many times, but so far without success. Whenever I can, I climb high on the Rock and throw green, glowing jewels to attract his attention. I just wish he would join me. Maybe one day he will."

Ewan was totally flabbergasted.

"This—this is unbelievable," he gasped. "I started my journey here because I saw a green light falling from the Rock! Jason was working close to the cliffs that night. *You* must have thrown it!" He was speechless and now suddenly confused. *It wasn't meant for me, but for Jason.* The thought was ghastly. *Then—I shouldn't really be here. The call was for someone else—and I claimed it instead!*

He paced the beach, agitated beyond measure.

"Penny, I'm so sorry," he said turning on her. "I—I don't know what to say."

"You don't have to say anything," she answered quietly. "Ewan, I'm glad you are here. Just glad that my efforts did some good." Seeing his distress, she added, "Listen, it's the way of the Rock. We think we know what's right. We do what's in our heart, but sometimes that's different from what the Rock wills. It's hard to cope with at first. But then, gradually, we come to see that he always brings good out of evil and hope out of disappointment. My stone wasn't wasted if it saved your life."

She offered a wan but encouraging smile.

"No, I suppose not," he said doubtfully. "All the same, it does seem unfair on poor old Jason."

"I don't think it's too late for him yet, do you?" she asked. "At least, I certainly haven't given up hope."

Just then somebody at the entrance to the gallery called Penny. She turned to Ewan. "I must be going. Don't worry about it, Ewan. I'm genuinely pleased to see you here. It was meant."

With that she turned and walked back to the cave.

"Penny, I—" he began. Then he realized she was right. What he really needed to do was to discuss it with the Rock. His thoughts turned to Sally. If Penny had tried to communicate with Jason, albeit with an unexpected effect, then Ewan wanted to send a message to Sally, too.

An hour later, after sorting the matter out with the Rock—having been reassured that, yes, the Rock had wanted him to come; and, no, he was not there under false pretenses; and, yes, he would be able to send a message to Sally in due course—Ewan lay down on the beach to sleep. It had been a long day, and his head spun with a thousand and one images—dramatic bas-reliefs, elegant figurines, poignant cameos, all alternating with blazing light and falling green jewels. He began to dream.

In his dream he saw a fiery boat speeding toward the Rock in full, burnished sail, and on its prow stood a radiant young woman clothed in garments of gold. She played a merry tune on a flute and danced and swayed to the rhythm.

As the boat drew near to where he stood at the mouth of The Sculptor's Gallery, its fire danced scarlet and vermilion over the Rock and the tune saturated the air with sounds of joy. At once, the myriad sculptures around him sprang to life and blazed with inner fire. Then they flew from the mouth of the cave and spread out all across the world, carrying the fire of heaven in their forms wherever they journeyed. In their place, thousands upon thousands of other sculptures formed, creation after creation repeating the process, until Ewan assumed that now they must have filled the world with their flaming beauty.

Then his dream transported him to a village marketplace. A small, curious group of people drew near to one of the fiery sculptures. It was a winged horse. At first they were cautious, but as their sense of wonder overcame their fear, they grew more bold. One man touched the horse. Immediately, a tongue of fire leapt from the animal and rested on the man's forehead. That started the ball rolling: moments later, others crowded in to touch the sculpture. Each one received the same touch of living fire as they did so.

Suddenly, Ewan's perspective shifted and he found himself gazing down from a great height. All over the world he saw people touching the sculptures, always with the same result. As he watched, the people then began to journey—men and women and children of all ages—each with the bobbing curl of flame on their foreheads. Soon a vast multitude was streaming across the earth toward the Rock. He saw millions pass through the cross-shaped entrance and come to The Haven of Souls.

The young woman continued playing her joyous music. Someone lowered a gangplank, and the throng began to pour onto the flaming boat. For a moment Ewan thought it must sink under the load, but this was no ordinary craft: as fast as the people streamed aboard, the boat enlarged to contain them until at last its size filled the screen of his dreams.

HE AWOKE to find it was dawn. Rising from the sand on which he had slumbered, he walked down to the sea. To his delight it was warm, and soon he was swimming under a blue sky and able to see for the first time something of the splendor of the Rock. Its benevolent, life-giving form throbbed and scintillated with living light as high and as far as he could see. Ewan sighed with joy.

"All's well!" he shouted.

To his infinite delight he heard above, beneath, and all around him the familiar voice of the Rock.

"Yes, all is well, my son."

This was going to be a good day, he decided.

Shortly afterward, he met Mark and Elizabeth at breakfast.

"So, what are the plans for today, then?" he asked enthusiastically.

"First, a cautionary tale, and then something very special," Mark replied enigmatically.

Elizabeth held her hands to her mouth and giggled at the delicious secret.

❖20❖

AFTER BREAKFAST MANY OF THE SCULPTORS GATHERED on the beach and began to sing in praise of the Rock. It was the first time Ewan had ever taken part in a corporate act of worship. He recalled ruefully that his previous efforts at singing had usually occurred under the influence of alcohol, and the subject matter had been far from holy.

At first he felt at a loss, partly because he was surrounded by strangers and partly because the songs were unfamiliar. But there was something attractive about the unity and genuine warmth of these people that overcame his initial shyness, and soon he joined in heartily, singing whatever words he felt were appropriate. He also realized that his relationship with the Rock was just as personal in the crowd as when he was alone. That encouraged him to treat the occasion as an opportunity for familiar address.

"Rock, you are marvelous," he sang. "I love your wonderful ways. I don't understand why I'm here, but I'm glad. Very glad."

It must have sounded raucous, but the words seemed to fit. He glanced down to see Elizabeth by his side, smiling up at him. She obviously thought it was all right, too.

The experience recalled to him something of what Mark had said about freedom. In this act, the worshipers chose of themselves to make a creative and proper response to the light. They neither contrived to attribute to it virtue where it had none, nor were they cowed by its sheer power. No, the Rock was *worth* worshiping.

Apparently this was a normal way of commencing the day, and in due course when the singing concluded, the sculptors, chatting convivially, returned to the cavern to continue their labors. Ewan remained on the beach with his hosts.

"Ready then?" inquired Mark.

Ewan nodded and they set off.

Their journey took them to a small headland which, when they had rounded it, revealed another cove no less beautiful than the one they had left behind; only here pieces of rock were scattered across the sand. Mark explained that there were hundreds, perhaps thousands of these inlets making up the outer perimeter of the Rock, and each one was home to a different community. All shared the same identity with the Rock, and that was the common bond uniting them. Ewan realized it might take him a lifetime to visit everyone. He wondered where he would be allowed to settle.

"You'll probably find the people we are about to meet a little strange," Mark warned as they tramped along the beach. "I think you are meant to learn something from them, though. That's why the Rock wanted you to make this visit."

Ewan replied that he was happy with whatever they arranged for him.

They had traveled about halfway along the beach before Ewan spotted the building. He viewed it with considerable surprise and wondered why it even had been erected, especially since they already had passed several very beautiful caverns on this stretch of shore. Why did the people not live in one of these?

Worse still was the architecture. Against the splendor of the Rock it looked drab and cheap—an unadorned, oblong structure built of ill-matched pieces of stone with poorly proportioned, niggardly windows and an unnecessarily pitched roof of cracked tiles. He voiced his feelings to Mark and Elizabeth.

"Herein lies the cautionary tale," Mark explained. "The people you are about to meet are one of the smallest groups you will encounter, but they have had arguably some of the best and clearest experiences of the Rock. Their creative potential is enormous, but they've missed the way."

Ewan was puzzled. "I thought somehow that everything would be perfect here," he said.

"Ha! I did warn you this wasn't heaven, now, didn't I?" Mark said with a twinkle in his eye. "That's the trouble with these folk. They are so anxious to escape from here and get to heaven that they see little point in investing time and energy in the present."

"So why do they bother at all?" Ewan asked. "I don't mean to be disparaging, but if that building is anything to go by, they should give up completely!"

"They still belong to the Rock," Elizabeth reminded him. There was a slight edge of rebuke in her voice. "I like lots of the people here as well, even if they are a bit funny."

"Lizzie's right," said Mark. "The point of meeting these folk is to learn about one or two of the pitfalls in The Haven of Souls so that hopefully you will avoid them yourself." He smiled at Ewan's glum face. "Anyway, let's take a look inside, shall we?"

After the splendor of the light outside, the building was exceedingly dull. It did nothing to raise Ewan's spirits. The lack of light was occasioned not only by the smallness and grubbiness of the windows, but also by the fact that the predominant color scheme was a tired brown and yellow.

"They don't like too much light here," Elizabeth explained. "It frightens them."

Through the gloom Ewan detected a number of people at work in little alcoves built out of rickety plywood screens. His interest was drawn to a man engaged at a canvas. Mark nodded, encouraging Ewan to introduce himself.

The man greeted Ewan brightly enough. His name was Reggie, and, in response to Ewan's inquiry, he explained with somewhat overenthusiasm that he was painting a parable about the Rock—a sublime realism, he called it.

Ewan, still smarting from Elizabeth's mild rebuke, tried politely to hide his distaste for the work. The canvas was no more than a piece of cardboard painted white—a fact put down to the expense of things and the need not to be extravagant. The picture consisted of a half-finished, crude representation of the Rock that conveyed nothing of its actual glory or magnitude. Daubed across the center was a large cross above which read the words, "Enter and be saved," painted in angry, fluorescent orange. A bucket with a winch handle turned by an angelic creature hung from a derrick at the foot of the Rock, and in it sat a man who evidently had just been pulled out of the water.

Emotionally the picture was lifeless, artistically it was crude, and the materials used were poor. Ewan wondered anxiously if this was what the renewal of his own artistic gifts would mean.

"It's the message that matters," Reggie said enthusiastically. "Every day is a day nearer the end of the world, so there's less time than there was yesterday. Ha ha! No time for self-indulgent fine art. Must get it finished. It may help some poor lost soul."

Not wishing to offend the man's evident sincerity, Ewan politely took his leave and looked around for Mark and Elizabeth.

Elizabeth had disappeared, but he did spot Mark. He was being harangued by a woman whose robe looked distinctly shabby.

"Nobody understands me," she said, her well-educated voice indicating a refined background. "That's the trouble with this place. No one appreciates the real importance of the arts. We artists of the Rock should be properly recognized.

It's time people here took notice and realized how valuable we are to society. After all, we are the ones gifted to express the truth, surely?"

Mark patiently tried to explain that artists were appreciated. After all, he was a sculptor himself. Many of his close friends were excellent artists, and none of them felt unappreciated as far as he could tell. Why did she feel the way she did? It was unnecessary to feel so in The Haven of Souls.

"But I'm a special case," she protested. "I simply know that I have been given a deeper insight than most. Why must I be rejected this way?" She sighed. "I suppose one day everyone will recognize my gift. But then it will probably be too late."

Ewan carefully avoided catching the woman's eye and sidled into the alcove where she worked. Her handiwork consisted of three crude circles of colored cotton yarns glued to a pale-yellow piece of card. He could make no sense of it.

Suddenly, to his dismay, the woman spotted him and rushed to him eagerly.

"Do you like it?" she inquired earnestly. "No, sorry, that's not what I meant. Do you understand it? Oh, dear no, not that either. It's more insightful than that, isn't it? A mystery. I've tried to catch the essence of the Rock. It's taken me days to do this. Oh, if only you knew what it's cost me—the agonies, the pathos!"

Ewan turned to her with a puzzled frown.

"I don't wish to be rude," he said, "but I find it hard to believe it's taken you that long."

The woman stepped back and clasped her hands theatrically to her throat. "Oh, not another one who doesn't understand!" she groaned. "Well, never mind. Go on—go away! Leave me to my art. I shall suffer alone. I may be misunderstood, but I do it all for the Rock. That must be my comfort, I suppose."

She shooed them out of her alcove.

"I'm extremely sorry," Ewan said to Mark. "I was rude, wasn't I? That's the second time today I've put my foot in it."

"Not really," Mark replied. "You told her the truth, that's all. The trouble is, she believes that artists like herself are a special breed and entitled to more recognition than others. She is actually quite a talented person. But her present work is crude and lacks craftsmanship because she creates from her own ego rather than from the life of the Rock."

"Then what is she—what are *any* of these people doing here?" Ewan was incredulous. "Have they bypassed all that I and you and everyone else has gone through to get here?"

"No, not really. Though they do puzzle me," Mark confessed. "I think the problem is that they've lost their real love for the Rock and replaced it with something lesser."

"But, how can they?" Ewan demanded, incredulous. Suddenly it dawned on him. "Is that a danger for me, too?"

Mark nodded. "For any of us. Freedom means that there will always be the temptation to substitute other things or people for pure love and service to the Rock."

He took Ewan by the arm. "I brought you here so you could see the danger—but also because I want you to hear something."

Elizabeth returned at that moment. "He's just started," she whispered.

"This way," prompted Mark.

At the far end of the building a number of people had gathered in a semicircle. An elderly man stood before them. Joining the circle, Ewan, Mark, and Elizabeth listened as the man began to address the group.

"The golden boat soon will come for each one of us," he said. "Life here is very fleeting. But there is more, much more than this vain life, my dear friends. For the day is almost nigh when the world as we know it will end, and when the Rock will transform himself into something new. The sea will pass away and all things will be made afresh. So we must be ready. Let no one get too comfortable here. All things will end soon."

All around him Ewan heard grunts of assent. Suddenly, the drabness and poverty and tawdriness of the surroundings and poor quality of the craftsmanship made sense to him: these people were not expecting to be here long. Evidently, it wasn't worth doing anything well because it all was destined for imminent destruction.

The man continued in a similar vein, and after listening for a while, Ewan indicated to Mark that he wished to talk.

"Outside," Mark whispered. Elizabeth nodded and led the way.

It relieved Ewan enormously to step from the depressing gloom of the building and return to the radiance of the Rock. "Phew!" he gasped.

"I did warn you," Mark said.

"But are they right?" Ewan asked. "Is everything really about to end? Will I have to paint as badly as Reggie? Why aren't you like that in the Sculptor's Gallery?"

Mark laughed.

"Serves us right for taking you there, I suppose!" he said. "Yes, it is true that the world as we know it will end, and all things will be changed and transformed into something even better. But it will not be as soon as the people in there like to think. A lot has to happen first."

"The Rock likes people," Elizabeth interjected. "He wants lots and lots and lots of them to escape from the Sea of Silly Billies before he changes everything round."

"That's the biggest reason why it won't all finish just yet," Mark affirmed. "Meanwhile, we're meant to celebrate our renewed life in the work we do. It shouldn't be second-rate if it's done to the glory of the Rock, even if you expect the world to last only another day. So to answer your particular concern, yes, you will be able to paint properly. In fact, soon you'll have the chance to paint better than ever before."

"I'm relieved to hear that," Ewan sighed.

"I think you're going to paint pictures that will help people find their way here," Elizabeth said. She looked up at him with large, steady eyes, and her words suddenly seemed very important.

"I would like to do that very much, Lizzie," he replied. "There are a lot of people I wish to see make it here. I have a girlfriend called Sally. I wish she would come."

"Then you will have to call her," said Elizabeth. "You can't come if you aren't called, can you?"

He looked at her wonderingly. Then—"Penny! Penny threw glowing stones. That's how I got started on my journey!"

"I know. She told me," Elizabeth replied. "You could do the same."

"Just show me how!" he said with enthusiasm.

Mark intervened. "Before you two think any more about that, there's the very special event I promised you at breakfast time."

Elizabeth clapped her hands to her mouth. "I'd forgotten all about that," she gasped. "Oops!"

"It's all right, we're not too late," Mark smiled. "But we'd best get a move on. It's quite a long walk from here."

"I'm intrigued," said Ewan. "Lead on!"

With that, Elizabeth grabbed his hand and they set off for the next cove.

21

HURRIED ALONG BY ELIZABETH'S EXCITEMENT, Ewan's sense of intrigue grew with each step, but neither Mark nor his sister said anything to relieve his suspense. By the time they reached the craggy tongue of rock that marked the far end of the cove, Ewan was bursting with curiosity. He had quickened his pace so that Elizabeth had to trot along to keep up with him.

"Hold on, Ewan," Mark cried from behind. "Whoa, Lizzie!"

Ewan hesitated while Mark caught up.

"Sorry to be in a rush," he said. "I'm just curious to know what's in store for me around the next bend. At least, I assume that's where it is. But you two have been so secretive that I really don't know what to expect."

"It's not your speed," Mark explained. "It's the fact that we aren't allowed to go any further with you. At least, not for the moment."

"What? But why not?" Ewan grew suddenly cautious. "Hey, just what is it that's waiting for me round there?"

"Oh, please don't be afraid, Ewan," Elizabeth chimed. She gazed up at him with big blue eyes and squeezed his hand reassuringly. "It's just that—well, it's something very personal, and we'd be in the way if we were there. The Rock says so."

"I'm sure there's nothing I'd want to hide from you two," Ewan replied. "Whatever it is, I'd like you to be there with me."

Mark smiled sympathetically. "We'll wait here and come along a little later, if you don't mind. Don't worry. The Rock will tell us when it's all right to do so."

Still Ewan hesitated.

"Oh, go on!" Elizabeth urged, and she gave him a gentle push that sent him on his way.

Still intrigued, Ewan with some trepidation began to clamber across the rocky spur that led into the next cove. To his surprise, however, he did not find another stretch of sand but came instead upon a small inlet. Here the sea ran among a jumble of boulders, and the light from the Rock was strangely muted.

He also heard music. It took him a few moments to ascertain its origin. Then he spotted the solitary figure of a woman seated on a boulder with the sea lapping at her feet. She held a flute to her lips, and from its keys flowed the most fluid and beautiful tones Ewan had ever heard. He stood stock still, entranced by the ethereal strains wafting toward him.

The melody she played was unknown to him, but it carried an unearthly, haunting quality that made him shiver from within. Trembling, plaintive, as delicate as the sheen on a butterfly's wing, the fragile beauty in the notes moved him to tears. Yet for all its tender pathos Ewan could not mistake the fact that the music was undergirded by an unassailable strength. He wondered at such a potent combination from a lone musician.

He stole a glance behind him. Mark and Elizabeth were out of sight completely. This evidently was the surprise they had kept so carefully in store for him. They presumably wanted him to meet this solitary stranger on the seashore in private. Mystified and not wishing to break the spell woven by the woman's playing, Ewan began carefully traversing the rocks toward where she sat facing out to sea. He hoped she wouldn't consider his presence an intrusion. Perhaps she even expected him.

He was within ten paces of her when something hit him like a gush of cold water. It almost shattered the enchantment of the music. The woman wore a white robe with a blue sheen, which left her arms and legs bare. It was her limbs that shocked Ewan to a standstill—for they were horribly and deeply scarred with the remains of many weals, as though she had been cruelly beaten or repeatedly slashed with a knife.

In spite of his astonishment, her music lost none of its power. The woman continued, lost in her playing and apparently unaware of his presence. Ewan simply marveled that one so marred could produce such a sublime melody. He crept closer until he could see her face. It too was terribly scarred, and her eyes were closed. Lines of a painful history surrounded them. He wondered if she also was blind.

By now he stood next to her. In spite of the scars, her spirit exuded an unmistakable greatness which stirred him to further wonder. It was a nobility tangibly expressed in her fluid, mobile fingers and the soaring melody that so patently triumphed over the pathos of her life. Whatever her hurt, he thought, she was far from broken.

Suddenly aware of his presence, the woman abruptly ceased playing and opened her eyes. Ewan was relieved to see she was not blind after all, and he was struck at once by the gray serenity of her eyes and the deep, inner resources that radiated from them.

She smiled, gazing at him long and quizzically. He felt suddenly awkward in her presence.

"Hello," he said stiffly. "Your music is very beautiful."

A slight tilt of her head acknowledged his compliment.

"Er, my name is Ewan," he stammered, "but you probably know that already. I expect Mark or Elizabeth, or—or maybe the Rock has told you."

She inclined her head again. He fumbled for words.

"Were you expecting me? I'm sorry if I interrupted you. I—I'll go away if you like," he blurted.

The woman looked him squarely in the face. In spite of her scarred and careworn features, her eyes danced.

"You don't recognize me, do you, Ewan?" she said in a mellow voice.

"No," he answered awkwardly. He was thrown by the question. "I don't think I do. I'm very sorry—should I?"

A warm smile kissed the corners of her mouth, and her gray eyes were full of love.

"You have grown well, Ewan. I am glad you have found your way here. Now look at me carefully—remember if you can," she said quietly. "Ewan, I am your mother."

Ewan was stunned beyond measure. Unable to string together a coherent sentence, he simply stared at her in amazement. When he did find his voice, he could do no more than stammer and fluster unintelligibly, much to her amusement. She broke into a brightly tinkling laugh of unqualified joy.

Ewan felt suddenly like a little child lost in a world beyond his comprehension. He wanted to cry. Sensing his plight, she ceased laughing and eyed him gravely.

"Come here, Ewan, my child," she said, and stretched out her scarred arms.

Obediently he drew close to her. He knelt down and gazed steadily, searchingly into her face.

Slowly, a recognition dawned through the multifarious, minute signals of kinship stored away deep in the recesses of his memory. "It is you," he breathed. "Mum, it is you."

He clasped her in his arms and wept uncontrollably. Her own sobs were no less restrained as the pain of the years rolled away and healing love flowed tenderly through their embrace.

At length Ewan lifted his tear-streaked face and looked into hers.

"How is it I couldn't recognize you?" he asked.

He recalled his last memories of his mother and felt suddenly ashamed. It had been years since they parted company for the last time. They had not done so in anger. It had been prompted by the recognition that he was old enough to find his own way in the world, and that way lay in a direction different from hers.

She had been younger then, and a very attractive woman. Tania the party-goer, always popular with the men. How he remembered that about her. He recalled the strange, unshaven men whom he came upon from time to time wandering around the kitchen in the morning and the afternoons when he was told to go play with his toys and not disturb Mum and her "friend."

Growing up he had learned first with incredulity—and later with shame hardened into cynicism—that the woman he had heard people talking about in suggestive tones was none other than his own mother. He had been disgusted with her then. What was he to make of this lone flautist before him now?

Some awful tragedy must have occurred since they had gone their separate ways. A terrible accident, a vicious assault had destroyed her beauty. He felt too awkward to ask or even to draw attention to her disfigurement.

She appeared to understand his dilemma and nodded encouragingly.

"When did it happen?" he whispered.

"All my life, Ewan," she answered wryly. "All my life. You see me now as I have always been, for here my spirit is made visible to you. No makeup, no glamour, no posturings, my son. Just the terrible, plain truth."

"I don't understand," he replied weakly.

Her eyes fixed on the far distance.

"All those years—and I am ashamed of them now—all those men, the parties, the high life. People think a woman doesn't get hurt by her affairs. After all, she's never meant to show it. Perhaps she doesn't even allow herself to see what's happening. But you cannot give yourself away like that and not be hurt. All lust is an assault on the soul, and we are wounded every one. My scars are my own doing."

"I've never looked at it that way," Ewan confessed. "I—I,"—and here he was ashamed—"I always saw you as so confident, so outgoing and popular. I was the one who felt hurt and rejected. I never saw that you were being hurt, too." He began to weep again.

"Hurt you were indeed, my son," she said, drawing him again to herself. "I am sorry for that—deeply, deeply sorry. Can you ever forgive me?"

His hands could feel the scars on her arms. "Yes," he sobbed. "Yes, Mum, of course I can."

She sighed, and they remained for a long time locked in the embrace of reconciliation. The soft light of the Rock began to caress their damaged relationship into wholeness.

"What happened then?" he asked suddenly. "How did you get here? What does this music mean? I don't remember you ever playing an instrument. And certainly you never liked this kind of music."

"I found my way into the Rock," she answered simply. "Just one day—like you, I assume—I discovered that there was life in the Rock. A falling jewel, you know. It filled me with despair when I saw it. I was so unworthy, so hopeless a case. There was no way I believed I could ever find what I longed for. The thought almost drove me to suicide. It was when I reached that point of desperation that I cried out for the Rock to help me."

"And he did?" said Ewan.

"Oh, yes," she replied with deep emotion. "Though it was not easy. At the time I was living alone on some decrepit commune shack, but a rich man wanted me to move in with him. It would have meant a very comfortable life if I had taken up his offer, though I see now it could never have lasted. Yet I knew if I accepted I would once more suppress the pain and longing in my heart. I went out on deck. We were close to the Rock on a calm night, and there was a strange phosphorescence to the sea. On impulse I cried to the Rock, 'Take me, save me, if there's anything there!' Then," she laughed, "I threw myself over the side and began to swim for it. You'd never believe what happened next on that incredibly calm night. A sudden freak wave caught me and threw me onto the Rock. I later found the cross-shaped entrance."

Ewan had been entranced. "Amazing," he whispered. Of course he identified with all that had happened, and he told her of his own experience.

"So how did you learn to play?" he asked.

"I never did," she answered. "At least, not consciously. What you hear is the music of my reconciliation. Somehow, the Rock healed my life as I journeyed through. It was wonderful. When I arrived here, some considerable time ago now, I found I could express my redeemed soul this way. I play to the Rock just to say thank you."

"But your scars—" Ewan began.

She smiled ruefully. "Scars are not open wounds," she said. "I am healed, and the scars are my testimony that I am healed. I do not even hide them, for in reconciliation they become part of my wholeness. They're a cause of glory to the Rock, not of shame to me."

"I can hear that in your music," Ewan said. "It is both strong and full of pathos. There's a—a poise about it, a balance. It doesn't deny the pain, but it has overcome. I can't explain it, Mum—but it moved me very deeply, and now I know why."

"I think I just call it experience," she replied with a smile. "Lizzie would say something simple like that."

Mention of Elizabeth reminded Ewan of his friends. He was about to say something to that effect when he heard Mark's voice. So engrossed had he been in conversation with his mother that he had failed to notice their arrival. He spun round to face them.

"We've come to say good-bye," said Elizabeth. She stood with her hands clasped solemnly in front of her.

"What?" Ewan began. Then he realized she was speaking not to him but to his mother.

"It is time for us to go, Ewan," Mark said quietly. "We have to say farewell to her."

"What are you talking about?" Ewan demanded. "We've only just met again after all these years." He felt angry and piqued. "I don't want just a brief conducted tour of this place. I've come here to live. This is my mother, for goodness' sake!"

His mother laid a restraining hand on his shoulder. "Mark and Lizzie are right, Ewan," she said soothingly. "It is time for me to depart. Look."

She pointed out to sea. Drawing near to the shore in full sail was a vessel of purest burnished gold, burning bright and fiery in the light of the Rock. Ewan's mother rose and turned to him.

"I must go home now, Ewan, my love," she said huskily. "My joy is complete that we should have met like this. Blessed be the Rock for his mercy toward us."

Ewan seized hold of her in desperation. "But you can't," he cried. "Not now—it's too soon! We've so much to share with each other."

"It is the decision of the Great King. See, his craft has come for me."

"Where are you going?" he asked earnestly. "I'll come with you."

She shook her head sadly.

"Not yet, Ewan. One day you will come, and we shall meet once more, and at that time, forever. But now I go to my home—heaven, you would call it—my eternal healing and everlasting joy. I go to meet the Creator Lord of all the worlds and the Reconciler of all things. Farewell, my son."

With that she kissed him gently, loosed from his now powerless grip and walked steadfastly onto the gangplank that had been lowered for her.

Ewan felt Elizabeth's hand slip into his. Tears formed in the little girl's eyes as she waved farewell with her free hand.

"Good-bye, Tania," she cried. "Godspeed."

Mark stood by Ewan and put an arm around his shoulders. "She will be fully restored now," he said quietly. "Blessed is she among women."

"Blessed is she among women," Ewan repeated. He thought to himself that he never would have believed anyone would say that of his mother.

Slowly, the gangplank withdrew and the ship pulled away from the shore. Ewan stood in silence with his two companions, watching until the ship disappeared into the misty horizon. As it sailed on, he heard drifting across the waters the haunting and ethereal notes of a flute. It was played by the most beautiful woman he had ever seen in his life.

❖22❖

EWAN REMAINED ON THE SHORE for many hours trying to probe the haze which screened the far horizon. His mother's departure had plunged him into a state of profound meditation. Somewhere, out of sight in that far realm of infinite possibilities, lay the ultimate meaning of life and eternity—perhaps the sublime mystery of God himself.

It was beyond his grasp, he decided. A person can handle only so much in his mortal capacity, and already his own encounter with the Rock had taken him beyond the scope of his wildest dreams. Heaven, paradise, eternal life—what did he actually know of such things? The reality must be so glorious that one could not even hope to comprehend it until he got there—and compared to which the splendor of The Haven of Souls itself could be no more than a generous hint.

However, far from producing in him a weary, fainthearted agnosticism, Ewan's acknowledged limits of present understanding served only to excite and challenge him to fresh hopes and longings. A yet farther country beckoned, and he knew his destiny lay beyond even this wonderful shore. Already he could feel its insistent tug. The day surely would come when, in the company of angels, the golden ship would bear Ewan Jones himself to the final haven that is no less than the heart of Divine Love. It was a heady thought!

Mark and Elizabeth must have slipped away at some point without his realizing it, for he suddenly became aware he was alone. Yet hardly had this fact registered in him when he was reminded of the love that had drawn him from the Sea of Futility to this distant shore. That same love guaranteed to see him safely to his final bliss.

All at once he felt overwhelmed with the wonder of his acceptance. He turned to face the Rock and slowly sank to his knees. Wave after wave of joy engulfed him as the life spirit of the Rock poured into his heart. He had never before felt such oneness and identity. Willingly, he allowed his pulse to beat to the rhythm of the Rock, and his thoughts and motivations quickly grew attuned to this all-consuming goodness. His will would gladly submit to that of the higher.

He remained in this blissful state for a long time, and he might have thought this would mark the end of all his strivings and difficulties. Instead, the experience triggered within him a strange and unexpected complexity of thoughts and emotions. After a while, it all came out as a question.

"What must I do, then?"

Ewan contemplated it with deep concern. "My will is yours and I am captive to your love. Yet, this is so strange. For reasons I can't understand, I feel restless—even though I dwell more securely than ever in the haven of your peace and love."

In response to his question he felt another emotional tide wash over him. This he could only describe as one of infinite pity, and it seemed to saturate every part of his being. He closed his eyes, lay back, and allowed himself to drift freely in its ocean depths.

DARKNESS WAS ALL AROUND him. He was underwater, but not drowning.

Somewhere in the murky distance, Ewan spied a small but insistent light. Drawn by its beauty, he swam toward it and came upon a glistening sapphire hanging from a slender gold thread which stretched away into the dark waters above. Its light illuminated a pale pathway, the beginnings and endings of which disappeared in both directions into the inky blackness. You would need to take that light with you, he thought, if you were to travel very far.

Pondering the significance of the scene, Ewan sat a short distance from the side of the path and waited. It wasn't long before he became dimly aware of another presence somewhere nearby; but the gloom hid whoever it was. Soon he heard sounds coming from the other direction. Moments later, he was surprised to see children emerging from the darkness. At least, the bodies were those of children—but with a start Ewan saw that their facial features were unmistakably those of adults. At first, he recognized nobody. Then he saw someone he knew. It was Sally's friend, Seamus Ferguson.

Ewan called out to him in greeting, but quickly realized that for reasons unknown the man could neither see nor hear him. Seamus reached the sapphire light and, with a shrewd gaze, gave it an experimental swing on its golden thread. Apparently satisfied with the result, he walked on. The other children, observing Seamus's actions, evidently had no such ideas of their own and ignored the light altogether.

Not long afterward Ewan saw Carl and Colette striding along the path. They consciously looked the other way when they passed by the light, seeming to be unnecessarily agitated by it. A whole army of children followed their example.

Frederick came next, morose and walking separately from everyone else. He saw the light and spat on it. It was a crude and futile gesture, Ewan thought indignantly. A crowd of ghostly, skeletal-faced children leered at the jewel as they passed.

With a start, Ewan saw that they were followed by Siegfried and Hilda. They shook their heads over Frederick's irreverence. Ewan had loved this couple. Earnestly he hoped and desired that they would take the light with them, but they simply bowed before it out of respect. Neither came close to it.

Another group of children with adult faces came into view. Ewan spotted Harp and Papa among them. They made fun of the light, Harp cackling, "Gleam, gleam, glitter, glitter!" as they walked by, much to the amusement of the other children. Realizing what was happening, Ewan now began to recognize many of his former acquaintances. He marveled at their responses. Jacques and Tim ran toward the light when they saw it, and Ewan hoped it might possess some meaning for them. But they quickly grew bored and turned decidedly away toward the adventures of the dark.

Baz, with his bright, searching eyes, was the last. The light drew him like a moth, and he stared fascinated at its beauty for a long time. Ewan thought that he would stay there and perhaps grasp it—but to his amazement Baz simply closed his eyes as though wanting to savor and capture a memory. He moved on.

Ewan's frustration knew no bounds. He wanted to cry out, "This is the light of life. How can you miss it? Why do you ignore it?"

But he knew they could not hear him.

Only then did he turn his attention in the other direction. To his dismay, just on the fringes, in the ambivalent region where light gave way to darkness, he saw standing by the path a shadowy figure wreathed in black and with a broad-rimmed hat pulled low over his features. Ewan knew at once who it was.

Strung around the Haunter's neck was a tray upon which burned many poorly made yellowish candles. These he offered freely to the children as they passed, and they snatched them up eagerly.

"Don't take them! He's conning you!" Ewan cried, his intensity disregarding the fact that they could not hear him. But of course it was to no avail. Ewan watched as by the pale, smoky light of these sickly candles the children followed the path into the gloom. Compared to the pure light of the gleaming sapphire they seemed such poor substitutes, but each child nursed his guttering flame as though life itself depended upon it.

Some seemed inordinately proud of their pathetic candles, while others fought to possess or quench the lights of those around them. No one appeared to heed or even be aware of the growing darkness as they moved down the path, farther and farther away from the still faintly visible jewel.

Then, to Ewan's horror, an invisible wind began to blow through this strange ocean, and the flames of the candles guttered even more. The hands he saw holding the candles were now old and gnarled, and in a panic they sought to shelter the flames. Anxious looks lit their lined faces.

It was no good. One by one their flames blew out. Terrible screams of despair and cries of deepest anguish greeted the ensuing darkness. Soon, all Ewan could hear were the groans and sobs of lost souls wandering alone in the endless, hellish darkness where no paths ran and no light illumined the way.

Ewan turned his gaze in the other direction. Others were coming now. With a start he saw that Sally was among them.

"No, not her, too!" he cried with alarm.

Before he could react further, the sapphire light suddenly blazed to such an incredible brightness that it swamped the entire scene and, before Ewan's astonished gaze, turned into a star of such splendor that he was almost blinded by its glory.

In the next moment, he was back on the seashore. Dusk was falling and the first lights of heaven were just becoming visible.

"Thank you, Rock!" he cried. "I know now what I have to do."

With that he set off in a brisk run toward The Sculptor's Gallery. There was no time to lose.

On his way he passed the building that he and his companions had visited earlier that day. Dim lights shone through the grubby windows.

"Why don't you share your light?" he panted half aloud as he ran past. For a moment he was tempted to stop and to try persuading them to join him, but the urgency of his vision drove him on.

"Either you get it, or you don't!" he muttered to himself.

Soon he reached the cove where the sculptors lived. The dusk was deepening.

"Lizzie! Lizzie!" he called as he ran along the beach. "I need your help. Where are you?"

He found her waiting for him at the entrance to the gallery. "Lizzie, thank goodness I've found you!" he gasped. "Listen, I've just had a terrible vision. I've seen what happens to people without the light. It's awful." He paused for breath. "I've got to reach Sally somehow, and all the others. What do I do? Earlier today you said something to me about stones. How do I do it?"

"I've been waiting for you," she said patiently. "I knew the Rock would speak to you."

He blinked in surprise at her evident awareness of what had been taking place. Her response confirmed that she was the right one to assist him.

"Can I go back to the people I've left behind? Tell me that," he urged.

"Yes, you can. But not the way you think," she answered enigmatically. "You can't just go and talk to them. They have to see."

"How?" he demanded.

"Come with me," she said.

AS DARKNESS SLOWLY DESCENDED, Elizabeth led Ewan into The Sculptor's Gallery. At her direction they climbed a long ladder and walked along a short tunnel until they reached a steep staircase that stretched upward as far as the eye could see.

Ewan gasped at the sight. "What, all the way up there?" he exclaimed.

"It's not as long as you think," Elizabeth laughed. "Look, you can just about see the sky at the top. It gets easier the more times you climb it. I've done it lots and lots of times!" She quickly leapt onto the stairs, leaving Ewan to follow.

By the time they reached the top, Ewan was gasping for breath.

"You'll have to get yourself fit like me," Elizabeth piped cheerily.

Ewan took in the surroundings as he recovered his wind. They were standing in a cleft of the Rock that by the chisel marks and chippings showed evidence of quarrying. They were not on the summit, for although it was almost dark, Ewan could see that the Rock soared behind them until its heights vanished into the clouds. He realized they must have passed right through the Rock and emerged on the other side. Below lay the Sea of Futility.

A glance over the edge confirmed his assessment. In the fading light he could make out the flat, silver sheen of the sea stretching away to a dull horizon. Boats of varying sizes dotted the surface, though it was too difficult for him to identify their names or ownership.

"We're here," said Elizabeth, somewhat obviously.

"So now what do we do?" he asked.

"We paint. Or, rather, you paint," she replied. "We're going to make some calling stones."

Light dawned on Ewan's puzzled features.

"Ah! You mean, like the one Penny threw to Jason—the one that drew me here?"

"Of course. That's what you want to do, isn't it?"

He assured her with all his heart that it was. Then, from a small bag, Elizabeth produced a hammer, chisel, and paintbrush.

Ewan laughed. "Now I know why the Rock sent me, a painter, to be among the sculptors. We need each other!"

"I'll cut the stones and you can paint them," she explained. "That way we'll both be doing what we're good at."

Lizzie began chiseling away at the Rock. Ewan watched, mesmerized as the little girl hammered away at the stone, her tongue sticking out in concentration. He marveled at her guileless intensity, and for a wistful moment he wished he had enjoyed a childhood like hers.

It was not long before she had produced a stone about the size of Ewan's hand. He was amazed to see just how well she had faced the sides so that it resembled a cleverly cut jewel.

"That's a good one," she said. "Now you can paint it for me." She presented him with the brush.

Ewan took the stone, weighed it in his hand, and looked around. "Have you remembered to bring any paint, Lizzie?" he asked.

She pointed to a small, bowl-shaped depression in the Rock. Ewan saw that it contained a reddish, powdery substance. "You can use that," she explained.

He touched the brush to the powder. "There's still one little problem, Lizzie," he said. "What am I to use for water? I can't do anything with this stuff as it is."

She looked at him squarely with her large, solemn eyes.

"You have to use tears," she said. "If you don't cry, you can't make calling stones."

Her reply left Ewan nonplussed.

"I—I can't just turn on tears," he protested. "I mean—it doesn't work like that for me."

Elizabeth came close to him, took his hand, and led him to the cliff's edge.

"Look down there," she said. "What do you see?"

"I see the sea and all the boats," he replied. "Some of them must belong to my friends. Some I don't recognize at all."

"What will happen to them?"

He recalled his earlier vision—the one that took place underwater. It began to sink in.

"They will all die and be lost in that dreadful darkness," he said slowly. "They'll never find the way to escape unless they see the light again. It will be such a horrible waste of their lives!"

Elizabeth did not answer.

From the rocky aerie, Ewan looked long and hard at the world below him. It was a sad, desolate place, full of pain and violence, eking out its futile existence through ever-growing despair and disillusionment. So many hurt and confused lives were at stake. Then he considered the wonderful love of the Rock, the joy he had discovered in The Haven of Souls—and the prospect of sailing the Sea of Infinite Possibilities. Tears sprang to his eyes. Quietly, he wept for a dying world whose few hopes were kept alive only by guttering candles given to them by an arch liar whose one intent was to prevent them from seeing the true light.

"I want to help," he cried out to them in anguish. "I want to tell you there's something better!"

"Now you can paint," Elizabeth said quietly.

Deeply moved, Ewan mixed his tears with the powder from the Rock. He then dipped the brush in the resulting red pigment and prepared for the first stroke. Elizabeth watched intently.

Tentatively, he touched the stone with the red. And before his startled eyes, the color sprang to life and began to glow with an uncanny phosphorescence.

"Go on," Elizabeth urged. "Do some more. This is good!"

Ewan applied further brush strokes to the stone. Slowly, as his confidence grew, he began to weave an intricate pattern of fiery color until the whole stone shone brilliantly like a fiery-lit ruby.

"It's become a living stone," Elizabeth said. "Let's see who we can throw it to!"

Ewan turned to her—she had a knowing look in her eyes.

They carried the glowing orb to the edge of the cliff and gazed downward.

Although it was dark by now, Ewan discovered he could see with exceptional clarity. His heart skipped a beat. Lying close to the cliff—dangerously close—he perceived the unmistakable lines of *Seaspray* and, by the faint glint of her blonde hair, he saw Sally standing near the prow gazing at the Rock. Why was she there? What was she thinking? Did she want to see the light for herself?

He and Elizabeth looked at each other.

"Together?" he asked.

"Together," she replied.

At that, they took the shining stone between them and, with a hope and a prayer, cast it forth in a high, shimmering arc into the darkness. They watched as slowly it plunged unerringly toward the sea—to where lay anchored the boat with the woman Ewan loved.

"Oh, Sally! Sally! Find the way," Ewan prayed. "I do so hope you find the way!"

"I hope you all do," whispered Elizabeth.

ABOUT THE AUTHOR

JOHN HOUGHTON originated from Baptist roots to become one of the most respected leaders in the independent and new church movements in Great Britain. He is the pastor of Living Word Community Church in Hailsham, East Sussex and currently serves as the chairman of East Sussex Bible Week, an interdenominational revival conference. He is the author of the most successful children's series ever published by a religious publisher in the U.K.—The Oswain Tales. He is currently working on another adult fantasy novel, and a non-fiction book, *Parenting Teenagers*, that he has co-written with his wife, Jan, is due out in August.